Rubi Ramos's Recipe for Success

Jessica Parra

WEDNESDAY BOOKS
NEW YORK

This is a work of fiction. All of the characters, organizations, and events portrayed in this novel are either products of the author's imagination or are used fictitiously.

First published in the United States by Wednesday Books, an imprint of St. Martin's Publishing Group

For information, address St. Martin's Publishing Group, 120 Broadway, New York, N.Y. 10271.

www.wednesdaybooks.com

Interior and case stamp designed by Devan Norman

The Library of Congress Cataloging-in-Publication Data is available upon request.

ISBN 978-1-250-86252-5 (hardcover)
ISBN 978-1-250-86253-2 (ebook)

First Edition: 2023

10 9 8 7 6 5 4 3 2 1

♥ ♥ ♥

To Cindy and Caro,
and to everyone creating new lives from scratch

♥ ♥ ♥

Rubi Ramos's Recipe for Success

Chapter 1

The Ban on Baking didn't crumble in one chomp. Instead, it ended with a thousand little bites.

The first one came that morning, when I leaned into the kitchen counter and chewed through the bolillo's crusty shell. The soft middle made me sigh. Licking the Nutella-coated crumbs from the corners of my lips, I dropped my gaze to the oven.

If hazelnut tasted this good slathered inside a bolillo, how would it taste between flaky croissant layers? Or blended with the sugar paste topping a concha? The moka pot brewing Cuban coffee gave a high-pitched whistle. A warning I'd tread into dangerous territory.

"Rubi, el café," my mother called from the laundry room.

"On it," I yelled back through the last mouthful of bread. I turned the stove off. The blue flames vanished, the baking ideas didn't. They never did.

I craned my neck toward the hallway. Still clear.

Darting across the kitchen, I grabbed a binder from the messenger bag slung on the back of the chair and pulled the pencil from the middle of my curls, wrangled high into a topknot.

Hazelnut croissants, I jotted in the margins of the Law and Debate binder. *And hazelnut conchas.*

Underneath the word *concha,* I drew a lopsided circle, striped its insides like the seashell the Hispanic sweet bread was named after. The dark and hurried scribbles gleamed against the rest of the blank, white page, daring me to keep going.

So I did.

The tip of the pencil scratched against paper as I drew a multiplication sign over the *and.* I added an equal sign after *concha.*

"Croncha," I said, writing in big, bold letters.

I didn't know if I could replace the concha's regular sweet bread with buttery layers of croissant dough. But I could almost taste the combination. The notion of a new pastry excited me more than spring break.

Then my parents' voices drifted in from the hallway.

The words Dad spoke were thick and exaggerated, like wooden spikes he drove through his Spanish to make sure his Cuban accent never went away. My mother's was more like the pictures I've seen of Havana's oldest buildings, falling away bit by bit. Crumbly, unlike the rest of her.

Striding down the hallway, my mother's pin-straight hair bounced down her back like a shiny, black cape only Darth Vader could envy more than I did. No matter how short he cropped them, Dad's salt-and-pepper curls still managed to boing and frizz. Exactly like mine did whenever I let them loose.

My mother made a beeline for the coffee. Dad started in the direction of the sliced bolillos. Only he was so focused on the kitchen table that he nearly slammed into the edge of the island. I followed his line of sight all the way to the baking notes dripping down the margins of my wide-open binder.

My stomach flipped. I almost snapped the lid on the contraband. But something about the way the corners of his lips curved into a smile made my fingers itch with the urge to hold it up for him to see. His eyes roved down the page. I swore he was salivating—and it had nothing to do with the warm bolillo he grabbed.

Mid-bite, he nearly choked though. Probably remembering who stood right next to him. Just as my mother turned to see what the commotion was, he pointed the bread at her.

I slammed the binder closed. Even if creating recipes wasn't technically breaking the Ban, baking-adjacent activities were still no bueno. I shoved it into my messenger bag. The croncha scurried into my heart, squeezed into chambers overcrowded with the rest of my in-the-margins recipes.

"The mail," said my mother, reminding me of the Recipe that mattered most.

- One acceptance letter from Alma University.
- Fold in pre-law major until smooth.
- Sprinkle in a dash of Ivy League law school.
- Set, and watch me rise.

They'd crafted it for me the moment I was born. Never asked me about adjusting any of the ingredients. Ironic, yes. But I also couldn't deny the Recipe was foolproof. If followed to a T, it'd yield my future success. My mother downed another cup of Cuban rocket fuel. "Did you check the mailbox yet? Is the mail here?"

The kitchen air felt suddenly thick. "I'll go check it now." Grateful for the chance to escape it, I breezed through the sparsely decorated living room, and out the front door.

Morning sun stirred awake, lighting up the hills and the already gridlocked freeways of OC. The ocean stretching beyond it glittered. I squinted. The faintest edges of Catalina Island came into view.

The sight made me wistful for something I couldn't place. Probably a spring break on the beach with Devon. Not freezing inside the auditorium with Madeline and the rest of the Law and Debate team. Swallowing hard, I walked down the driveway to the mailbox.

Our postman, Samuel, approached ours. He shuffled through a stack of mail. Paused at something thick. Chunky enough to be Alma U's acceptance package.

My heart pounded, spurring my feet to do the same. I sprinted forward, arms outstretched. Ready to finally receive the key ingredient in our Recipe for Success.

"Whoa, Rubi. Nothing from Alma today."

Soles of my flip-flops squeaked to a halt. Heart did too. "Nada? You sure?"

He shook his head. "Only these."

The pile of mail thudding between my palms masked a huge sigh. As if it wasn't totally weird I sometimes (lots of times) stalked the mailbox, he asked, "Same time tomorrow?"

Not trusting my voice to hide my disappointment, I nodded. Whoever said patience was a virtue obviously never applied to colleges before. Never mind living inside the pressure cooker of making sure their Big, Shiny Future stayed on track.

I riffled through some bills, *USA Today*'s Best College Rankings—and ooh—the latest issue of *Baker's Dozen*.

I flipped through Dad's magazine, fully intent on borrowing it to read at study period, like always.

Then my breath hitched.

The announcement written across the page jolted me like a defibrillator. Every recipe housed inside my chest pounded. Stilled heart fluttered to life again.

Orange County's First Annual Bake-Off: Four challenges. Two acclaimed judges. One prize of a lifetime.

Dough you have what it takes to be OC's best amateur baker?

I glanced up the driveway to the front door, ready for my mother to burst free and catch me red-handed. I pulled the phone from the back pocket of my uniform khakis. Opening the message thread with Devon, I snapped a picture of the ad, added a few question marks, and hit send.

"Dough you have what it takes?" I whispered to myself, nearly dropping both the magazine and my phone when it started buzzing in my palm. The phone was only halfway up to my ear when Devon's voice trilled, "Rubi, you have to try out for this! You *dough* have what it takes to get in!"

My mouth twitched into a smile. Just like Devon showed me every single one of her fashion sketches, I showed her every new baking idea. Except while Devon was actually allowed to make her creations, the Ban put a wrench in baking any of mine.

Was baking like riding a bike? With Devon squealing in my ear, I very badly wanted to find out.

Then again, the whole point of my parents working so hard in the bakeries was so I didn't have to. Not to mention the last time I tried riding a bike, it didn't go well.

"Oh, come on, Rubes! I can feel you smiling," she sang-shouted.

"No, I'm not." Only damn it, I was. "But let's say if I hypothetically got in, you know my mother would actually kill me if I competed."

"Only if she knew about it," she said, egging me on.

Luckily, there was enough good daughter left in me to try to fight the fire Devon was fanning. "But I'd know about it."

"We're seventeen! Hiding things from our parents is in our DNA. It's our teenage duty, or something."

There were lots of other teenage duties I hadn't partaken in. Like despite knowing the tongue was the main organ in the gustatory system, I'd never actually used it to kiss anyone. Never spent a full day at the beach even though I lived pretty close to one. Considering my DNA was so different from most teenagers living in Pelican Point, my duty was to make sure my parents' sacrifices amounted to something.

Like making damn sure I got into Alma.

"Don't you think I should at least wait until I get accepted into Alma before trying to get into Bake-Off?" I snuck another peek up the driveway.

"It's not your fault Alma still uses snail mail. Your acceptance package is probably on its way as we speak."

I glared at the mail tucked underneath my armpit. "It's not."

"It will be. In the meantime, just do this thing, Rubes. Today's the last day to submit an application."

I looked down at the magazine again, wide open in the palm of my hand. Arguments against at least trying out began to drain away. Maybe my mother sensed it because the front door creaked open. "Dev, I got to go. The Boss is coming."

"Fine, but if you don't sign up before second period, I'll force you to do it then."

I ripped the ad from the magazine, and shoved it and my phone into my back pocket right before my mother popped through the front door. "Honorio, hurry up." Her shoes clicked forward. I tucked the magazine under my armpit between the other mail.

"Nothing yet?" she asked when she reached me.

I shook my head.

Her forehead wrinkled and her face darkened with disappointment. "Entonces what are those?"

"Oh these?" I held them up like they were nothing substantial. "College rankings. Bills." *Act natural*. "Oh, and one of Dad's magazines too."

He walked from the house then with my messenger bag over

his shoulder, a thermos in one hand and a bolillo in the other. He kicked the door closed and rushed down the driveway to meet us.

My mother snatched the baking magazine from my hand, swatting him with it. "How many times do I have to keep telling you these should really go straight to the bakery, Honorio?"

He pulled her in for a hug. "Until it gets through my thick skull." He winked at me. She didn't see me return the gesture because her eyes closed as she hugged him back. Probably relishing in the sound of her favorite nickname or the warmth of the parental PDA.

When they finally peeled apart, she honed in on the other magazine. Plucked it from my hands. I wanted to tell her she didn't still have to keep subscribing to it. But I couldn't. Not when she pressed the magazine to her chest and smiled like it was Christmas morning.

Finding out Alma never dipped below the top ten, and that I was almost in, was undoubtedly her idea of the best gift ever.

As if she wanted to give me a little present of my own, she grabbed the bolillo from Dad and handed it to me. "Now eat up. You won't be able to learn anything on an empty stomach. Get moving or you'll be late. Same goes for you too, Honorio." And with that, she walked to her car and drove off.

"Gotta love the Boss," Dad said. He took a sip from his thermos. At least she'd left him with some sustenance.

"Want your bolillo back? I already had one."

"You keep it. I'll eat at the bakery." He slung the bag over my shoulder then patted it.

"Oh, and Dad? Thanks for the save back there."

"No worries, kiddo." He brought his face down to my ear and lowered his voice as if letting me in on a secret. "Since you have a half day today, are you coming in later? After your shift, you can tell me what the croncha is all about."

A chance to riff baking ideas again? "Of course!" When it came to Alma ushering in the next episode of our family's future, my parents were always on the same page. As far as the Ban though . . . While my mother would never even entertain the idea of me breaking it, Dad sometimes looked the other way for a slight bend or two. "I'll head over right after debate practice."

I looked to the magazine in his hand, then touched my back pocket. He smiled super wide, as if knowing Bake-Off's ad was hidden inside it.

"Okay, kiddo, let's get moving before we get in trouble."

That's the trouble with bending. It was impossible to know how far to go before you broke.

Chapter 2

School went by in a blur. I studied Bake-Off's site between classes. During classes. Jotting down notes about each challenge instead of following along with the lectures.

Ideas for Bake-Off Challenges:

1. *Chewy or crispy for the Cookie Try-Out Round?*
2. *Should I put my own spin on a bread or a cake recipe for the Signature Bake Challenge?*
3. *Omigawd. A Mystery Challenge. All bakers will have to bake the same recipe—except the details of said recipe will be announced upon arrival. Yikes (but also yay)!*
4. *Last. But. Not. Least. The Jaw-Dropper Challenge . . . what jaw-dropping feast for the eyes and taste buds could I make for this one?*

Thinking about all the delicious possibilities made my mouth water, filling it with a phantom sweetness. My stomach growled.

The last bell rung, masking most of the grumbles. AP English textbooks slammed shut. Classmates bolted from chairs and spilled into hallways. I cut through the crowds, winding up the bricked and cobblestoned walkways paving every courtyard and corner. Temptation throbbed throughout my body. And inside was something deeper.

A longing to bring my unbaked recipes out of the margins.

"Rubi! Wait up." Devon's voice echoed through the campus. She shouldered through the throng of plaid Catholic school uniforms. Torie, already clad in her Immaculate Heart softball jersey, followed closely behind.

Devon nudged me in the ribs. "So, did you do it yet?"

"Not yet." We shared a conspiratorial smile.

"You hear that, Torie? Everyone knows 'not yet' is an inch away from 'yes.'"

"I mean there are only *four* challenges." How time-consuming could they possibly be? I pulled the phone from my pocket and handed it to Devon. Torie leaned over to take a look.

"Wow. Celebrity judges? Do you know who they are yet?" she asked. "Any scoop on the Prize of a Lifetime?"

As if *Dough you have what it takes?* wasn't intriguing enough, now I was salivating for more info. I snatched the phone back and refreshed the site for the millionth time. "Nope. Nothing yet." I slipped it back into my pocket and quickened my steps, trying to outdistance my impatience.

The bottoms of my flip-flops slapped against the pathway. Devon's heels clicked and Torie's cleats scraped as they kept up with my mad dash to debate practice. Devon wiggled her eyebrows at me. "Do you need my kitchen to film the 'show us your baking skills' part of the application?"

Both the phone and the ad burned through my uniform. "I mean, I have a shift at the bakery later." I paused at the front of the auditorium doors. "I could film something there." Low-key, of course. "My shifts don't technically violate the Ban . . ." Neither would applying to Bake-Off. Right?

Devon's smile went wide. "You don't have to convince us, Miss Master Debater."

"Yeah, Rubi. This isn't one of your matches."

At the mention of Law and Debate, I reflexively went into rebuttal mode. "Then again"—I glanced at the doors I was about to walk through—"the tournament is weeks away."

The smart thing to do was use all my free time to prep for it. "Not to mention the Trig midterm." Ugh, math. The one stain on my otherwise spotless GPA, and the barrier keeping me from the top 5 percent of my class. "I could try to raise my solid B to an A minus."

Devon and Torie sighed in exasperation, knowing full well without some miracle tutor, raising it wasn't going to happen anytime soon.

"Okay, fine." I leaned into Devon's honey-blonde hair. Whispered the only argument meaty enough to keep me from applying to Bake-Off. "But what about the Recipe?"

Devon knew about my predetermined Recipe for Success. She knew mostly everything about my family's past and my future. A part of me wanted her to do a complete one-eighty and talk some sense into me.

Instead, she said, "Some recipes are begging to be tampered with."

I swallowed hard. "Not this one." Never this one. Plus, without Alma's acceptance letter in hand, I didn't even have the key ingredient yet to even attempt some tampering. And just like that, my priorities settled over me like a dusting of powdered sugar. "I'll see you two later."

"Rubi—"

I pushed through the doors so fast I got light-headed. Though I wasn't sure if that's all that made me dizzy.

Whenever it got close to debate tournament season, Sister Bernadette moved our practice sessions to the auditorium. Holding them here did add an extra layer of gravitas. The only downside was hauling all the theater pieces backstage and lugging our debate equipment onstage.

Teammates scraped tables and chairs into place. All the cardio should've counted as an extra period of PE.

Carolina dragged one of the podiums across the floorboards. I hurried to help her. "Sorry I wasn't here as early as usual to set up," I said. "I got caught up in a little mock-debate sesh outside." Technically, true.

"A captain's work is never done."

I cracked the teeniest smile, fingers tensing against the podium. Today, I'd spent zero minutes on *debate* debate. What was wrong with me?

Heart, do not answer that.

Except it did—pounding and pounding. "Let me go grab more chairs." I darted away so she—and the entire team—wouldn't hear it.

Pushing through the backstage curtains, I jumped back, barely avoiding a head-on collision with the murder-wasp-in-queen-bee's-clothing herself.

"Jeez, can't you ever watch where you're going?"

I reined in an eye roll. "Sorry, Madeline."

She dusted the front of her blazer even though I hadn't actually knocked into her. "Yeah, you should be."

Whether she wanted me to apologize for snagging the captain spot on the debate team, a seat in the FLOC, or my general existence, I couldn't tell.

Oh god. Her scowl was turning into a smirk.

Whatever crap she wanted to stir, I had no time for it. Sister Bernadette would be here any minute. I grabbed two chairs and moved toward the stage.

Madeline's heels stomped behind me. "I ran into your little friends outside."

"Uh-huh."

"I asked Devon about Parsons . . ." One look at Devon and most people would think she was a model instead of someone wanting to design clothes for them. "She said she got in three days ago."

"I know." A squeal flew from my lips and I whipped around, almost hitting her (again). "We celebrated by going to the Mix." Even Madeline nodded like it was the best food hall in OC. "Then we had a dozen chocolate-dipped strawberries for dessert—"

I almost let slip that I'd made them for her too, but I turned away. Set one chair at the end of the table.

Most of the team was here now. Shuffling through index cards, reading outlines, muttering arguments from behind the podiums.

"Victoria," Madeline continued, "or Torie, as she likes to call herself, is still deciding between UCLA and USC." Under the bright auditorium lights, her smile gleamed poison-apple red. "A total mood." Then her voice got syrupy. Chemically sweet, like cancer-inducing saccharine. "I haven't been able to decide between Harvard and Yale myself."

The humblebrag garnered a handful of head shakes. I walked to the other end of the table and set the last chair down. "Looks like the debate team has a Rory Gilmore on their hands," I mumbled, slinging my messenger bag over it.

Carolina glanced up from her index cards. "More like Azula Barbie."

I bit the sides of my mouth to keep from laughing. All laughter evaporated when Madeline plopped herself into my chair. "Uh, hello? I was going to sit there."

Madeline said nothing. Proceeded to adjust the silk hairband crowning hair so blonde it shone silver, and settled into the chair as if it were her throne.

A throne a long line of ancestors had warmed for her before passing on the birthright. Ha! As if birthrights were the only paths to thrones. Hadn't she ever heard of wars and rebellions?

Save it for the stage, Sister Bernadette's voice boomed in my head.

Considering she'd storm in here any minute—fine.

I grabbed my bag and stomped to the other end of the table. Took out my Law and Debate binder. Nothing like reviewing affirmative and negative resolutions of paying college athletes to cool down.

Except my glaze bypassed the arguments and zeroed in on the croncha brainstorm instead. I turned the page, but the outline of it bled through to the other side. Daring me to craft another shell-inspired pastry . . . Ooh, like a madeleine.

Traditionally these little sponge cakes were made from ground almonds. I snuck a peek at Madeline and my handwriting exploded. What about swapping almond flour with semi-ground Cap'n Crunch? Because these treats definitely would shred the roof of one's mouth.

"As I was saying." Madeline reached into her python-skin Hermès briefcase and pulled out her iPad. She tapped on something and began scrolling. "Junko chose MIT. Stacey, Brown." She mumbled some of the other FLOC members' names, rattling off Ivy after Ivy. "This morning Ella settled on Juilliard."

Underneath Cap'n Crunch, I wrote: *shards of glass could work too*. "What's your point, Madeline?" I peeled my face from my binder. "This is debate practice, not a FLOC meeting."

"I really wish you'd stop using that disgusting acronym. It makes the Future Leaders of Orange County sound like a flock of birds."

"That's exactly what we are. A group of birds flying to the best colleges in the US." We locked eyes. "A FLOC, if you will." Duh.

Carolina's spray-tanned skin got blotchy. Her body shook with laughter. "Birds of a feather . . ." She trailed off, laughing. Her laugh was so loud and infectious, it made me crack up.

Nina did too. Nat pressed their lips together as if trying to stop themselves from joining in.

Madeline didn't. She was too busy shooting us—me—a look. "Not all the same feather."

Every ounce of air left the auditorium. All eyes landed on me. I was very conscious of my feathers, darker than any of theirs. Much darker than most of the past debate (and FLOC) members too.

Carolina opened her lips as if to protest. Nat pushed their neon-green glasses up the bridge of their nose. At least my team had my back.

Leave it. I'm fine, I mouthed, afraid if I used my voice, even a little, I'd yell so loud it'd permanently damage my vocal cords.

"Circling back to your question, Rubi." Madeline crossed her arms. "My point is, any updates from Alma?"

Despite the AC blasting through the auditorium, I got clammy. Clammier when every gaze turned in my direction again. I didn't blame them. They simply wanted to know if they had a captain capable of making landfall . . . We'd made it to the OC tournament, after all. They were probably wondering if now was the best time to jump ship. Or even worse, mutiny.

Over my dead body.

"I told you I'm still waiting for my acceptance package to arrive in the mail," I said.

"BTW, I think they're phasing out acceptance letters and sending emails instead." I raised a brow. "Or maybe sending both. My aunt's on the board." Madeline was from one of those types of families where each member was on a board of insert-prestigious-institution. "I think she mentioned something about it last night. Since Alma was never on my radar, I wasn't paying much attention." She smiled. The pointed tips of her canines sparkled against her lipstick. "I can text her right now and see *if* you got in."

I hated how she kept doubting me. Hating more how her doubts always managed to tug at mine. All my academic accomplishments were proof I wasn't the token brown member of the FLOC or the debate team, and yet. In that moment I wished for Alma's unconditional acceptance to appear in my hands. Not only because it was the main ingredient in the Recipe. But because it'd finally shut Madeline up. It'd shut up any doubt monsters lingering inside of me too.

I put on my captain face. "Our SAT scores are nearly identical. My GPA is a 4.1—"

"Easier to do when you're two math courses behind."

Not wrong, but ouch. As I shrugged off the dig, Carolina grabbed the stopwatch from the middle of the table. Her eyes flashed between me and the on button.

I nodded. Showtime. "I've done more community service than any of our illustrious past-FLOC members. We're on the same debate team. Last year, I took us to the finals—"

"We didn't win it."

"Did you forgot I got us into the tournament this year too?" Madeline's lips flapped open to say something, but I jumped in first. "We will make it to the final round and I'll make damn sure we win." I straightened my spine. "It's not a matter of *if* I get in, but when."

Carolina clicked the stopwatch and clapped. Nina made air horn sounds. My heart pounded the way it did after winning a debate. I guess I just did.

Against Madeline. Against my doubts. As my arguments echoed in the cavernous room, it hit me. I'd also crushed the last bits of hesitation over applying to Bake-Off.

The acceptance letter *was* coming. Bake-Off wouldn't pose any risk to Alma now.

"Whatever." Madeline rolled her eyes. "I was only trying to help." She flipped through an outline, droned on about the pros of fracking.

Go frack yourself, buzzed on my lips. I pushed out, "Thanks, but no thanks," instead.

Under the table, I pulled out my phone. Bake-Off's application lit up its screen.

Somewhere backstage, clogs pounded floorboards. All chatter around the table and podiums evaporated. Even the blasts of AC ceased to hiss. The swish of Sister Bernadette's habit was more powerful anyway, prickling all our arms with goose bumps.

My fingers outpaced her march. Most of the application was filled out by the time she took command of the stage. Black habit whipped to a halt. She pushed her headpiece back a few inches, revealing a swath of hair so silver it shone like metal, forehead lines as deep as trenches. "We are only a few weeks away from the tournament." Pacing between the two podiums, she clapped and rubbed her palms together. "Are you ready to win it this year?"

The entire team erupted into cheers. Well, almost. With

my fingers glued to the phone, I couldn't clap until my palms stung. Much less do that fingers-in-mouth whistle thing Nat was doing. Sister Bernadette's voice boomed louder than any mic could. "Team, I said: Are. You. Ready?"

All the applause lifted my heart higher and higher. I snuck one last peek at the brainstorms in the margins. At Bake-Off's application.

YES. A million times, yes.

Chapter 3

I slipped in through the bakery's back door. The prep room buzzed with mixers whisking at different speeds. Metal scraped and chopped at baking stations. Bakers and decorators bantered in Spanish.

Then there was the smell of bread. Punctuating through all of it.

Notes of sugar and yeast billowed from cooling and mixing vats. The tang of dairy and spice rode on invisible currents of heat radiating from oven doors, both opened and closed. The scents followed me as I dodged bakers hauling fifty-pound bags of flour and decorators balancing multi-tiered cakes, exchanging nods and holas on the way into the employee break-slash-locker room.

I stepped to the steel trough sink. Washed my hands. Checked the whiteboard to see where I was stationed for my shift. Wrangled all wayward curls back into my topknot. Slathered lip gloss across the jack-o'-lantern-sized smile spreading across my face.

Time to shoot the application video. If the coast was clear, of course.

♥ ♥ ♥

I took my spot at the far end of the long wooden dividing table. Rubbing my hands with a thin layer of flour, I dusted the residue onto the table's surface. The dough had already been made and proofed by bakers on an earlier shift. Now Rafa, my bolillo partner for the day, and I had to shape it into loaves and bake them. "Don Rafa, discúlpame por—"

He cut off my apology for being late with a raised hand, revealing calloused fingers. The texture and color of his skin reminded me of walnut shells. "Estás aquí, eso es todo lo que importa."

I didn't think he cut me slack because I was the boss's daughter. He cut me slack because he'd watched me take notes whenever he tweaked ingredient ratios. SoCal didn't really have seasons. But in the un-air-conditioned prep room, triple-digit heat made doughs rise faster than double digits. Even the rare rainstorm could throw off calculations. With every baking-related question I asked, I'd let him glimpse inside my heart's secret chamber.

He'd seen it because he had one. Dad did too.

Speaking of Dad, I snuck a peek toward his office, tiny and tucked midway between the prep room and cake decorating room. The blinds looking out into the prep room were half-drawn. He slumped in his chair, his face behind a thick stack of papers filled with charts and checklists: inventory.

It always took him forever. He probably wouldn't get through it before my shift. Let alone get a chance to work in the prep room. The baking gods *really* wanted me to record that video.

I flinched at Rafa pounding a ball of dough onto the table. Flour blew off the table in every direction. White flecks floated down, flashing brightly as they caught the light in the room.

Exactly the type of content I needed for the audition video.

But by the time I yanked out my phone, the flashes were gone. Rafa lifted a brow at me.

"Um, está bien si grabo esto?" I asked. Explaining it was for social media. It really sucked to (sort of) lie to him, but sometimes the ends really did justify the means.

A moment of hesitation was followed by a limp shrug.

"Gracias." I tucked the phone between a mixing bowl and a bag of flour. "To prop it up correctly," I said in Spanish. Never mind it also obscured the phone from most of the bakers' views.

I hit record as he slid the ball of dough down. Catching how it slowed, then stopped, right in front of me. I squared my shoulders. "I'm Rubi Ramos, a full-time student at Immaculate Heart High and part-time baker at Rubi's Bakery in Costa Mesa."

I said nothing about the Ban on Baking. Or how these shifts were the only loopholes around it. Freshman year, I'd convinced my mother to let me work on weekends and school breaks. That way I could add Rubi's Bakery on my CV. Showing Alma's admissions board both my Cuban-immigrant parents and my first-generation status without telling them about it in my personal essay. My personal essay would be reserved to tell the story of what a great fit I'd make with Alma. My mother and I shook on the compromise. And even though it hurt at first not to experiment on new bakes at the R&D table with Dad anymore, some baking was better than none.

I dusted my fingers with flour and rubbed my palms together. "Today I'm going to be making some bolillo. Lots of people think they're like mini Hispanic baguettes. I guess they have some similarities." Dipping my hands into the dough, I squeezed it, testing for tautness with just the right amount of spring. Perfect.

I dusted my bench knife with flour before cutting the dough into symmetrical portions. With as few motions as possible, I folded and flipped the dough. "In reality though, these are their own thing." I leaned into the phone and whispered, "I can't show you the recipe. That'd be violating trade secrets."

I stepped back and adjusted the camera so the bakers working on Dad's other recipes were out of frame. "But I can show you how we still make these mostly by hand, especially how we get the crust to be more delicate and the inside even flakier than a baguette."

I stretched the dough into the beginning of an oval. "Careful here," I said. "I don't want to manipulate it so much to push out the gases or tear the gluten strands formed during kneading and proofing." I cupped and pulled the ends of the dough, molding it into a more precise oval. Then I flipped it over again, picked up the sharp chef's knife, and slashed a line down the middle of the dough. Hours of practice made it possible for me to cut long and deep enough. "This makes way for the oven's hot air to expand them, crust the outside, while preserving their signature soft middle." I looked up into the camera. "Since I'm at work, I have to keep making more, so I'm going to hit pause until I have some finished ones to show you."

I slipped the phone back into my pocket.

I repeated the process all over, and for the next few hours, I lost myself in the rhythm of baking.

I slid the last baking sheet into the rolling rack. They weren't all perfectly symmetrical. Still, their shapes looked pretty good, and they smelled mouthwatering. Grabbing onto the metal edges, I rolled my last batch to the ovens. The wheels squeaked against the floor. Rafa caught up beside me, pushing another full rack.

As I opened the oven, waves of hot air pumped out from inside. The heat flowed up our arms, over our faces. Rafa and I took out the baked ones, placed them on cooling racks. Then we started stacking the unbaked ones onto the rotating trays inside. Rafa patted me on the arm when they were all in. The stamp of approval melted me more than the rush of 400-degree heat. "Te veo en quince." He pulled a small digital timer from his pocket, setting it to fifteen minutes.

I nodded, keeping my eyes on the seconds ticking off his clock. Time was running out for me to upload the video. Instead of following him outside for a break, I pressed my back against the oven. The sounds of the prep room faded until all there was left was the oven's motor, thrumming inside my bones.

I visualized what was happening on the other side of the oven's door. How the loaves of dough were hardening, transforming into bolillos because of chemistry and heat.

Broken down to its smallest particle, baking was edible alchemy. A communal combination of science and magic.

And when I got into Alma, I'd have to give it all up.

But if I got into Bake-Off, I could hang on to it a little bit longer.

I moved to the tray of cooling bolillos. Melted butter and the tang of yeast gave me a final boost of confidence. I pressed record. "Well, guys, what do you think? Dough I have what it takes for Bake-Off?"

Please say yes.

Later that night, I'd planned to pro and con trade embargoes for Law and Debate. Instead, I edited my bakery footage, uploaded it to the site, and hit send.

The entry flew into the internet with a *swoosh*.

It reverberated inside of me with a bang.

Chapter 4

Perched on the corner of my bed, I toggled back and forth between Bake-Off's website and my inbox. The corners of the unfinished Law and Debate spreadsheet peered from behind them like a guilty secret. Not now, you. I clicked it away. Checked my email again. No news yet. Just like with Alma.

I exhaled and dropped my laptop onto the mattress, changed out of my pajamas, and threw on *Lord of the Rings* leggings and a Rubi's Bakery polo. At least my shift later would keep me away from the screen for a few hours.

Grabbing my phone, I was about to refresh the inbox when something metallic clicked outside my window.

The mailbox snapping shut louder than ever before.

Storming through my house, I threw the front door open in time to see Samuel hop back into his idling truck. "Sammy," I called out from the porch, panting. "Anything from Alma U?"

Samuel glanced back slowly. So slowly, I wondered if his head was caught in an invisible bowl of batter. Then our eyes met. He stepped on the accelerator and hurtled down the road.

A chill spread up my limbs, crystallizing into two realizations. Alma U had finally sent news. And it was anything but good.

Dear Rubi Ramos,

We appreciate the thoughtfulness and hard work you put into your application and acknowledge your strong interest in Alma University. After careful consideration and a thorough review of your candidacy, we are offering you a place on our waitlist.

Your application demonstrated great promise, and you are a part of a select group to be reevaluated by the admissions committee. It is important to know we rank students on our waitlist and you are in the top 5 percent. The strong potential in your application was evident and we will accept additional information such as current semester grades, extracurricular achievements, recommendations, and/or interviews within the thirty-day reevaluation window.

We appreciate your patience and willingness to be flexible. I hope you understand how impressed we are with your application and how much we value your interest in Alma University.

Sincerely,
Addison Teague
Dean of Admissions

I stepped away from the mailbox, away from whatever dimension I'd inadvertently stumbled into. A blur of black flew overhead. Discordant sets of caws screeched with it.

The letter slipped from my hands, landed noiselessly on the driveway. The spray of crows kept circling. Shadows shifted one way. Rays of sun scudded another. It all made the driveway—no, the letter—ripple with otherworldly light.

Somehow, I whipped up the courage to crouch down and pick the letter up. Against the bone-white page, the words stayed the same.

Alma had waitlisted me.

Why did this happen? *How* had it happened? I'd followed all the steps in the Recipe so far. Captain of the debate team . . . a member of the FLOC . . . I was supposed to be a shoo-in.

I turned the letter over, looked for an explanation. My fingers moved across the page's edges, double-checking for the magic button to scramble all the words to make them right.

The only thing that did was give me a paper cut. A single drop of blood welled onto the corner of the page. And because the same blood flowed in my parents' veins, their blood spilled on it too.

Oh my god. What was I going to say to my parents?

What were they going to say to me?

When the blood stopped welling, tears threatened to take its place. I blinked fast to keep them back. It only made the letter look even more ripply, strobing. One word seemed to strobe brightest of all.

"Reevaluation." My voice was ragged, with the tiniest tinge of relief.

Reevaluation was not flat-out rejection.

Alma had given me thirty days to persuade them I was worthy.

Law and Debate's last tournament would take place during this time frame. So would my Trig midterm. If Madeline—holy crap, I was going to have to tell Madeline.

My cheeks burned with the fire of a hundred ovens. Here was her chance to publicly humiliate me in front of the FLOC. And crawling back to her, asking her to talk to her aunt on my behalf? The very thought sent me to the brink of dry heaves.

Deep breaths. There had to be a way to bypass the dragon

altogether. Find another FLOC member who knew someone on Alma's board willing to sit down with me for a last-minute interview.

Hope tiptoed in. So did Devon's advice from earlier. *Hiding things from our parents is in our DNA. It's our teenage duty.*

My mother's plate was full with the newest bakery they'd recently opened in Santa Ana. Dad's too since he now ran the original Costa Mesa location. A good daughter wouldn't dream of piling on more. Especially since I had a shot of fixing this without them ever knowing.

Not telling them was the right thing to do for them.

Considering I couldn't stomach seeing them look at me like their worst investment ever, it was also the right thing to do for me.

With that settled, the time had come for another impromptu debate: What's the best way to destroy the waitlist letter—sudden death round.

Burning it on the stove? Nope. My mother's nose would definitely pick up on the scents of charred paper and failure. Trash? Even ripped into a million little pieces and scattered throughout the house (hell, the neighborhood), she'd somehow piece them back together. Trash disposal? Absolutely not. The magnitude of the letter would probably break the motor.

I rose from the driveway on shaky knees.

Maybe it was the Gollum leggings I wore. Or how a few seconds ago, the letter had gotten all glowy with shadow and light. Because when I looked at the letter again, I thought about the Ring.

"Fire," I said. My voice echoed Gandalf's at the council to destroy the Ring. Maybe burning was the best option. Only not inside the house. Because Matteo Beach's firepits were the closest I was going to ever get to Mount Doom, I got into my car and drove.

♥ ♥ ♥

I pushed forward to the firepits, flip-flops crunching on wind-crusted sand. Even though it neighbored Pelican Point, the wind blew stronger and the waves grew taller here in Matteo Beach.

At a firepit, I read the letter one last time. Committed it to memory. Grades, extracurricular achievements, interview. I dug my hand into my messenger bag. Smooth edges of binders grazed my fingertips. So did the textured spines of AP textbooks—and the curves of the cake mold I always had with me. Unbaked recipes pounded against my heart again.

It felt dangerous to keep touching its cool steel. Nowhere near as dangerous as walking into the bakery in less than an hour with Alma's waitlist letter still intact, so. "Come on. Where are you?"

Finally, my fingers made contact with the lighter I'd used last week to light Devon's birthday cake.

I pressed down on the wheely thing with a *click*. A weak flame flickered in the salty breeze. I dipped a corner of the waitlist letter into it.

The breeze tried its best to snuff out the fire spreading across the page. I fed it fresh flame after fresh flame so it wouldn't go out. One by one, sentences charred and curled. Mid-page, I let go.

The fire became hungrier inside the firepit. Eating the page until nothing except bits and pieces of crumbled ash remained.

Relief vanished in a rush of dread. Pulling the phone from my pocket to call Devon, I had to keep my fingers from tapping the inbox.

What the hell was wrong with me? Was I seriously about to check if Bake-Off had accepted me? Now? When I was on the verge of Alma's rejection? Get it together.

Devon's number went straight to voicemail. I tried Torie's

next, considering all their recent hangouts. Only Torie's went to voicemail too. Without my friends to comfort me, it was easier for the weight of the morning to creep in and surround me.

It pressed down on my shoulders. Squeezed my lungs. Dragged me down to the sand.

I drew my knees up like a shield. Wrapped my arms around my legs, gave myself the hug I so desperately needed. While the rest of the beachgoers frolicked in the sun, I had to tell the FLOC what'd happened. And I needed one of them to be able to come to my rescue.

Mortification and insecurity poured from my fingers as I sent text after text. Within seconds, lines of gray bubbles appeared on my phone. All of them turned into variations on *sorry that sucks, sorry don't know anyone,* and worst of all, *Madeline does.*

My palms got so sweaty the phone nearly slipped from my hands.

Yesterday I'd basically told her to shove it. Today, I had to swallow my pride and ask—maybe even beg—for her help.

I wanted to unleash my wrath at the irony. Maybe even cry about it. I tried to take a breath, but the mouthfuls of briny air kept getting stuck in my throat. As if I needed even more salt to rub into this wound.

Hey Madeline, remember how you offered to contact your aunt for me? My fingers trembled as I typed. Would you still be down to do it for me? Ask her if she's willing to set up an interview? Alma waitlisted me.

The text sent a spasm of humiliation through me so fierce I thought I was going to be sick.

Minutes stretched further than the island in the distance, further than the entire swath of sea. And just when I thought I was SOL, the phone buzzed with a text.

Of course. The phone pinged again with another. I'd love to

help. One more chime. I'll email you a plan in a few. Each text felt like a stab to the stomach. Then she went in for the kill.

A winky-face emoji. Its open eye glinted in the sun so bright, I had to glance away.

True to her future politician self, Madeline's "help" would undoubtedly come at a cost. Wondering whether I'd be able to pay it pushed my already ragged breath to the edge of hyperventilation. Seeing how I didn't have any paper bags handy, I dragged my messenger bag closer and pulled out the next best thing.

The cake mold.

I lay on the sand and covered my face with it. Under the mold's dark gray steel, I took one deep breath and then another. I inhaled deeply. So deep, for a split second, when I breathed in, I could smell traces of past bakes.

The soggy attempt at a tres leches. Double-tiered vanilla caramel. A huge corn mantecada muffin. I kept inhaling, going further and further until I hit on the very first one.

That day, my mother had given me a plastic red pail and yellow shovel. We'd just moved from Anaheim to Pelican Point. She'd told Dad to bring me down to the beach, maybe even to a spot exactly like this. I'd grabbed a handful of sand. Loosened my fingers a bit.

I sifted the sand between them like I'd seen him do so many times with dry mixes inside the prep room. The sand sprinkled down in a rainbow of colors. Rock-sugar pink. Tan oat. Gingerbread brown. "Are you sure sand isn't flours and sugars and spices all mixed together?" I asked in Spanish. He smiled. Lines formed around his eyes, making it look like they were smiling too.

"Sí, mija." He hunched over and gave me a kiss on the head. "Pero, shh. Es nuestro secreto."

From that day on, we swapped the pail and shovel set for an

old cake mold. Instead of building sandcastles we baked sand cakes. And even though it'd been years since we last used it, I always kept it close.

Nostalgia? Some sort of lucky charm? Now it felt like I'd held on to it for this exact moment.

The roar of the ocean rushed back in. So did the footsteps of people stepping around me. The warm sand began to melt some of the knots in my muscles. I patted the sand next to me. Latching onto the hard edges of my phone, I pressed the button on its side and said, "Open text thread with Devon."

The phone pinged with the sound of the thread opening. My fingers flew reflexively over the keyboard, and without removing the mold, I typed, Call me 911. The text flew through the air with a *swoosh*.

"And here I was beginning to think superheroes were just figments of Stan Lee's imagination." The voice boomed from somewhere above me. Slowly, I lifted the mold off my face.

Two silhouettes blocked out the hard sun. The shapes came into focus as my vision adjusted to the light. One of them revealed itself to be a longboard. The other, the smoking-hot, dripping-wet guy who'd surfed it.

Chapter 5

"Can you only see through metal or other things too?" he asked.

Forget metal. I wanted to be able to see through his wetsuit. Surfer boy must've read my mind because he reached behind him and pulled down on something sounding like a zipper.

Oh my god. It was a zipper.

He freed his arms from the neoprene sleeves. Rolled the top of his wetsuit down his torso, slinging drops of salt water in the process.

A few hit me. My skin sizzled on contact. It heated up when he sat next to me. Hotter still when he leaned back on long, sculpted arms. Beads of water and grains of sand breaded his biceps. Down the length of his sinewy torso too, making surfer boy sparkle under the sun. AP Anatomy hadn't prepared me for a body like his. AP Physiology even less for the way mine was responding to his.

A smile wriggled to the corners of his mouth when he caught me staring. Curling my toes into the sand, I took my attention somewhere safer—his hands. A streaky coat of sunscreen let a smattering of freckles on the backs of them peek through. The same colored freckles dotted other parts of him too.

A spray of them across the bridge of his nose. *Stop looking.*

A trail of them started at his belly button and went down. *Keep looking.*

He caught me staring. Again. Making his smile grow wide enough to flash all his teeth.

I cleared my throat. Tried to find the right words to rebut his assumption that I was checking him out. Considering I was totally checking him out, only half of my brain cells were firing. So, I thought it was a good idea to go with "You got me totally wet by the way."

We stared at each other, processing what I'd said. The beach closed in around me. I wanted to bury myself in the sand for the rest of my days.

Thankfully he burst out laughing, with a few snorts so deliciously loud and hilarious I couldn't help but join in. "I meant my shirt." I blotted the spots where he'd drizzled me during his striptease.

"My apologies." He lay on his side, propped his head up with an open palm. Stared at me with cilantro-green eyes flecked with copper specks. The reddish color almost perfectly matched his hair. Even while wet, it made me think of fire. "Although you should know by now getting wet is a foreseeable hazard of close proximity to the beach." His lips twisted into a grin.

"Moot court or debate?" I hoped he didn't hear the edge in my voice. As soon as I'd gotten into Immaculate Heart, my mother "suggested" I explore "real" extracurricular activities outside of experimenting with bakes at home. When I made the Law and Debate team, the suggestion turned into the beginning of the Ban. "I'm on debate myself," I said. As much as I loved it, my relationship status with it had always been complicated. "At Immaculate Heart."

He looked at the stitching above my polo's pocket. If he

wondered why it spelled out Rubi's Bakery instead of Immaculate Heart, he didn't mention it. "Moot court at Lazarus High," he said. "What gave it away?"

"Only future lawyers use 'foreseeable,' 'hazard,' and 'proximity' in one sentence."

"To know that means you're a future lawyer too. Plus, you can see through metal? Impressive."

"Future lawyer, yes. But why do you think I can see through metal?"

"Because you had that over your face." He motioned the cake mold beside me. "While you were texting. I'm Ryan, by the way. Ryan O'Reilly."

He extended his hand. A cluster of freckles on the back of it looked like they formed the Orion constellation. Huh, so this guy was apparently made of fire and stars. I took his hand and shook it. "Rubi Ramos."

"Total superhero name," Ryan said.

"Like yours isn't?"

"I'm not the one able to see through metal."

"If you must know, it's steel. Not metal." I yanked my hand away before it permanently glued to his. "Steel distributes heat evenly. This is why it's preferred amongst bakers, even if it requires more maintenance than, say, aluminum." I hadn't meant to get all Martha Stewart on him. With thoughts of Bake-Off apparently still lingering, it just poured out.

"Whoa," Ryan said, crouching closer. "So you're a baker too?" There were no hints of condescension in his voice, like Madeline. Or tones of disapproval, like my mother. Only curiosity and genuine interest.

"Yes. No." I took a deep breath. "I mean sometimes I work at my parents' bakery. Rubi's Bakery. They have two. The new one in Santa Ana opened a few weeks ago, but I work at the original one in Costa Mesa."

"Awesome."

"Tell it to my mother," I said, but had only meant to think. I flicked my gaze away, to the crowded pier hovering above the sea. When I looked back up at Ryan, his eyes locked on mine.

"So yours too, huh?" Ryan pushed back the damp locks sticking to his cheek. They tumbled over half of his face again when he lowered his chin. He stuck his index finger in the sand. Started drawing circles within circles.

Despite cutting into thousands of grains of shifting sand, the circles were nearly perfect in their symmetry. If I hadn't been watching him so intently, I would've missed the way his hand twitched on the last one.

Something about it, about how the fire in his irises dimmed at the mention of parents, made me think maybe he had a secret wall around his heart too.

I wanted to ask him when he'd built it. So badly wanted to see what he kept locked inside. Whatever it was, did it sometimes try to pound its way out? How often did he have to reinforce the walls' sides to make sure it didn't?

I pressed my lips together though. The weird mix of family, sacrifice, and duty that went into those questions made them AP-level difficult to answer. Let alone try to explain to someone he'd barely met.

Then his stomach growled. His cheeks got red. At least my brown skin concealed the way I undoubtedly blushed too.

Ryan reached into some hidden pocket on the side of his wetsuit, and opened a Halloween-sized bag of Peanut M&M's. He offered the candy to me first.

"My mother taught me never to take candy from strangers," I said, smiling.

He smiled right back. "Good thing we're not strangers."

He was right. We didn't feel like strangers. Not anymore.

We ate the M&M's, popping them into our mouths one at a time and chewing slowly, as if wanting to stretch out time. The bursts of sugar and chocolate and peanut made me think of the croncha again. I wanted to tell him about it. About Bake-Off.

Instead, I watched his hand flick another M&M into his mouth. "Has anyone ever told you the freckles on the back of your hand form the Orion constellation?"

He stopped chewing. Looked down at his hand. A big, irrepressible smile spread across his face. As if he'd been waiting his entire life for someone to notice. "Only you," he said.

"If you were a superhero your alias could be Orion."

"What would my superpowers be?"

Bright sun glinted off his hair. Salt-stiffened tousles of reds and rust weaved through the rest of his damp hair like flames. "Something with heat. Something with fire."

"Because of my hair?"

I shrugged. *Yes, but because of your everything else too.*

"Orion," he said, testing the alias out.

"Super cheesy, I know, but I like it."

"I like it too." The lilt in his voice made me think he'd really been talking about me. I hoped he'd really been talking about me.

"Next time, I'll have an alias ready for you too."

Sure. Next time.

As if I could spare extra hours for a "next time." Inside my bag, the phone vibrated between the books and cake mold, jarring me out of self-pity.

I peeked into my bag. Devon's name flashed one more time before it vanished from the screen. Then a text from her popped up. RUBES WHAT HAPPENED??!! The devastation of the wait-list letter broke over me again.

"Hey, is everything okay?" Ryan asked.

"No, yes. I mean, um, I have to go."

"Like right now?"

If I didn't leave now I'd be late for my shift at the bakery. And because I was never late for my shift, Dad would ask why. Today of all days I needed to avoid arousing parental suspicions. No matter how much I'd loved this detour with Ryan, I rose to my feet. "Like right now."

"Okay. Let me at least walk you to your car." He started to get up.

I waved him down. "It's cool." If he walked me to my car we'd probably end up exchanging info. As much as it pained me to admit, the last thing I needed right now was a distraction. "Thanks for the candy."

Slowly, I turned and walked away from him. I didn't know if I really could feel the heat from his gaze burning between my shoulder blades. The nape of my neck. The backs of my thighs. Or if I simply wanted to feel it.

My whole body yelled to turn around and check. Only nothing good came from getting one last look for the road. Thank you, Greek mythology.

So I kept dragging my feet across the sand. I texted Devon back, told her all about the disaster. Then I fixed my gaze straight forward. Or as my mother would say, pa'lante.

I took one step, pa'lante. Then another, and another. Until I stepped off the sand and disappeared into the crowds of downtown Matteo Beach.

Chapter 6

Flour hung in the air outside the bakery's back door. Its wire mesh let the rise and fall of voices and equipment through. The sounds swelled with each step closer.

A ping of a new email drowned them all out.

Whatever Madeline had finally sent cracked thick and heavy over me. I stopped midstep, tapped my inbox to face it.

Orange County Bake-Off: Congratulations, Bakers! Welcome to OC's 1st Annual Competition!

Whatever dread had been curdling in my stomach began to melt. I blinked and blinked and yet, the words in the subject line stayed put. *Congratulations, Bakers*? I tapped the email to make sure this meant what I hoped it did.

The email opened to a photo of what looked like an entire bakery stacked on top of a table. Tiered cakes towered high atop porcelain platters. Loaves of bread piled on wooden cutting boards. Trays covered with every type of cookie imaginable. The weight of it all sank the table's legs into caramel sand.

Three people stood behind it. Their smiles were big.

The one spreading across my face, bigger. I enlarged the photo to read the orange piping written across the chocolate cake they all held. "Welcome to OC's Bake-Off," I squealed, loud enough that several people moving through the parking lot cocked their heads my way.

I waved the screen high for all to see.

So what if I was causing a scene? This was no waitlist. It was a huge, unconditional serving of *yes.*

It didn't just make me proud or excited. Under my feet, I could almost feel the world tilt itself upright, its core starting to spin again. In the right direction this time.

I pushed my shoulders back and scrolled down the email's text: *The competition will consist of four bakes. Each will be tasted and judged by International Pastry Diva Madame Aminata Terese and the Bad Boy of Bread Johnny Oliver.*

International Pastry Diva? Bad Boy of Bread? I licked my lips, huddled even closer to the screen. Instead of asking myself, *What if I entered?* I dared myself to wonder, *What if I won?*

I tilted my chin toward the prep room's door, breathed in the possibilities. Unbiased proof of my baking abilities. The courage to tell Dad I missed concocting bakes with him. Showing him all the bakes that only lived in the margins of my notebooks—or inside the chambers of my heart. My mother seeing baking in a different light. I turned back to the phone and kept reading.

For the Cookie Try-Out Round, the judges knead to know if your recipes and Bake-Off are a batch made in heaven. Bring us your tried, tested, and tastiest cookies this Sunday at 1 p.m. to find out.

Sunday. Only two days away.

I dialed Devon's number as the prep room door opened. Rafa held the door open. Out came Dad. He carried a stack of pink boxes piled so high they covered half of his face—and conveniently also hid most of mine from his view.

"Hi, Dad, bye, Dad," I said, "Have a good delivery. See you when you get back."

He might've mumbled something, but I'd already stepped into the prep room and left him on the other side.

♥ ♥ ♥

"Dev, I know I've left you a million messages already." I glanced at the large clock above the doorway. Only two minutes before Rafa needed me back at the carrot cake station. "But I did it, Dev. I got into Bake-Off!" I sucked in a mouthful of air. "I just got the official email and I'm in. Did I mention I'm in?!" I sounded as giddy as I felt. "Call me back." I plugged my phone back into the socket. I turned around, the unexpected sight of Dad standing in the doorway made me almost jump out of my flip-flops. "You scared the crap out of me!"

He fanned his face with a stack of papers. Aside from the smile tugging the corners of his lips, his face showed no signs of him having overheard my voicemail. "How's school going?"

"It's going." Vague wasn't lying. Neither were omissions. Those were some of my favorite tricks from Law and Debate. "As much as I'd love to chat, I gotta rush back to grate those carrots or else Rafa's gonna kill me."

Dad too if I told him the truth. Because as much as he loved to let me bend the Ban, this was certainly a parabola too steep . . . even for him.

"Not so fast, Rubi." He crossed his arms across his chest. "Isn't there something we need to celebrate?"

A lump formed in my throat. Oh no. Had he heard the voicemail? "Nope. Nothing to celebrate here."

He grabbed me by the arm. Pulled me through the doorway.

My lips parted, ready to ask him why he was dragging me into the prep room. He beat me to the punch by speaking—no—shouting first.

"¡Todos! Rubi acaba de ser aceptada en la Universidad de Alma."

At his announcement, every single head in the prep room pivoted in his direction, mine included. WHAT?

My heart hammered against my eardrums. It was nothing compared to the thunder erupting from every corner of the prep room. Bakers I'd known my entire life rushed over to us. They shook hands with him. With me. Every clap, every pat on the back felt like a bee's sting. After the swarm lifted, comprehension dawned.

So he *had* heard me on the phone with Devon. Or at least the last part when I'd gushed, *I'm in*.

Rafa elbowed his way through the small crowd of bakers. He pulled me into a tight hug and asked in Spanish, "Rubi, why didn't you tell me when we were grating carrots?" There was no accusation or suspicion in his voice. The knots in my stomach doubled. Tripled. And whatever came after quadruple.

"I-I um," my voice left me. Fabiola, the head cake decorator, yanked me away for a hug of her own. My confession stalled for a moment longer.

I peeled away from her and conjured all the courage inside of me to tell everyone Dad had misunderstood. I lifted my head up, hoping the monologue for the truth was written somewhere on the ceiling.

When I brought my gaze down, all eyes were on me, waiting.

In the bright lights of the prep room, I read their expressions so clearly. Pride. Happiness. Excitement.

And something else harder to translate, but it was there, flashing beneath everything else: gratitude.

They looked at me like they were grateful I'd honored the risks and reasons they'd come here. As we worked together in the prep room, it was both impossible and easy to forget the majority of them had immigrated here. Like my parents.

Now I was living proof that the American Dream could be real. For them. For their kids and grandkids.

I dropped my gaze to my feet. I couldn't stomach faces shattering with disappointment when I told them proof would have to wait a little longer. They couldn't bottle this moment just yet.

Timers rang out through waning cheers. Bakes demanded attention and bakers began making their way to different parts of the prep room. The moment to correct the misunderstanding was slipping away.

I let it.

I buried my face into Dad's arms. From the outside, it looked like one last celebratory hug. In reality, I sought asylum until I figured a way out of this mess.

I tightened my grip over him. Like an amateur father-daughter tango duo, I steered him out of the prep room and nudged him toward the office. We stumbled through the door.

"Enough dancing for one day, Rubi." He chuckled. "I can't believe you didn't tell me the second you found out." He sat on the edge of his desk. "Then again, I should've figured you wanted to wait until tonight when the Boss came home so you could tell us the good news together."

Tell. Us. The. Good. News. Together.

My soul left my body then. Because the only way this mess could get any worse was to involve my mother. The air went from warm to oppressively thick. "Dad." I unclenched my jaw, tried to find the words to tell him the truth. "When I said—"

A set of arms wrapped around us from behind. They smooshed me deep into Dad's armpits. Smothered out the rest of my confession.

In the space between his arm and his torso, I found the hands that held us together.

Her fingers were calloused, her nails perfectly manicured. The skin on the backs of her hands, yearbooks of manual labor, and yet . . . The raised nicks and pink divots etched into her skin showed off her resistance to flames. Showed off how she'd stitched herself back together each time the world tried to break her.

Spidey had his suit. Cap, his shield.

Rosa Ramos had these scars.

My eyes flicked from her scars to mine.

A tiny spot of pink. A few dark beige lines that blended more naturally on my tan skin. A haiku compared to her anthology. But they were there. Inextricably connecting us. And I loved them for it.

"I knew you'd be able to do it, mija." Every word rose in pitch, swinging wildly between accents. "Pa'lante!" She spun me around, drew me in for a rare hug. "How does getting into Alma feel?"

My shoulders contracted under the weight of my epic failure. Somehow, I found the courage to look her in the face. To cobble together bits and pieces of the truth and spit out the confession once and for all.

Her smile spread. Dimples deepened. All at once, her face unleashed images of an unfurling rose.

Rosa. The name fit her so perfectly in this moment.

I didn't know whether her petals had fallen off slowly over time. Or whether they'd been sheared off in a single clip. Right now though, because of me, she was blooming.

I wanted to make sure she stayed that way. "Better than I ever dreamed."

The lie tasted bitter. It went down sweet.

When I got home, I barreled into my room and slammed the door. Maybe the lie and the guilt would be trapped on the other side of it.

Nope. They were already waiting inside my room. I kicked the rug by my bed, as if shooing them under it. Forcing them back to the place where all monsters were supposed to hide during the day.

I crossed my room to the small desk against the far window. Plopping into the chair, I did the only thing I could. I picked up a pen and got down to work.

Recipe for Getting Off the Waitlist:

1. *Nail interview with ~~someone on Alma's board of admissions~~ Madeline's aunt*
2. *Win Law and Debate tournament*
3. *Break into the 5 percent of my class by acing Trig midterm*
4. *Hire math tutor (see above)*

I tore the plan of attack from my Law and Debate binder and held it up to the open window. Late-afternoon light shone through it. The orangey glow highlighted a key ingredient: I didn't have an entire semester to accomplish these tasks.

On account of it being mid-April—and spring break—the best tutors would probably be incommunicado until the end of next week. Whittling away Alma's thirty-day window to twenty-three. At best.

My hand quivered from the weight of it all. I lowered the list and slumped against the chair. The hardwood didn't steady me. If anything, it felt like my back was up against a wall. With thoughts of walls, my mind went to the worst possible one. Not being able to crack through the one surrounding Alma U. It was impossible to scrub my mother's joyful face—everyone's faces—from my thoughts.

I stuffed the list back into the binder, yanked the laptop from my bag. *I will get off the waitlist. I have no other choice.*

Flipping the laptop open, I decided to start crossing off the tasks with the hardest one. The interview.

My fingers flew across the keys, asking Madeline what her ETA was on her plan. Before I hit send, her name popped up in my inbox, right next to the subject line: *Emergency Future Leaders of Orange County meeting this weekend*. I tapped the email.

Dear Future Leaders,

Alma University has waitlisted Ruby Ramos. Understandably, this situation is cause for concern. Concern for Ruby's future, but more importantly concern for the reputation of the Future Leaders of Orange County. Such a turn of events could tarnish our club's twenty-two-year history of 100 percent acceptance rate. As Future Leader president, I am hard at work to make sure this doesn't happen.

For those of you enjoying the tropics or Rivieras during spring break, please continue doing so. Post pics please :) For those of you staycationing, I'm calling an emergency meeting this Sunday at 3 p.m. to discuss Ruby's situation. See some of you there.

Very Best,
Madeline Crowley

I stared at the email. Ground her words through my teeth. Madeline claimed she was hard at work. But hard at work doing what exactly?

Spelling my name wrong? CC-ing the entire FLOC to show them what a good ally she was being by helping me fix the screwup? Or convincing them I was the screwup?

So what if the rest of the FLOC had gotten into their Ivies on their first shot without complications. It didn't mean I wasn't as smart or as good as the rest of them. Right?

I slammed the laptop shut.

After a few ragged breaths I heard Sister Bernadette's voice. *Save it for the stage*. She was right. I shouldn't let Madeline's crap get to me. Not now. Not with everything on the line.

I flipped the laptop open again. Deleted her make-the-FLOC-great-again crap from my inbox.

Which made Bake-Off's email rise to the top.

I couldn't help but read it again. Only this time, the rose-colored glasses were off. A drum solo started in my chest. I immediately fished Madeline's email from the trash, scrolling to the end.

She'd set the meeting for the same day as Bake-Off's first challenge. Two hours later. Plus, the Ban threw a wrench into having to bring a batch of cookies to the competition.

I slumped against the chair. Deleted the right email this time.

"Well, that's the way the cookie crumbles." I closed the laptop. The afterimage of Bake-Off's email blinked behind my eyelids. The details grew hazier and hazier, then vanished, along with the last few stirrings of hope.

I tugged my binder closer. Back to Sister Bernadette's list of assigned Law and Debate topics: the electoral college, binge watching, and censoring offensive language in books. Pro and conned each side until the pages blurred. My breath caught in the back of my throat, which always happened before I cried.

I told myself I had nothing to cry about, and yet. I cradled my head between my hands, pressed my thumbs into my temples, and blinked back tears. Of all people, I should've known it was impossible to have my cake and eat it too.

Chapter 7

Without Bake-Off, the bakery needed to be my consolation. Before hunkering down to study for the rest of the day, I went in to work an early shift. Finishing cutting sheets of chocolate sponge, I took them to the refrigerator so they could cool down before the decorators piped them with whipped cream and ornaments.

The fridge was really a room the size of most walk-in closets in a Pelican Point master suite. Only instead of protecting tall heels or huge handbags, it slowed the rise of fermented doughs, and kept eggs, dairy, fruits, and flowers fresh. I placed the warm sponge on the racks next to finished cakes ready to be picked up.

If summer brought weddings, then spring brought bachelorette parties. I walked to the shelf holding all the cakes rated PG-13. And R. One cake was essentially a fondant chiseled torso. I stepped close enough to count the muscles. Hmm, these abs had nothing on Ryan's.

"I have a pencil and paper if you want to take notes," a voice said from behind me.

I whirled around, mortified, to discover Fabiola holding open the refrigerator room's door. Her hair was pulled back into a bun at the base of her neck. Teal eyeliner traced lashes batting against eyes filled with laughter. She let go of the handle and walked in. "With all the money tus papás are spending on your fancy school, you'd think they'd teach you basic anatomía."

"This is not basic anatomy." I tried joking off my humiliation. "No one really looks like this." Except Ryan of course.

Maybe I could go to Matteo Beach again and "bump" into him. The very notion of it was enough to send flares of heat through me. The swooshes of cold air, mixed with an enormous helping of common sense, iced the idea. Any distractions needed to wait until after I got into Alma.

"And besides, I go to a Catholic school, remember? You can't blame me for being a little curious."

She chuckled and patted me on the shoulder as she made her way to the stand of flowers. "I guess not, mija." She combed through several buckets, probably searching for the perfect combination. "Speaking of school, you'll be able to feed your curiosity soon enough." Fabiola glanced back from the flowers and winked.

I looked at her, blinked and blinked.

"Rubi?"

And then it hit me. "Alma! You're talking about Alma."

"Yes, silly." She tapped her chin and watched me through narrowing eyelids. "It's only a few months away. There will be boys there."

"Right." I chewed my lip. "Sorry, the last twenty-four hours have been such a whirlwind, I still can't think straight." I forced a laugh, trying hard not to choke on it.

Her real laugh mixed with my fake one. "Of course you can't, mija, you got into Alma! A million congratulations again."

My cheeks burned. The cold air did nothing to cool them

this time. I turned around so I didn't have to keep holding her gaze.

"So why do people order these?" I nudged our conversation back to neutral ground. "I mean I appreciate that they do." My mother did too. She used the sales of bachelorette cakes to project the sales of wedding cakes and budget accordingly. A true Boss through and through. "But they're just so—"

"Fun, Rubi. They are fun y necesarios."

"Necessary?" I watched her pluck white roses and pink peonies from the containers of flowers. My fingers itched to give her some herbs to add to the mix.

"People need to go out with a bang."

I exploded with laughter. "If people went out with a bang, I think the wedding would be canceled."

Fabiola bopped me on the head with the flowers. "Fine. Not *bang*. ¿Pero cómo se dice? ¿Una última celebración? A last hooray?"

"I think you mean a last hurrah."

"Pues, eso." She placed the flowers on a counter and moved to the racks with round sheets of vanilla sponge, checking the order form hanging above them before pulling two out. "One last hurrah. A celebration to say goodbye."

I'd always assumed parties and cakes were meant to celebrate the beginning of something. Not the end of it. Maybe it was important to celebrate both.

"Bueno," Fabiola said. "I have to go finish a cake before José picks me up."

"Wait." I sprinted across the room to the shelf holding all the fresh herbs. "What about these?" I plucked and held up sprigs of fresh rosemary and sage. "They'd look good bunched up with the flowers on top. Or cascading down the side. Adds more color and texture, don't you think?"

Fabiola took the sprigs and held them next to the roses and peonies. She grinned. "Has anyone told you you're good at this?"

♥ ♥ ♥

When it was time for my lunch break, I nabbed a slice of the chocolate sponge I'd baked, topped it with a slice of flan. I poured myself a cup of Cuban coffee. Grabbed a white chocolate and macadamia nut cookie from one of the display cases, and headed out back.

On Dad's reserved parking spot, he'd set up a small table and chairs for the employees to use on breaks. I plopped into a chair at the empty table to work on a 2,500-page essay on the life of Pythagoras for Trig extra credit.

Every now and then, the squawk of a gull or the crunch of tires on the gravel would pull me out of my essay. I'd take a bite of the cookie, a sip of the coffee, then lower my head and get back to writing.

Until I heard the slap of flip-flops round the corner. They were loud, determined.

I craned my neck up. Obviously, the day's heat—and emotional whiplash—were getting to me. Because there was no way RYAN WAS ACTUALLY CROSSING THE PARKING LOT RIGHT NOW.

I bit the inside of my cheek as if that would bring me back to my senses, make this delicious mirage disappear.

Thankfully, it didn't. Ryan only moved closer. And closer.

He blinked against the sun, against the damp and dry tousles skimming his eyelids. His gaze fell on me like spotlights. And even though the table covered half of my body, I felt him take all of me in.

He stopped at the table. Surveyed my outfit . . . from my seafoam painted nails to my mass of hair. I'd thought the unwashed, two-day-old curls spiraled too big against my back. From the way Ryan smiled though, maybe not.

"Rubi Ramos, we meet again."

"Ryan, what are you doing here? I mean I'm super—" I bit my lip. The sun made the reddish flecks in his irises burn brighter. My cheeks—my everything—flamed. I fanned myself with the half-finished essay before I caught fire and set off every single fire alarm within a five-mile radius. "Is it just me or is it super hot today?"

"Super hot," Ryan said. "Even hotter than yesterday." Spots of pink mottled his neck, which made me wonder if we were actually talking about the weather. I smiled hugely in case we weren't. "Can I sit?" He gestured to the empty chair.

"Where are my manners? Of course. Yes. Please."

He slid into the chair. "Well, to answer your first question, I was on my way to get a coffee down at Sun Goat when I saw your place." He tucked some hair behind his ear. "The lady up front said you were on your break. Figured I'd be a gentleman and ask if you wanted to grab one with me." Despite sitting, my knees wobbled. "It's right down the block."

He draped an arm over the back of the chair. I identified the contours of his deltoids, rhomboids, and triceps. Each one of them perfectly filled and stretched the cotton fibers of his green shirt. Too bad I needed a math tutor and not an anatomy one.

Ogling, the pen slipped from my fingers.

He bent over to pick it up.

The bottom hem of his shirt rode up, exposing a swath of skin on his lower back. Allspice-colored freckles dusted it. Sparsely though, in the same casual way they flecked the backs of his hands, the high cheekbones cutting the planes of his face. They looked more like tiny embers than freckles. Embers kindling the flames that were his hair.

His fingers grazed mine when he handed the pen back to me.

Yup. Ryan's superpower definitely involved fire.

"Well, what d'ya say?" he asked. "My treat."

"I, um." I took a tiny sip of my coffee, desperately wanting to get another one with him. And then, I chugged the rest in one gulp. Caffeine, please wake me up to what really matters.

The waitlist required a distraction-less me. And Ryan—as much as I wanted to convince myself otherwise—was a walking billboard for Distraction City. "Sorry, I just finished this one."

He frowned a little, then brightened up. "Fine, but before I go, can I at least sample some of the goodies you have there?"

I pushed the plate of flan-topped cake and what was left of the cookie across the table. "I can go grab you another cookie and fork if you want."

He smiled, shook his head. Cut a perfect square from the slice of cake stacked with flan. The flan's caramel sauce drizzled over the sides of the cake, pooling at the bottom of the plate. Ryan scooped the forkful to his lips. Groaned through a mouthful. "What is this deliciousness and why haven't I had it before?"

"I call it choco-flan cake." I puffed out my chest (mostly) because I was proud of this old-school creation of mine. "It's a secret menu item I keep insisting should be an actual menu item." A breeze blew past, carrying with it pieces of conversations from inside the prep room. Dozens of different scents too. Vanilla and caramel wafting from the cake. Bread being baked on the other side of the wall.

Ryan's scent mixed with them. It was salty and tropical and oily in a good way. Plucked at something weirdly familiar. "Coppertone Water Babies," I blurted out.

Ryan stopped mid-chew.

This wasn't the lasting impression I wanted to make before

"bumping" into him again. "I wasn't trying to smell you or anything weird like that." A bark of awkward laughter. "Full disclosure, I have an off-the-charts sense of smell."

"You do, because I am wearing Water Babies." Ryan leaned into the table, propped his elbows on top. "Is the super sense of smell something you built up from working here?" He took another bite of the choco-flan.

"Good question." I didn't know if my sense of smell was inherited or something I'd worked on like a muscle. If the latter, would it wither away when I stopped working in the prep room? I slumped in my chair a little.

"So besides X-ray vision and a super sense of smell, are there any other superpowers you're hiding?"

I shook my head and laughed. Laughter was better than dishing about the real things I was hiding. No way he'd stick around if he discovered the truth about my lying ways.

"No water-bending abilities?" Curiosity and excitement slipped from his voice.

"Nope."

His face reminded me of Devon and her tell-me-every-detail look. "What about fire?"

I rubbed the tips of my fingers, still warm from his touch. "No, that's you, remember?"

He shrugged like he didn't believe me. "I promised I'd come up with a superhero name for you. It's going to be hard if you don't give me anything to work with."

Even though this was only a silly game we were playing, a part of me did want a superhero name. A superhero name could provide some placebo effect, give me that extra boost to help me crush Operation: Alma. "Fine," I said, in faux annoyance. "Let me think." I actually tried too, but nothing came.

"Would closing your eyes help you concentrate? That always helps me visualize things."

"Okay, Yoda." I grabbed a cookie to hide my smile, took a bite, and closed my eyes.

The cars speeding down the street revved like mixers. Car doors slammed shut like ovens. Even the squawking of gulls reminded me of the prep room's banter. I took another bite of the cookie. This time, I let the flavors roll over my tongue long enough to envision them in a cupcake.

Baking. The word blared so loud in my head, it muted the sounds of the parking lot.

I parted my lips to tell him. "I—"

Only the words dissolved on my tongue like cotton candy. Without Bake-Off to test my skills, I didn't know how good I actually was. "Hold on," I told Ryan. "Let me try again." I pushed baking to the side and reached for the set of abilities that had been tested.

Skills that helped me beat Madeline for the team captain spot. Taking the Law and Debate team to regionals four years in a row. Skills to help our team finally nab the gold at the tournament. And off Alma's waitlist.

One day, those skills would turn me into a lawyer. Which would transform my family from blue collar–wearing to white. The ability to do that had to be a superpower. Intending to dazzle Ryan with my intellect, I said, "I'm a master debater."

Only it didn't sound that way.

A car chose that exact moment to honk its horn.

The blast had drowned out the "de" part of "debater."

My eyes shot open. Just in time to watch Ryan almost put the "choke" in choco-flan.

Kill. Me. Now.

"No! No! What I meant to say is—What I actually said—" Humiliation swallowed the rest of my explanation.

The cringe lasted forever. In that slice of eternity, the corners of Ryan's mouth twitched into a smile. My shoulders vibrated with laughter. Ryan's did too.

At the same time, we burst into laughter. Soon, we found ourselves bent over the table, dissolving into the all-out guffaws reserved for best friends and the truly mortified.

Our laughter tapered off. Teary-eyed and gasping for breath, I felt as if I'd broken through the surface of an ocean I hadn't known I'd been drowning in. Breathing freely for the first time since I'd opened Alma's letter, I wiped the curls from my face and turned to Ryan.

I resisted the urge to look away.

Not the impression I'd planned to make. Then again, because I had to wait until after I got off the waitlist to see Ryan again, there was no way he could possibly forget me now, so. Mission haphazardly complete?

"To superpowers." He lifted another forkful of choco-flan and tapped it against my last piece of cookie. As I popped it into my mouth, his gaze refused to leave mine. "Although you might have a tough time getting into the Avengers with that one."

"Guess I'll have to try my luck with the triple-X-Men." Wow. I couldn't believe I was flirting away my faux pas. I couldn't believe I was flirting, period.

Ryan's cheeks flushed. The reddening spots on his face made his milky skin glow even brighter. *I'm making him blush.* The realization set my own cheeks on fire. When the breeze stirred past us, I pressed my face into it, grateful for the sudden jet of cool air.

The air lifted a handful of curls and blew them across my face. A ringlet got stuck in a layer of clear lip gloss. I blew, trying to nudge it loose. When it refused to budge, Ryan leaned across the table and freed the curl himself.

He tucked the stray curl behind my ear. His Orion-freckled hand lingered on the side of my face.

Suddenly, there was no parking lot, no idling cars, no embarrassing honks.

Only us. And right when I thought the world couldn't contract any further, it did. The universe reduced itself to the inches between our lips.

He leaned closer, parting them. I didn't know if those things were actually happening. Or if I wanted them to. Either way, his mouth was within kissing distance. If I was braver, I'd tilt my chin, press his lips against mine.

Then the door slammed behind us.

Fabiola came bursting through. She nearly tripped over herself when she saw us.

I looked at her—or, more accurately, all the wheels turning inside her head. Back to Ryan. Then at the cookie crumbs scattered on top of the unfinished math essay.

The spell was broken. Priorities settled back in place. We scooted back into our chairs.

"Rafa is looking for you," Fabiola said. She gave me a knowing smile, like catching me checking out cakes in the fridge room finally made sense. She hopped into the waiting car and mouthed, *Está guapo*. Hell yeah, he's hot.

"Ryan, my break is over." I peeled myself from the chair. "I got to go."

"Well, do you want to grab food sometime this week?"

Yes. And every single week after. "I can't." A huge sigh. "This week I'm swamped with studying and homework. Math and Law and Debate especially."

"Debate homework or 'debate homework'?" He wiggled his eyebrows.

"Ha, ha, ha." With an exaggerated eye roll I bent my head into the persistent breeze, and started cleaning up the table. "I'm Miss Master Debater. Or that's what my bestie calls me. I'm the team captain."

His smile dialed up to ten. It felt good to get his attention for something I'd worked so hard for.

"We made it to the regional championship tournament. This year, the pressure is super on for us to win." There was a quote about pressure making diamonds. In my case, it better make a gold trophy. Alma depended on it. So did the Recipe.

Ryan must've noticed the way my eyebrows furrowed because he asked, "Uh-oh, what's wrong? You don't work well under pressure?"

I shook my head. "You know what? Actually I do. Is that weird? Because sometimes when I get onstage . . ." I trailed off. "Or when I have to speed bake a cake for a last-minute order or shape another batch of bolillos for the lunch crowd . . . everything else falls away."

"That's exactly how I feel when I'm surfing. Also when I'm—" His voice broke off. Red crept up his cheeks. Setting mine on fire again.

"When you're what?" Gravel crunched under our shoes as we set off to the prep room's back door. "When you're playing a sport or something?" I figured basketball on account of his height. Or maybe something echoing the cost and exclusivity of his high school, like golf.

"I don't know. Do you consider mathletes a sport?"

My head swung hard in his direction. "Did you just say mathlete?"

"Super nerdy, I know. But math runs in the family, I guess."

My jaw lowered another inch. Was this a chance for me to tweak my tutoring plans? "Rubi, please say something before I start worrying being a math geek is a deal breaker for you."

"Actually, I'm in the market for a tutor. Specifically a trig tutor to help me ace the midterm." The fact that my class ranking depended on it was on a need-to-know basis. "I never really understood geometry, and now, some of its concepts are coming back to haunt me."

Ryan brought a hand to the back of his head and scratched it. "It's been a while since I've done trig, let alone geometry." Great, was every senior in OC enrolled in AP Calculus except me? Right before my shoulders slumped below sea level, Ryan said, "But I did ace both when I took them. Very fortuitous for you." He swallowed hard, then added, "For me too." *Swoon*.

Nothing sounded more perfect than tutoring sessions with Ryan. I was still waiting for one of Devon's recommended tutors to call back after all. Hiring him in the meantime was totally the smart thing to do. An alarm blared through the door. If it was a sign from the universe warning me to stop the idea from taking root, I ignored it.

"Does this mean you're up for the challenge?" I asked.

"Only if you are." Without taking his gaze off my lips, he licked his. My limbs went all melty, and if I was being completely honest, so did my brain. Since the moment we met, that constellation on his hand had been steering me toward Distraction City. Thankfully, I still had enough sense to know I couldn't afford an extended stay there, but a teeny-tiny pit stop . . .

"Yes," I said, finally. "I am."

Chapter 8

I sat at the kitchen table hunched over an old geometry textbook. Chewing on the end of my pencil, theorems glared at me from the page. Ryan had recommended brushing up on some of the fundamentals in preparation for tomorrow's tutoring.

Three problems later, my answer checked out with the right one in the back of the book. Hope fluttered inside my chest. I powered through more problems until my concentration faltered. I leaned back in my chair, closed my eyes to reset my focus.

A flashback to our tutoring negotiations met me instead.

Once you've had my cookies, you'll never want anyone else's.

"Why?" I groaned into the empty kitchen. "Why the hell did I have to say that?" I collapsed into my notebook, covered the back of my head with my arms as if to shield myself from the shame. I couldn't help but laugh a little too.

Well, you do know what they say, Rubi. The way to a man's heart is through his stomach.

So we'd come to an accord. My cookies in exchange for his math tutoring.

I really needed to thank my lucky stars because this mix could totally work. Baking. Ryan. Math.

Glancing at the next problem, I wrote the Pythagorean theorem but heard one of the philosopher's quotes instead.

Salt is born of the purest parents: the sun and the sea.

Exactly like Ryan's skin and his salt-stiffened hair.

"Sea salt. No. Sea salt flakes."

My fingertips tingled with the beginnings of a new brainstorm. I pushed away the math and reached for the Law and Debate binder. Truth be told, this thing was quickly becoming my go-to notebook for bakes.

"Sprinkled on top of chocolate-chip cookie dough. Ohhh, and crunch." I scribbled in the margins. Added a little sketch of six-pack abs. On account of Ryan's muscles, the cookies needed some snap.

Not too much though. That day on the beach, a shadow had flickered across his face when we touched on the subject of parents. So the cookie needed some softness too. I tapped the pencil against my lips.

Chewy middle? Some crumbliness? I wrote. *Ahhh and some cinnamon pasilla chile or a dash of chipotle.* Whichever complemented the sweet and salty combo best. Because when it came to Ryan, an element of heat was essential.

The brainstorm spilled from the margins and leaked all over the page. Sure, the half-finished arguments on whether video games should be considered a sport (obviously yes) were muddled now. To the point of incomprehension. But whoa.

These flavors, the techniques buzzing in my head to make them in real life . . . Should I pour all of this into Bake-Off's Cookie Try-Out Round? Baking cookies for Ryan was the safer choice, sure.

Except the longer I stared at the page, the wilder my heart thumped. Pulsing in Morse code: *Dough you have what it takes?*

The front door slammed shut. "Rubi," a voice called from the front of the house. "I'm home." I froze. "Rubi?" Dad's voice floated farther away, like he'd probably gone looking for me in my bedroom. A few more seconds to set the stage for my performance.

I snapped the Law and Debate binder shut. Tugged some of the math textbooks closer, slanted some binders diagonally.

"Earth to Rubi." He breezed into the kitchen.

Ah! "Oh, hey, Dad." I kept my voice steady. Since I hadn't finished debate homework, the least I could do was practice some techniques. "Did you just get home?"

He paused, brows drawing together. "Yes. Didn't you hear me calling you?"

I gestured to the study materials scattered all around. "I must've been in the zone. There's a Trig midterm next week. I really want to ace it."

Have to ace was more accurate.

Suddenly, I couldn't keep holding his gaze. It drifted to the one spot on the table not covered by textbooks. But, sadly, there was no escape. The shiny surface reflected his face perfectly. Showed how it filled with admiration with every tome he scanned. When he got to the math ones, he flinched. "Matemáticas and I don't mix."

"I'm sure you would've figured it out, Dad."

"I don't know." His voice was far away. Maybe as far away as Cuba and his childhood, where he'd left school at twelve to help his mom raise his younger siblings. "If there is a bad math gene, Abuela Carmen gifted it to me. I'm glad I didn't pass it down to you."

I hunched over the pages, packed with as many right answers as wrong ones. The math gene was definitely passed down. As was the one for dark skin, out-of-control curls—and so much more.

"Rubi, is everything okay?"

No. "Yeah, why wouldn't it be?"

He leaned closer. His gaze burned across the side of my downturned face. "Because you're acting strange."

"I *am* strange." I winked. He chuckled. The tension diffused enough to let me continue with my everything-is-fine act.

"Strange, yes." He squeezed my shoulders the way a boxing coach did to their prize fighter. "But you just got into Alma!" His voice rose with excitement and pride. "I figured you'd be in a happier, more celebratory mood." He drumrolled his palms against the table. "Ooh! How about we put your letter in a frame before the Boss gets home?"

My knuckles twinged against the pencil I was holding.

Damn it. Not again. In my zeal to pretend nothing was wrong, I'd completely forgotten to act as if everything was right.

More than right. Perfect. "I dropped it off to have it professionally framed for us." Apparently, lies were just like potato chips. Impossible to stop after one.

"Nice thinking, mija. She'll love that. Well, you deserve a break from studying. At least for spring break, don't you think?"

Guilt churned in my stomach. "Dad, no." My voice came out louder than intended. I exhaled slowly. "What I meant is, I have to maintain my GPA. Alma could rescind their acceptance if I don't."

He frowned. "I didn't know colleges could do that."

"If I screw up, they can do whatever they want." I flicked my gaze down. Hating myself for using his inexperience with higher education against him. For whisking together parts of the truth to bolster the lie.

The kiss he planted on the top of my head nearly singed off my locks. He headed to the fridge. "So, no rest for the wicked, eh?"

I let go of the pencil before it snapped in half. "Exactly. No rest for the wicked."

For my sake, there better be redemption.

The fluorescent glow of the refrigerator edged his body in light. For someone as stocky as he was, he never ceased to amaze me with how far he could push himself inside.

While he rummaged for appetizers, I stirred our main course, potaje de garbanzos, simmering in the Crock-Pot.

Frying pans, Crock-Pots, and pressure cookers were our personal chefs. Meals prepared while at work or school, or as soon as we got home, were our go-to dishes. Not exactly the catered or coursed meals typical in most Pelican Point homes.

And I couldn't care less.

The scent of pork, garlic, and spices pulled me closer to inhale the stew. Dark red broth bubbled around garbanzo beans. Cubes of malanga, quartered baby potatoes, and round slices of chorizo simmered.

Cuban food and drinks were all about improvisation. Indigenous, Spanish, Chinese, and African ingredients came together out of both necessity and creative thinking. It was a bonus they tasted so good.

"What time is the Boss going to join us?" I placed the lid on the Crock-Pot. It fogged up instantly. "The stew is almost done."

"If she doesn't come home soon, I'll call her to get an update." He motioned me over to the fridge, handed me a jug of agua de tamarindo, a sweet yet acidic drink reminiscent of lemonade, but with earthier notes courtesy of the tamarind pods.

I took the iced tea–colored jug to the table, pushed some of my books to the side to make room. When I glanced back at him, his face was back in the fridge. "In the meantime, what about a treat to tide us over?"

"I thought you'd never ask," I said.

Dad set two grapefruit-sized mameys, mismatched plates, a knife, and two forks on the table. He plopped into the chair across from me. Let out a long sigh. Every line on his face relaxed. This was probably the first time all day he'd been off his feet. My heart walloped for him.

"Glasses," he said. "I forgot the glasses." His voice was slow and slurry, like honey dripping off a spoon. Gravity dragged on his head. His head of cropped curls lolled over the back of the chair. Sweat slicked his forehead. Under the bright kitchen lights, his cheeks glistened with a fine coating of flour.

"Don't get up. I'll get them." I sprang from the chair before he did. Opened the glassware cabinet and mulled over which cups to choose.

When I turned back around, he was fast asleep. I tiptoed back to the table. If I couldn't tell him the truth about the lie, the least I could do was let him power nap and peel the mamey.

Between my palms, the brown skin of the tropical fruit felt scratchy yet soft. Somewhere between the texture of soft bark and sandpaper. I pressed down on the knife. The fruit gave easily under the blade as I cut lengthwise around its circumference.

Circumference. The term surprised a smile out of me. Ryan's geometry refresher was apparently sinking in. Hopefully, tomorrow's session would make other concepts sink in just as fast.

Math concepts, I reminded myself. Not chemistry concepts. Sadly, not anatomy concepts either. With those two rules in place, I brought my focus back to the fruit, turning the two halves of the fruit clockwise then pulling them apart.

The fruit's flesh was a bright, pinky orange. Redder and

creamier in consistency than a papaya. A sweet aroma with notes of almonds drifted from the fruit, hinting at its honeyed and earthy taste. I plucked the dark, oblong seed embedded in one of its halves and released it onto a plate. The seed chimed on the porcelain. Loud, but not loud enough to wake Dad.

I resumed my task by cutting into the flesh again. Usually, I scooped the flesh straight from the fruit and ate it by the spoonful. Since my mother would be joining us any second, it'd be best to eat in a more civilized manner.

I ached to see her. Was wary to see her too.

Maybe tonight's family time was a mistake.

She took stock of people the way she inventoried the bakeries. Efficiently and never missing a thing. I didn't blame her. She needed to protect her investments. Me being her most valuable one.

The knife slipped in my hand. I swerved the blade in time to avoid sawing off my thumb. *Crap!*

The blade glinted against the lights. I waited for my heartbeat to slow down, for my fingers to stop trembling.

When they did, I cut symmetrical lines into the side of the fruit. I pushed the knife up and laid the strip of fruit on the plate. I repeated the process until there was a small mound of tropical fruit rising from the plate.

"When did you get so deft with a knife?"

I froze at the sound of his voice. "You're awake." I glanced back at the mamey. The compliment sunk in. "Wait, you really think I've gotten better with the knife?"

"The strips are all uniform in length and width. They would look great on fruit tarts."

The compliment swelled my chest. I tilted my head to study the fruit. He was right: they'd go nicely on tarts. "Totally. Like lattice striping on top of the custard tarts to make them look like a piecrust."

He pulled the plate closer. Plucking strip after strip, he weaved them into small lattices on another plate. He grinned. And like that, we were bending the Ban again.

Only this time we arched so low it also felt like we had somehow opened a portal.

Transporting us back to our makeshift R&D table in the prep room.

Before the second bakery, before the debate team; when I'd spent every weekend in the bakery. Back to the times when the Boss bossed and Dad baked.

But then I'd made Law and Debate. And my mother whittled away the hours I could spend in the bakery. For a while, Dad and I moved the R&D table here. But when she found out, she banned it too.

No more distractions, Rubi. Not now, we're on the fast track to Alma. And no, don't even think about minoring in their culinary program.

By that time, I was well aware that baking was no longer part of my future, but . . . being around students that *did* bake? Walking by the building housing the kitchens, whiffs of bread, snippets of new recipe ideas on the way to classes . . . Obviously, secondhand baking wasn't everything, but it wasn't nothing either.

Our chairs scratched against the floor when we scooted closer to the table. Dad patted his pockets. I gave him my pencil, tore out a piece of paper from my binder, and handed it him.

Enrejado de fruta para las tartas, he wrote in hurried and slanted letters. "Okay, I got your fruit lattice down. What else?"

Excitement rushed through me. So did nervousness.

We hadn't done this in so long. I didn't want him to see how rusty I was. My eyes veered over to the Law and Debate/baking notebook. Maybe there was something to Ryan's hypothesis of my X-ray vision. Because even though it was shut tight and layered with pages of math, I visualized hints of the brainstorm for his cookies.

Whispers of so many other bakes too. All those margins exploding with so many recipes.

Just because I hadn't riffed baking ideas with Dad in a while didn't mean I hadn't been riffing this entire time.

When it came to baking ideas, maybe I wasn't as rusty as I thought. Maybe I was golden.

I opened my lips only to be interrupted by his cell phone. He pulled it from his pocket. THE BOSS flashed on its screen. "Are you on your way?" he asked in Spanish. "It's acting up? Again?" He massaged the back of his neck. "How much is it going to cost?" He slumped against the chair for a moment before springing from it. "Okay, I'll tell her." He cast a quick glance at me and mouthed, *One minute, Rubi.*

Judging by the way his face had darkened, it was going to take a lot longer. I nodded anyway and he walked out of the kitchen.

With each shuffle of his feet down the hallway, the portal to our R&D table kept shrinking.

Then it was gone.

When he came back, he probably wouldn't even remember what we'd been talking about. If he came back at all.

A few minutes later, he poked his head into the kitchen. Told me he needed to go to Santa Ana and help the Boss with one of the ovens. It was probably best not to wait up. We'd celebrate Alma soon.

I didn't know how long I stayed at the kitchen table. Long

enough for the mound of fruit to start toppling over. The strips falling apart made me feel as if something inside me was coming apart too.

I wiped my eyes with the back of my hand. Rushed to the cabinets and found a Tupperware container large enough to hold the mamey. They'd need a snack when they got back home. I slammed the fridge's door shut. Out of sight—and out of mind.

Or so I told myself.

Chapter 9

"Ryan, are you home?" I craned my neck through the half-open door.

"Yeah. Come in." His voice boomed from what sounded like the second floor of his beach house. "I'll be down in a sec. Barely got back from a surf. Let me shower real quick and throw something on."

If Ryan had to "shower" then "throw something on," it meant he was about to have *nothing* on. My cheeks—my entire body—flushed. "Abso-freaking-lutely!" I cleared my throat. "I mean, no worries. Take your time." I shook my head, pushed the door all the way open, and stepped over the threshold.

Wooden beams supported high ceilings. Super-polished marble floors. Glass walls. Real flowers in every vase. This foyer was straight out of *Architectural Digest*, and the focal point was definitely the staircase. Wood-carved handrails and glass banisters framed a set of stairs circling upward.

"Whoa." No wonder Ryan was a mathlete. He lived in a museum devoted to mathematical principles. Closing the door behind me, I noticed a pair of wet, sandy flip-flops next to the doorway.

I slipped off my own sandals, stepped deeper into the house. The phone vibrated in my back pocket.

Devon's face flashed on my screen. Her hair was tucked underneath a red cap with a huge *A* in the middle. I was about to tease her about suddenly becoming a baseball fan, when I spied my bookshelves and unmade bed behind her. "Wait, are you in my room right now?"

"Yeah." She nearly tripped on the small mountain of clothes on the floor. "Jeez. Were you doing *all* of your laundry this morning?"

"No." Never mind I *had* tried most of it on. It took me longer than expected to decide on an outfit for today. Ultimately, it came down to the dress with the map of Middle-earth printed on it (geeky but low-cut) versus shorts paired with a Spider-Man tank (geeky but tight). The latter won. "Dev, I got to go."

"Why are you whispering? Are you at the bakery?" My stomach growled. Nerves had made it impossible for me to eat breakfast. "I'll swing by to get you," she continued. "I'll help you go over debate stuff, and you can be my model for the new swimsuit I'm designing." More like guinea pig. "Then we can drive to the FLOC meeting together."

"I can't. I'm about to have my first tutoring session. I'll meet you there later."

"Oh cool. So Brunhilda finally called you back? My cousin said she's got this British no-nonsense charm you'll eventually come to love."

"No." I didn't want to love *her.* "I found someone else." I glanced up the staircase. Devon raised a single brow.

"Who?"

"His name's Ryan." I bit my lip. "He goes to Lazarus. He's a surfer."

"A jock?" Her mouth hung open. "Really?"

"Says the person wearing the baseball cap."

Her hand flew to the cap. "Yeah, about that—" She shook her head. "No, you will not throw me off, Miss Master Debater. Details on this alleged surfer. Now."

"'Alleged'?" I stole another glance upstairs, dared to imagine what was happening a floor above my head. "Not with a body like his." Devon pretended to gag. "And for your information, he's not only a surfer. He's a mathlete too. A super qualified one in everything up to AP Calc, thank you very much." I dug a hand into my bag. From underneath the bags of flour, brown sugar, and other ingredients needed to make Ryan's cookies, I fished out the shiniest tube of lip gloss I owned. Proceeded to slather my lips with it. "This is strictly for academic purposes."

"Uh-huh." Her stare darted all over my outfit. If I didn't love Devon as much as I did, if I didn't know how uncomfortable she felt in her comic book–proportioned physique, I might've felt jealous I looked like *this* in the mornings, while she looked like *that*.

Rainbow print spelled out BEACHES LOVE ME across her tank top. One strap hung loose against her shoulder, surrendering to the weight of her ginormous boobs. I glanced down at my own tank.

Contrary to the curvy Latinx stereotype, no big boobs here. Just the words SPIDER and MAN above my small ones. I sighed and daubed more gloss.

"Whatever you say." A laugh-snort. "Sure. Academic purposes."

"I'm serious, Devon."

"If you don't raise your Trig grade, you'll miss making the top five percent of the class, so yeah. You should be."

I flinched, so startled I dropped the lip gloss. The tube

crashed ridiculously loudly against the floor. I picked it up, dropping it between the baking supplies and the textbooks. "Is it so wrong to try to mix something I need to do with something I want?" I whispered more to myself than to her.

The tension in Devon's jaw loosened. "Wow, you really like this dude, don't you?"

Yes. "I mean he's cool, but not so much that I'll screw this up. I promise."

She did that duck-lip thing, a dead giveaway she was trying hard not to smile. I counted to three, and right on cue, she flashed all her teeth. "Check this out. If you lower one of those straps like this . . ." She pulled one of hers down, modeling. "You'll be academically purposing in no time."

Uh-oh. Thinking about kissing and *actually kissing* were entirely different things. What if I (no pun intended) sucked at it? What if he did? Wait. All this assumed he even wanted to kiss me in the first place.

Devon laughed. "I'm so going to screenshot what your face is doing right now and make it your contact photo."

"Dev!"

"Seriously, Rubes. As long as you keep your promise to work hard, I totally support you playing hard too."

"But Devon—"

"Byeee!" She smooched at the screen and hung up before I could say anything else.

My lips tingled. It was probably all the chemicals in the ungodly layers of gloss. Not nerves. I stepped deeper into the house, googling *how to French kiss someone* just in case.

"Almost done drying off," Ryan shouted from upstairs.

"Okay," I shouted back, finding a tutorial that had 9.4 million views. So I wasn't the only one completely clueless on the topic. "Don't rush!"

I was about to play the video when the sun hit the back wall. Wow.

Golden and mahogany frames blinked in the sunlight. There had to be at least one family photo embarrassing enough to water down my nervousness over what may (fingers-crossed) or may not (sigh) happen. Not to mention cancel out those images of Ryan, soaking wet.

Except it wasn't a wall of family portraits. It was a wall of family diplomas. Calligraphy and gold embossed the Ivy League logos of undergraduate degrees. A med school diploma hung right next to it. As I followed the trail of his parents' diplomas, it hit me.

If—no, *when*—I got into Alma, my diploma would be more than a degree on a wall. It'd be the first rung of a ladder taking me as high as I wanted to go.

A sheet of wax paper suddenly came between duty and desire. I pushed the logistics of kissing to the back burner. Freshly focused for my math lesson, I slipped my phone back into my pocket. Backed away from the wall, only to crash into Ryan's rock-hard pecs. The force of our collision sent waves of tingles—er, *stings*—all over me.

"Apologies for sneaking up on you like that. You looked so absorbed with . . ." Ryan motioned to the wall. "I didn't want to disturb you."

My eyes roved from his chest, to the hollow of his throat, up to his mouth. If I moved my face a few inches closer, our lips would meet.

Whoa. Suddenly, that back burner flared again. Only this time I wasn't boiling over with nerves. In that moment, all I wanted to do was follow Nike's great words of wisdom and Just Do It.

"Are you okay?" Ryan placed his hands on my shoulders,

keeping me steady. Leftover sun lingered on his skin. The heat flowed down his fingers and through my body, like a mug of Abuelita hot chocolate on a winter morning. "I hope you didn't twist anything?" His brows drew together.

Maybe my priorities. "No. All good. I simply need to be more careful." I steadied my legs and stepped back. Immediately missing the heat from his hands. "Watch where I step."

"Yeah, you do." He turned his attention up the steps. Remnants of wet footprints slicked the edges of the spiraling staircase. "Because I set up for tutoring upstairs. Here, let me help you."

He extended his Orion-freckled hand. Whether he intended to help me onto the first rung or guide me up the entire way, I wasn't sure. All I knew was if I took it, my legs would probably give way again.

So would my focus.

I took the handrail instead. Edged around him and hiked up.

Halfway, I paused, turned back.

He remained on the first step. A smile unfurled slowly across his lips. It threatened to pull every atom of oxygen from my lungs. Somehow I managed to ask, "Well, O-Ryan? Are you coming up or what?"

He blinked hard as if waking up from a trance. My heart sped up, finding the notion very appealing. "Lead the way," he said.

Though I only had a vague sense of where I was headed, I did.

At the coffee table we'd selected as our study space, Ryan talked about theorems the way I talked about ingredients in recipes. Like they were close friends instead of creations of some long-dead genius. Maybe If I started looking at the formulas like they were my friends too, something would shift.

Ryan untangled theorems. I followed his explanations. Some of them even began to stick. The way the concepts connected and built on one another reminded me of a world I understood: baking.

Only these mathematical recipes seemed to be written in a language I wasn't quite fluent in yet. I crossed my legs and scooted closer, careful to avoid bumping into him. I nodded when he explained how he was going to find the surface area of the next tetrahedron. And when he turned the page to work out the problem, I slapped my hand down on the page. "Wait, let me try this one."

Ryan kept his hand planted on the page, refusing to release it to me so easily. "Are you going to find the area with Trig or PT?"

"Is this supposed to be a trick question, or something?"

"I don't know." Ryan grinned. "You tell me." He uncrossed and recrossed his long legs. Except he wasn't as careful as I'd been. His knee knocked into mine. It felt like touching a hot stove.

I scooted away and refocused. "Well, the area of one face of the triangle can be found with either trig principles or the Pythagorean theorem," I said, surprising myself with my budding mathematical fluency.

Ryan took his hand off the page. "My Padawan is a fast learner."

I could've swooned over how he'd used the *Star Wars* word for apprentice. Over how he'd used a possessive adjective to modify it. Or how the light streaming through the glass walls caught in his hair like fire.

Instead, I turned back to the problem at hand. Like Devon had so bluntly reminded me, Alma depended on raising my class ranking. Acing the midterm was the only way to make that happen.

Swooning must wait.

"All right," I said. "Here goes nothing."

Four rows of numbers and symbols later, I arrived at an answer.

I presented the page to Ryan for his inspection. He glanced at my answer, bit down on a smile. Picking up his pencil, he worked out the problem for himself.

I liked that he did this instead of simply checking the answer key in the index.

I liked that he was a kinesthetic teacher, preferring to use his hands to tutor me. A callus bulged from the side of his right, middle finger. I glanced down at my own hand. Spotted a matching one on mine.

"The sides are all . . ." Ryan's voice grew distant as my gaze drifted from the callus to the tiny baking scars on my skin. "The height is . . ."

I shifted on the ground, trying to concentrate. The sharp lead point of his pencil scratched on the page. His hand moved fast.

Almost as fast as the hands inside the waterproof watch strapped around his wrist. They ticked closer and closer to 1 P.M.

Until now, the study session had kept thoughts of Bake-Off at bay. I turned my attention back to his hands, but there was something about how they moved down the page that tugged at something deep inside my belly. The growing enthusiasm on his face only made my stomach pull harder. Then I felt it; a cold splash of déjà vu.

"So the tetrahedron must be—"

"Bake-Off." The moment I said it, I froze.

Ryan lowered his pencil. "What's Bake-Off?" Silence hung between us. If I could take the words back, I would. "Rubi?"

Again I tried to hold back. Except, as I looked around the living room, the glass walls begged me to be as transparent as they were. When my gaze landed on Ryan's face, I found it equally as open and safe as the rest of the room.

"It's this baking competition. I got accepted a few days ago." My shoulders rose before falling. "The first challenge is in a couple hours."

"Then why are you here working on this instead of there, baking?"

"It's not one of those baking-on-site type of competitions. Probably because it's their first year doing it so it's not nearly the scale of a big, reality-TV baking show." I sighed and kept going. "I mean, the judges are supposed to be famous, and there's even supposed to be a *Prize of a Lifetime*." I could never say that part without licking my lips. "But the contest itself has more of an OC Fair vibe. You know, the ones where you bake at home and bring it with you to the competition? The first challenge is a Cookie Try-Out Round, so."

"So you're freaking out about what the judges will say about your dessert?" He tapped his pencil against the textbook.

"No." My stomach tightened. "I'm not competing."

"What?" He looked as bummed as I felt. "Why?"

I considered dishing everything. Alma's fresh waitlist. How I didn't have a carbon copy of myself. One to send to the FLOC meeting while the real me competed in the cookie challenge. But no, that wouldn't work either. The real me was bound by the rules of the Ban. "It's complicated," I finally said.

He leaned back, braced his back against the sofa behind us. "Huh." His voice burned with a wistfulness not there a moment ago. His eyes drifted across the room to the longboard propped up against the corner. "I know all about complicated." Okay,

Ryan *definitely* longed for something off-limits, exactly like I did. "There's this surf trip to Indo right after graduation. Pops knew I wanted to do it but he lined up an internship at the attorney general's office for me instead." He scoffed, picking at his calloused finger. "Probably why he set it up."

"So you're not going to take it?" I scooted closer to him, to this super-familiar conversation. "The trip, I mean."

"I don't know." His green eyes narrowed. "It'd be a mistake not to do the internship."

I glanced at my bag. I didn't need X-ray vision to see the baking mold and ingredients tucked away inside of it. "But it also feels like a mistake not to do the trip, right?"

"Yeah." He swallowed. Loudly. "Funny thing is, I'm not good enough to go pro or anything. And I don't want to be. I guess it's technically a hobby, but I don't know. It also feels like—" Ryan's voice broke off. He took his gaze out the window, to the pier caught between an endless ocean and a cloudless sky.

I took mine further, all the way to the blurry edges of Catalina way out in the distance.

"More," I said. "It also feels like more."

"Yes. Exactly." He turned back, flashed that smile. Had he caught a glimpse of the walls around my heart? Was he happy to discover they sort of matched his? "It feels like more."

I leaned across the table, reached for my messenger bag. Yanked out the Law and Debate binder and flipped through the pages until I found the Ryan's cookies recipe from last night. "Look at this." I handed it to him.

Ryan took the binder with both of his hands. Inched it closer for a better look. He scanned the page, witnessing for himself the way underbaked debate prep battled ingredients for dominion of the lines. "Sea salt, crunch, chewy middle," he said, in almost a whisper. With a finger he traced the word *heat*. The corners of his lips hinted at a grin. "Are these the cookies you're going to make me?"

I pulled the binder back. "*Was* going to make you. Truth is, I even brought the ingredients to make them here. That way you could have them fresh." Not at all because of the Ban or anything. "But I don't know. I shouldn't be anywhere near baking right now. I'll pick some cookies up from the bakery for you. My dad's oatmeal raisins are super good."

"Not the deal we made. Plus, I—"

"Plus, nothing. You've seen for yourself how baking hijacks my concentration. I doubt Sister Cornelia will be as understanding as you if I turn in my midterm and it looks like this." I pointed to the page. "Or write 'Bake-Off' for any of the answers."

He shrugged, unconvinced. "Master debate me." He shot me a lopsided grin.

"Fine." I thumbed back through some pages. "Since you don't believe it's a serious problem, take a peek at exhibit A."

He examined the recipe and its corresponding sketch. "What's a croncha?"

"The love child of a croissant and a concha, a Hispanic sweet bread that looks like a seashell. After the bolillos, my dad's conchas are the next bestsellers."

"Awesome. You're thinking of ways to level it up. Exactly the reason why you should do the competition."

"Not awesome."

Ryan angled his body closer to mine, the expression on his face screaming, *Really?* "Okay, maybe a part of me does think it's cool, but part of me is also scared." I drew in a shaky breath. "You know the quote about the two wolves?"

"The ones fighting?"

I nodded. Alma and Bake-Off were fighting inside me right

now. But I couldn't tell him because that'd mean spilling the beans about the waitlist. And I still wasn't ready to repeat the story out loud again. Especially to him. "The wolf who wins is the one you feed." I only had to turn a few pages until the next baking idea. "Exhibit B. Undeniable proof I need to stop feeding this wolf."

Ryan said nothing about starving wolves. He only took in the page and said, "Exhibit B's freaking amazing."

A small gasp escaped me. "Really?" I pulled the binder closer.

Even inside the tiny spaces of the margins, the sketch was pretty intricate.

An arrangement of roses crowned the top of it. Petals and glaze cascaded down the sides of round tiers. Three tiers in total, each one less wide than the one stacked beneath it.

In the middle, I'd drawn a slice, exposing the inside of the cake. Thick layers of sponge sandwiched alternating layers of mousse and buttercream.

Ryan was right. The cake was pretty amazing.

"No wonder you're grasping these concepts as quickly as you are." He picked up his pencil. "This cake, with its lines, angles, and circles . . ." He pointed to the edges and angles of the sketch. Turning the pages back to the croncha, he said, "And this." He circled the diameters and ratios in the recipe. "Your recipes have trig written all over them."

"Huh," I said, spotting triangles, cylinders, surface areas, and volumes where before I'd only seen imaginary bakes. I traced the shapes and measurements, hoping he was right.

If he was, it meant I'd been speaking math this entire time. And maybe I was more fluent than I gave myself credit for.

The possibility of acing the midterm started to crystallize. Alma felt one step closer. "Maybe it's clicking because of the baking." I paused. "Or maybe it's because I have a really good tutor."

"Does this mean I still get your cookies?"

I snapped the binder shut and shoved it back into my bag. "It's too dangerous. Bake-Off's like a poisonous spider or something. It's bitten me and I need to suck the poison out before it's too late."

"Or . . ." He motioned to my bag, then my shirt. "You can let the poison become part of you. You know, let the poison become powers you can use to your advantage."

I scoffed. "Peter Parker got bitten by a radioactive spider. Not a poisonous one."

"I think radioactive material still counts as poison."

I shook my head. "The point is, I can't let this poison become a part of me." I wanted to tell him how my parents would see me becoming a baker as treasonous. Even more so on account of them fleeing Cuba to give their future (and sole) offspring a better life. But I kept the explanations inside, hermetically sealed along with so much else. "Baking can never become a power."

"Why not?" His voice wasn't judgmental or accusatory. It was filled only with genuine concern.

I swallowed hard. If Ryan didn't understand why he'd be applauded for following in his doctor-and-lawyer parents' footsteps, while I'd literally been applauded in the prep room for *not* following in my parents' footsteps—then I wasn't going to Brownsplain it to him.

"Look, I appreciate you listening. I really do. But you're like one step away from getting all Oprah Winfrey on me when all I want is for us to get back to trig."

"Oprah Winfrey, huh? And here I thought I was more of an Obi-Wan."

"Same difference."

Ryan laughed. "Touché."

"So back to work?"

"After something to drink. I completely forgot I got us coffee. It's in the fridge though."

I stood. Ryan didn't seem like the type of person who cooked for himself, let alone baked. I doubted his parents did either.

His kitchen, I told myself, was safe.

Chapter 10

Metallic pullouts adorned white cabinets flanking the king of all residential ovens—a stainless steel Thermador dual fuel range. My mouth watered for cookies I wouldn't be baking.

Ryan walked past the oven and brought his hand over a panel on the wall. A soft click brought the chandelier to life. Hundreds of tiny bulbs poured angled beams of light all over the kitchen, but most of them shined down on the island in the middle of the room.

I sidestepped the counter stools lining one side of it, examining the chandelier closer. Different lights blinked at me with every step. Shadows shifted one way, stretched another. "Wow," I whispered. So much creativity and craftsmanship had gone into creating something so intricately beautiful.

"Pretty cool, right?" Ryan said.

"Definitely. It looks more like a cumulus cloud made of silver than a fancy lamp. Who knew hands were capable of making something like this?"

As soon as I heard my question though, a voice answered.

You know.

And just like that, images of Dad's expert piping and meticulous handiwork rushed over me.

He too could take simple elements and whip them into clouds of meringue.

Maybe I could too.

"You said you had drinks?" I needed something cold.

"Yes. They're probably extra watery by now." He closed the refrigerator with his elbow and walked back to the island. "They're from the coffee place by your bakery." He blew a tuft of hair from his face. "The one you refused to go to with me the other day." He held out the cup.

"Wanting to do something and not being able to are two different things, you know." We locked eyes. That smoldering look sent me to the verge of spontaneous combustion.

"So you *did* want to go with me." A grin played at the corners of his mouth.

I brought mine over the straw. Bit down so the smile stretching across my face wouldn't break a Guinness World Record. I took a sip.

The melted ice cubes diluted the acidity of the espresso, letting the sweetness of the milk chocolate explode more powerfully over my taste buds. A creamy flavor followed it.

"Oh my god." Another sip to identify it. "Is this a *malted* mocha?"

He nodded. "It's from the secret menu. Do you like it?"

I was too busy guzzling the rest of it down to answer. Too busy tasting memories of afternoons at the bakery. "When I was little, before my parents could afford day care, they'd bring me to work."

Early reader books were my babysitters, bakers on breaks my

playmates. Homework got done at Dad's desk, with legs swinging from the chair like a conductor trying to keep up with the sounds of the prep room.

"Every day, someone there would make me a shake. Mamey, mango, guanábana."

Ryan leaned into the island. His eyes pools of green so calm and deep, I dove in and swam. "My favorite was this one made from condensed and evaporated milks. Blended with chocolate ice cream and a splash of Malta Hatuey."

Ryan tilted his head up, curious.

"It's a Cuban drink. Dark brown, fermented malt. It sounds weird, but it tastes like caramely molasses. Trust me, it's good."

"I don't know if I can trust you." He angled his body closer. "You've broken the terms of our deal already."

"Ha-ha. Well, it is." I placed the empty cup on the island. I ran a finger over the sparkles of light reflected on the bluish-black surface. "Whoa, on this, the chandelier looks like a nebula."

"I always wondered how long it would take someone else to notice."

"What? The cosmos in your kitchen?"

"Something like that," Ryan answered with a grin. I returned the gesture.

It didn't matter whether extravagant chandeliers or fluorescent rods hung overhead. Baking was inherently an act of creation. Prep room–size or small, the cosmos was always in kitchens.

I turned to the oven. The stainless steel caught the hundreds of lights, blinking. No—winking—a double dare. My stomach growled, begging me to accept it. Ryan must've heard it because he asked, "Are you sure you don't want to make those cookies?"

I turned back to him, cheeks flaming. The rest of my defenses melted away. "You wouldn't happen to have any condensed milk or malted milk powder handy, would you?"

We scavenged the pantry, fridge, and cabinets until I had all the ingredients to make Malta Condensada Chocolate-Chip Cookies.

It was Ryan who found a KitchenAid Pro Line stand mixer. He tore off the tape sealing the box. Pulled the mixer out and eased it onto the island. It gleamed a shade of copper like wet sand.

"KitchenAid's biggest and most powerful home stand mixer." I didn't add it also happened to be the most expensive of the home-use models. "With this baby we can double the amount of cookies we make."

I glanced down at Ryan's watch. He caught me staring. "What time's your competition?"

"In a few hours." Hope buoyed me. Reality plunged me down again because (sigh) so would the FLOC meeting.

As much as Madeline turned up her nose at baking as a profession, she never shied away from multiple servings whenever I brought pastries to meetings. Any extra cookies could probably even butter her up, make her more willing to help set up the Alma interview.

Priorities in place, I grabbed the wire whisk. Tried to lock it into place too.

I tried and tried, huffing as I twisted it every way. Only it refused to latch into the attachment hub.

Ryan's hands cupped over mine.

He gave them a sharp twist to the right. The whisk locked with a metallic *click*.

The red strands in his hair weaved through the brownish ones, ready to catch fire.

Or maybe it was just me. Because with his hands layered over mine, Ryan's heat ignited my own.

I allowed myself to stay like that for a moment longer. Before I melted completely, I peeled away to plug in the mixer. "Oven's ready."

Ryan looked at all the ingredients, baking utensils, and bowls strewn across the island. "Okay. How can I help you?"

No way was I going to turn down help when time ticked closer and closer to the FLOC meeting. "Double the ingredients for the dry mix. I'll start mixing some of the wet."

The stick of butter fell with a *thwack* into the mixer's stainless-steel bowl. I flicked the mixer's shift from zero to stir. The transition was so seamless, even I had trouble keeping the knob from revving at full speed.

The whisk spun around the bowl, elliptically, powerfully, and thoroughly. No ingredients went to waste with this baby. "Motor's no joke," Ryan said.

I laughed. "It really isn't." I pushed the knob a little farther. The motor revved louder, beating the butter until creamy.

I added brown and white sugar. Cranked the mixer's speed up another notch. When it was perfectly fluffy, I lowered the speed all the way back to stir. Added a splash of vanilla extract, a few tablespoons of condensed milk.

"Can I try? It looks super fun."

"It is fun. You can mix the dry and wet ingredients." I turned off the mixer. "Did you notice if there was a flat beater in the cabinet where you found the mixer?"

"Flat beater? Is that something different than the whisk we're already using?"

What a sweet summer child. Biting down on a grin, I dropped down to the cabinets and rummaged through for the flat beater attachment. "Technically, the whisk could mix the cookie dough.

Since we're using larger and heavier ingredients though, it'd have to spin for longer to mix everything properly." I kept searching.

"That's a bad thing?"

"In this case, yes." I pushed away expensive equipment still in boxes, never-used-before copper pots and pans. Reminders that—regardless of our similarities and sprouting of something-more-than-friendship—in OC, there were families who ate the meals and families who made them.

I was supposed to be studying to switch my trajectory. Here I was though, baking instead.

Sure, the Ban was still in place. But Ryan's kitchen was a world—a universe—away from mine. Baking here didn't feel like a crime.

"The longer the whisk rotates through the flour, the more strands of gluten it'd develop. Meaning the cookies would come out tough instead of chewy."

I didn't want to make tough cookies. I wanted to make perfect ones.

"Aha!" I grabbed the beater. "Found it."

"Do I drop the dry stuff into the bowl of wet stuff?"

"Yup." I rose up. "And mix it." As soon as the words left my mouth, I froze at the sight of Ryan's fingers squeezing the shift knob. The tendons under his skin moved. Made the Orion freckles sway like they were gearing up to go full throttle.

"Wait!" Only I yelled it at the same time the 1.3-horsepower motor roared to life.

The max speed detonated a flour bomb.

It mushroomed up and out the sides of the mixer, still spinning at full speed.

Panicked, Ryan lurched his hand forward. Then backward. Gunning the motor only shot the flour cloud to new heights. More revs from the motor. A handful of curses from Ryan. Probably assuming the mixer was equipped with an automatic shutoff mechanism, he flung the mixer's head up.

Splattering our already floured faces with chunks of cookie dough.

I jumped to the edge of the island. Globs of dough pelted my head as I grabbed the mixer's cord and yanked it from the socket. The whirring slowed, then stopped.

Coughing and gasping for air, I wiped the chunks of dough from my eyes. "You saved my life back there," Ryan said, breathless. "The way you flew across the kitchen. Definitely a superhero move."

Ryan's height had saved the top half of his face from the mixer's line of fire. The same couldn't be said for the lower half. Or his neck. I pressed my lips together to keep from cracking up.

"Don't let it go straight to your head, O-Ryan. I mostly did it for the cookies."

"Too bad." He let out an exaggerated sigh. "Most of them are in your hair now."

"Oh no!" The lost batch of cookies stung more than the undoubtable mess that was my mane. "Like how many?" I pulled the hair tie from my topknot. Curls sprung loose and hit my shoulder blades. A small flour cloud puffed out of them. I flipped my hair forward to inspect the damage. "Ahh!" My heart skittered inside my chest. "This better not be over a half dozen!"

I sprinted across the kitchen to grab a paper towel.

"We can always make more. Plus . . ." Ryan paused, filled his voice up with teasing. "Most people wouldn't look this good covered in cookies."

I wiped off some of the biggest globs. "Well, I'm not like most people." Even though it came out sounding flirty, in reality, it was a variation of one of my mother's favorite mantras: *We're not like most people in Pelican Point.*

"Trust me, Rubi, I know you're not like most people."

When my mother said it, she made it sound like our differences were burdens to overcome. Ryan managed to make my differences sound like assets I should be proud of. Yes, he was probably referring to my overall weirdness, not any socioeconomic difference or racial otherness, but still. For the first time in my life, a part of me wanted to wave the weird flag high for everyone to see.

I stopped wiping off the cookies.

Ryan rounded the island and stepped right next to me. "Hmm, let me check if you got them all." He tore the last paper towel from the dispenser, wrapped it around a curl. "You missed this cookie." He slid the paper towel down, wiped away the clump. "Another one here."

I expected him to keep wiping my hair. Instead, he brought his hand under my chin and tilted it up. With a thumb, he traced a line up my cheekbone. His skin was calloused, his touch was soft. He lifted his thumb.

A bit of dough stuck to the bottom of it. His gaze went from the dough, to me, then back to the dough again. A smile spread across his lips, and he pushed the dough back onto my cheek. As if it belonged there all along.

Without thinking, I wiped away the dough smearing his bottom lip. The touch of his lips melted most of my nervousness. I tiptoed forward, finally following the pull on my own.

Ryan's hand moved from my cheek to the nape of my neck, moving me closer. Here it came. My first kiss.

There were handfuls of forehead collisions. Some breaking away to giggle. Coming back to finally press our lips together. Movies did nothing to prepare me for the teeth gnashing. Nose bumps. Or where to place all those limbs.

Fresh out of a math refresher though, we shifted to different angles.

Better.

Way better.

Whoa.

Behind my eyelids, the kitchen started to burst with neon colors. I burst with them. I kissed him again. The scent of the ocean filled my nostrils. Sea salt cookie dough exploded over my tongue.

The combination untethered me. I wrapped my arms around his shoulders to anchor myself. Ryan latched his fingers onto my waist, like he too felt gravity begin to slip away.

After what felt like both forever and not long enough, we pulled apart. Sucking in mouthfuls of air, he said, "Wow." His cheeks got all red, as if he couldn't believe he'd said that out loud. I giggled. "Um, what I meant was, you know that thing you said about having the cosmos in kitchens?"

"Yeah."

"It's not just the cosmos."

"Nope." I inched my face closer. "It's the entire freaking universe."

Chapter 11

I drove through Matteo Beach, riding high on the kiss.

Kisses. Dozens and dozens of kisses. My lips still tingled . . .

Everything still tingled. A car horn blared behind me, bringing me back down to Earth. I sighed and pressed my foot on the gas pedal.

Green light after green light made it easy to keep it there. Perfect, because I needed to get home and shower before the FLOC meeting. As much as I wanted to stay in these cookie-splattered clothes forever, I couldn't stride in looking like a literal Cookie Monster.

Madeline would hate that. And I couldn't have her hating even more things about me. Not now.

I switched into the next lane, gunning the engine to make it through the next light. When I approached the intersection, it blinked yellow, then red.

It stayed red for a while. Long enough for me to glance at the cookies riding shotgun.

Golden-brown edges shimmered under the plastic lid of the dessert carrier Ryan loaned me. The middles were lighter, softer.

with mounds of chocolate chips spread symmetrically across the surface. The math lesson had paid off in more ways than one: the cookies' circumferences all matched.

Sure, these weren't the original cookies I'd planned to make Ryan.

They were even better.

And instead of sharing them with the International Pastry Diva or the Bad Boy of Bread, these cookies were going to Madeline and her minion.

I checked the dashboard clock—2:17 P.M. My forehead dropped, thumping against the steering wheel. Bake-Off's first challenge was well underway. Probably even wrapping up.

By now, the judges had likely tasted all the cookies. The locals had probably seen every type under the sun . . . Well, except for a batch of Malta Condensada Chocolate-Chip.

A car honked behind me.

I pressed on the gas, turned left instead of right like I was supposed to. It wouldn't hurt to drive by Bake-Off's setup. A quick peek. Nothing more.

Except every ounce of me knew better.

There was a very specific reason I'd picked a study spot that also happened to have a kitchen. Paid Ryan with cookies. Drove down this road versus the other . . .

As much as I wanted to pretend otherwise, the fact was, of course I wanted to take this route. I wanted to be here, on my way to Bake-Off's first challenge.

All lights flashed green again, as if the Bake Gods were rewarding my honesty. But the real prize was there. In the distance, above the traffic lights.

The white peaks of a huge tent. A tent exactly like the one in Bake-Off's email. My heart sputtered against the seat belt.

The last light before the tent flashed red. My knuckles went white against the steering wheel. If I kept it steady, the car wouldn't drift into the parking lot. Or toward the sign all roads and detours had led to: a huge BAKE-OFF banner paired with big arrows pointing at the tent's entrance.

White cloth draped the sides of it. They billowed. Beckoned.

Pretend it's a wedding tent. That's all it was. The last shreds of Good, First-Gen Daughter yelled at me to keep trying. Only the conversation with Fabiola in the fridge welled up instead.

If bachelorettes needed one last hurrah before they walked down the aisle, maybe I did too. That way, when I walked down the red bricks paving Alma's pathways, ready to proclaim my commitment to higher education, I'd do it without cold feet.

No more pining for baking. No what-ifs over Bake-Off.

Was there any chance left of competing? Since I didn't have X-ray vision like Ryan teased, there was only one way to find out.

Chapter 12

Artificial grass padded my steps as I made my way through the tent. The crowd was thick. Way thicker than I expected for a first-time competition. People clustered at the kitchen racks and cabinets. Gathered around every island, chattering.

Painted in every shade of pastel, the furniture displayed magnificent collections of porcelain teacups and saucers. Copper pots and pans. Glass jars filled with different types of flour and sugar. Fruit platters at the center of every island, brimming with oranges.

The oranges were one clue I wasn't standing in the middle of an English countryside kitchen. Other clues came from the bright streamers of light running up the sides of the tent, all the way up to its peaks. Dangling from their center, a marquee of LED letters spelled: OC BAKE-OFF.

In less than an hour, I had to be at the FLOC meeting. In spite of it, my senses pulled me deeper into the tent.

Whiffs of gingerbread, sugar cookies, peanut butter, apples, and coffee wafted from every island, the scents emanating from all the cookie trays, platters, carriers, and baskets strewn across countertops. On closer inspection, they were completely empty. And their respective bakers fell into one of two groups.

Those gushing into cell phones or to people clustered around them.

And those standing silent, blinking back tears.

Backstage at Law and Debate tournaments looked a lot like this, a pendulum swinging wildly between celebration and defeat. My breath left me in a rush of panic.

If bakers were already celebrating or crying, if most of the cookies were MIA . . . the judging was over. My fingers trembled against the cookie carrier. For the millionth time in the last couple of days, Bake-Off slipped between them.

A woman's voice boomed from speakers set up throughout the tent. "Last batch of bakers! Please make your way to the judging table at the front of the tent." Every conversation ceased. The air in the tent thickened. "The final round of judging will commence shortly."

I raced forward, faster than I ever ran before.

I took a spot at the end of the line. Ten bakers stood in front of me, all to apparently check in with a woman holding a clipboard at the base of a platform. I craned my neck over a pair of broad shoulders. The platform led to a mini-stage! A handful of skipped heartbeats, and my turn finally came.

"Rubi Ramos." I lifted to my full height.

With a black marker, she went down a list names. Flipped through a couple of pages before bringing the marker to a stop in the middle. "Ah. Here you are." Only she didn't check the box. Why was her Sharpie paused on the page? "You never checked in."

"Is it too late to check in now?" A wave of coldness went through me. "Please, please, please don't say it's too late." In a desperate attempt to gain sympathy, I gestured to my hair. "As you can see, I had some technical difficulties with a mixer."

She finally looked up from the clipboard. Eyebrows rose to her hairline. A moment's deliberation was followed by a chuckle. "Up the platform and down the table, kiddo. Take whatever space you can find." After more laughter, she handed me the Sharpie. And a wet wipe. "Write your name on the place card and put it in front of your bake."

"Thank you." I slipped the pen into my pocket. "You have no idea how much this means to me."

Breathless, I took the open spot at the end of the long table. Set the carrier onto the palm tree–print tablecloth while trying to ignore how some of the bakers cocked their heads at my sudden appearance. Or maybe just my appearance, period.

I lifted a hand to my face, wiped at spots of flour or cookie dough I'd missed. Or Ryan hadn't kissed off.

The flush of heat brought a much-needed surge of confidence. The lights dimmed. A metallic *click*. Spotlights fell onto three antique-looking refrigerators several feet in front of us. They were huge, Drax the Destroyer huge, and they swung open in unison.

Out stepped the judges. Madame Terese and Johnny Oliver waved at the crowd. So did the tall blonde trailing them. She must be the competition's host. Lifting a microphone to her glossy lips she yelled, "Are you ready to see how these cookies crumble?"

The roars were so deafening, I turned back to make sure the crowd hadn't suddenly quadrupled. It hadn't.

If baking had the power to make people feel like *this*, why were prep rooms tucked away in the backs of buildings? The only thing that could make this sweeter would be if my parents were here, witnessing this magic for themselves.

Would this remind Dad of his reasons for loving baking? Would it force the Boss to reconsider all her reasons for loathing it? I smiled so wide, my cheeks burned.

"That's more like it, beautiful people. One more time, I'm your host, Summer Rae." The blue sequins on her dress sparkled like wave tops on her strut down to the judging table, Madame Terese and Johnny Oliver close on her super tall heels. "By now you're well aware of how this works. Every week for the next four weeks, your bakes will be tasted by International Pastry Diva Madame Terese and the Bad Boy of Bread Johnny Oliver." She paused to let the cheers taper. "Between the two of them, our judges have decades of experience, four bestselling books, and two Michelin stars. For the last time of the day"—Summer Rae swung her arms through the air like she was starting a car race—"show us your cookies!"

*Whoosh*es and *pops* flew through the air as bakers pulled away cloths and snapped off lids to reveal their bakes. A collective hush fell over the crowd when images of the bakes were projected onto the sides of the tent.

A batch of what looked like classic chocolate-chip spilled out of a weaved basket. Another of gingerbread people, wearing icing-piped Hawaiian shirts, displayed on a surfboard platter. Sugar-dusted almonds poked out of white chocolate–dipped biscotti slices. Perfectly bent and crisp fortune cookies rose from a gold tin. Gem-colored jams glistened from the middles of thumbprints.

Whoa. My mouth watered at the sight of so many gorgeous—and gorgeously presented—cookies. Then again, this was OC. Presentation was key. Wait, had all of the cookies today been this good?

I craned my neck to take a peek down the judging table.

Red splotches crept up necks, spread onto faces. Several bakers cleared their throats. Sweat pinpricked most foreheads. Behind us, the crowd stilled.

I gulped. Hard.

So the best had, in fact, been saved for last.

I slumped back to my spot at the table. I hadn't even uncovered my bake yet. Caught up in the excitement, I'd forgotten. Apparently, the woman next to me forgot too. She was too busy checking out the competition, probably wondering, like me, whether she still had a shot. When she caught me staring, she peered at me down her nose—not the warm reception I expected from a fellow baker. Then she shot me a look.

A look I was familiar with thanks to Madeline.

It was judgment and condescension rolled into one. And it went through me like a heat-seeking missile aimed straight at my confidence.

She hovered a perfectly manicured hand over her bake. A flick of her wrist, a blur of pink silk, and her cookies were unveiled.

Star-shaped, white chocolate–dipped, and decorated with tiny pearls, her cookies were perfectly arranged in stacked layers that formed a pyramid. I smiled at the beauty of them, making a mental note to tell Ryan he'd been right. Math *was* in baking.

Words of congratulation buzzed at my lips. They evaporated the moment she snickered.

While I'd been checking her cookies out, she'd been checking mine out too. Eyes like lasers burned through my container's plastic top. She raised her pointy chin. Smirked as though pleased that my plain-looking cookies made hers shine that much brighter.

I stood there, at another table where most people looked nothing like me. Maybe a part of me had longed to compete in a game I thought I knew. With baking, I didn't need an exclusive school to teach me the rules. I didn't need a FLOC to show me which secret ropes to grab when the rules weren't enough to win.

My head sagged in defeat, giving me a perfect view of my cookies.

I was an extension of them. So was Ryan. So was everyone in the prep room and the entire bakery itself.

My spine straightened. I yanked out the blank place card and black Sharpie from my pockets. It squeaked against the paper as I wrote RUBI RAMOS in big, huge caps, set it next to the impeccable cursive that read KATHERINE REED.

I snapped off the cookie carrier's lid and pushed my bake up, parallel to hers. Parallel to everybody's. Katherine narrowed her eyes. If she was looking for any hidden tricks, she was fresh out of luck.

No tricks. Only a dozen pieces of me.

♥ ♥ ♥

"Beautiful piping." Under the spotlights, Johnny Oliver's slicked-back hair gleamed like a black motorcycle helmet. He lifted a gingerbread man from the surfboard-shaped platter and scratched the bottom of the cookie with his thumb. "But raw batter is not fun."

"Neither is salmonella," Madame Terese said through a French accent.

"And they're back, folks," said Summer Rae. A ripple of applause and laughter from the crowd. Mid-clap, my palms fell to my sides at the judges moving one baker closer.

Johnny Oliver examined the purple-and-blue-haired baker's slice of biscotti. "Powder puffs and soda spreads. You used baking soda instead of baking powder for these, right?"

Because of my shifts at the bakery, I knew which recipes used baking soda and which ones used powder. Only I simply followed the recipes, never questioned why one worked better in some situations than others.

The baker chewed her lip, slowly nodding. The crowd seemed to hold its breath again when the judges clustered together to examine the biscotti. I tipped forward, curious to see if I'd be able to spot what they did.

The slices of biscotti *did* look a little flat. Like they hadn't risen to their full potential.

Powder puffs and soda spreads.

Excitement stirred inside of me as I stored this tidbit of knowledge away.

"Moving on to the next batch." Madame Terese stepped sideways and gestured to the fortune cookies with both hands. "Perfect shape and color." The knit-sweater-vest-wearing baker with glasses beamed.

The beam turned into a defensive glare the second Johnny Oliver bit into a cookie and declared, "Great look, but they lack the proper snap."

The judges tasted more cookies, gave more feedback. It lacked any sense of inhibition and their breadth of baking knowledge went deep. I was so busy taking mental notes that I didn't notice how close they'd gotten.

Only two more bakers and then it's my turn. If the judges continued to speed through the cookies—and I sped through green lights afterward—I'd be able to get their feedback *and* get to the FLOC meeting on time.

I dipped my hand into my pocket. Pressed my phone. The time lit up the screen.

Okay, maybe not.

I crouched over the platter, grabbed its edges. I tried to pick it up and leave. But no, I simply couldn't do it.

Not with all the invisible ingredients sparkling between the chocolate chips: stories of sugar harvested from cane fields in Cuba, my first kiss. I let go of the platter, folded my arms behind my back.

"These are absolument délicieux." Madame Terese chewed on a thumbprint cookie. "Sydney, is this bergamot coming through?" The baker reminded me of Devon's grandmother. Tall, curvy, and wearing a fabulous silk lounge set.

"Yes, Madame Terese. The bergamot ones are my grandson's favorite. The amber ones are spelt, rhubarb, and cinnamon. All organic, non-GMO, and sustainable, of course. If you'd both indulge me, I'd love for you to give those a nibble too."

Madame Terese and Johnny Oliver both reached for another cookie.

Hipster Granny, I'm running out of time! Wait. We're allowed to speak to the judges? Ask them to take another bite?

What would I say if they asked me about my flavors? They were probably accustomed to traditional ingredients and refined inspirations. But Malta Hatuey? Prep room offices? I wiped away the sweat pinpricking my hairline, only to discover more cookie dough. Great.

The judges stepped in front of Katherine. She puffed out her chest. A feat of flexibility considering how cosmetically "puffed" it already was. Johnny Oliver plucked a cookie from the top of her tower, examining it from all angles before taking a bite. After a brief pause, he said, "Excellent, color, shape, taste. You checked all the boxes with this shortbread."

Ugh, really?

"And the presentation . . ." Madame Terese scooted in for a closer look at the pyramid's construction. "Spectaculaire!" Apparently, the cookie platter supporting the cookies could spin too. Katherine gave it a twirl. Oohs and aahs broke out all over the tent. Of course, the cookies looked great from every angle.

"These are the best cookies we've seen all day." Summer Rae's cheeks flushed red over her pink blush. "Um. What I meant to say is: the judges have quite the variety to pick and *chews* from, am I right, folks?"

The crowd cheered. At the judging table, bakers gave stilted claps. Dreams of winning the competition faded into the horizon.

Dreams of winning the competition? What's wrong with me?

Johnny Oliver extended a fist across the table to bump Katherine's. The crowd roared. "Johnny O! A fist bump? Somebody pinch me before I wake up!"

Uh-huh. Her words were pure saccharine, lacking any real astonishment. Let alone actual appreciation. *If you give me the trophy now, we can miss rush hour and make it to the Ocean Club for happy hour* was what she probably wanted to say.

I stared off to the side of the tent where her cookies were projected in HD on the white fabric.

The judges *should* just hand her the trophy. The tower of shortbread stars was pretty amazing. Plus, if Bake-Off ended right now, I'd make it to the FLOC meeting with a few minutes to spare.

All I had to do was back one foot up and then the other. Ignore the pang inside my stomach. Give up on the misguidedly romantic notion of cementing my past before forging into my future.

Notions of advancing in the competition would simply cease to take up space in my head, make more room for everything Alma related.

With everyone fawning over Katherine, no one would even bother to notice my absence anyway. But she had to twist back and wave. Her hand movements oscillated between former beauty queen and professional window washer, though her skin looked too smooth to have ever dabbled in any form of manual labor.

I snorted. Yes, the reaction was a little OTT but she triggered images of Madeline. And my pent-up frustrations with that bruja stretched deep. Katherine threw eye daggers at me. The judges turned in my direction.

All at once they stood before me.

The high-def photos on Bake-Off's website hadn't done Madame Terese's beauty any justice. Cherry-red lipstick matched her mini-dress. The cap sleeves showed off toned arms and flawless skin the color of coffee without any cream. Heavy, black bangs framed wide-set eyes staring at me intently.

Judging by the way she looked at me, Madame Terese would *not* sugarcoat her feedback. Not on account of my age, sex, or skin tone. "Last but not least."

Johnny Oliver hunched over the table. He studied the Malta Condensadas closely, before studying me closer still. Teal-blue eyes burned with the intensity of a hundred stovetops.

I blinked down, to thick wrists and muscular hands corded with stories of long shifts at bakeries. Exactly like my parents, sans the tattoos.

Bold lines and bright colors colored the rest of his arms, all the way down to his fingers. I zeroed in on his bicep's centerpiece. A whisk, dough scale, and bread loaf held together by a scroll. The inscription inside it said: *Life Is What You Bake It*.

He picked up a cookie. "Very symmetrical. All uniformly colored, so I suspect a good bake. But the presentation is disappointing and the choice of chocolate-chip cookies, though classic, is maybe too safe for this competition."

My chest rose then fell. Yes, the cookies had chocolate chips in them, but they weren't only chocolate chip. They were afternoons in the prep room, the people working in them. And "safe"?

Everything I risked standing here piled together and jammed deep inside my throat.

While Johnny Oliver still examined the cookie, Madame Terese brought one to her lips. I bit the side of my mouth, but I kept my chin high. Begging the cookies to convey everything I, in that moment, couldn't.

Madame Terese chewed. "Nice slight chewiness in the middle and good crisp around the edges." Her mouth went slack. After a moment, she swallowed. Loud. "Malt." She angled closer. Voice dropped to barely a whisper, as if only speaking to me. "Mon Dieu, I haven't tasted malt since I was a girl. After ballet class."

With these cookies I wanted to capture the bakery. I'd never considered they were capable of capturing more. While I'd tasted bakeries, Madame Terese tasted her childhood studio. My chest struggled to contain a galloping heart. In the thumping, I felt something unfurl.

The flutterings of being a baker in my own right.

Johnny Oliver finally took a bite. "By the looks of the cookie, I certainly wasn't expecting that choice of ingredient either." He bit into the cookie again, chewed slowly as if savoring—or testing—the flavors. "Did you use dark brown sugar instead of light?"

"Yes, sir." Thanks to debate, I knew how to keep my voice steady. "I wanted these cookies to have notes of molasses. There wasn't any at my boyf—" I stopped for a millisecond to correct myself because Ryan wasn't my boyfriend. "Tu—" Ryan wasn't purely my tutor anymore either. Not after what we'd done in the kitchen.

My cheeks went hot. The judges' and Summer Rae's eyebrows slanted at various angles. I cleared my throat and continued. "I didn't have any Malta Hatuey handy either. That's what I originally wanted to use for the sweetener. So I opted for dark brown sugar instead to give the cookies the deeper, almost molassesy taste I was going for."

The judges stood in silence. Summer Rae pursed her glossy lips. "What's . . ." She gave an exaggerated tap to her chin.

Here it came: she's going to ask what Malta Hatuey was.

Would I stop with the tagline, *It's a Cuban soda*? Or give her the Wikipedia version? *It's a Cuban malt soda, named after the country's first national hero, Hatuey, the Taino chief who fled Hispaniola to warn his Taino cousins that the Spanish were coming.*

Probably too heavy for a baking competition. Though now, standing at a literal platform, I felt an urge to use it. I parted my lips, ready to give them the more detailed explanation.

Summer Rae jumped in first. "What's your boyftu?" she asked. "A secret ingredient or something?"

I flushed at the question. The mix of shock and embarrassment completely disarmed me. "Um. Well. The truth is. I started to say 'boyfriend' but meant to say 'tutor.' I guess I ended up combining the two?" Kill me now.

"So which one is it? Your secret's safe with us." She winked to an already giggling crowd. Some of the bakers were cracking up now. Madame Terese was too.

"Both. I think." *Both, I wanted.*

Much to the chagrin of Katherine, laughter and cheers broke out around the tent. And even Johnny Oliver's fiery stare cooled to low.

At least the humiliation was worth it.

"Well done," said Madame Terese. "On the lucky guy, but most importantly, on your bake."

Johnny Oliver nodded. "Working with what you've got to make what you want takes creativity. Grit." He took a step forward.

And extended his fist!

"Give it up for the third fist bump of the day, ladies and gentlemen," Summer Rae said. Loud cheers erupted from every corner of the tent. I bumped Johnny's fist harder than necessary, mostly to check this wasn't a dream.

It wasn't.

Chapter 13

Summer Rae led the judges back through the giant refrigerators for deliberations. The lights dimmed. A single spotlight poured over her, and the whole tent fell silent. "Only twenty contestants will advance to the Signature Bake Challenge. Here, bakers will have the chance to put their special spin on a classic bread or cake recipe."

My chest swelled. After Devon, bread was my bestie.

She turned in a telenovela-esque swish of sequins. "Only now they'll be doughing it LIVE!" The tent erupted with cheers. "That's right folks, starting next week, every bake will take place inside this tent!"

The applause was deafening. Louder—almost—than my heart beating against my rib cage. So maybe baking in the tent wasn't technically a breach on the Ban. It *was* a huge step in bending it though. No matter how much this made my stomach flip, the sparks beneath every flutter said it all.

Pushing against the Ban was 1,000 percent worth it. As much as I loved my shifts at the bakery, baking there meant sticking to my parents' recipes.

Here, I could bake whatever I wanted. Inside this tent, I'd be free.

"For those who can't stick around to find out which bakers are rising to the top, please check Bake-Off's site for the results." She gave an exaggerated wink. "We may also be posting info on the Prize of a Lifetime."

I looked down the judging table, around the tent.

I came. I competed. I wanted to stay and mingle. Find out if I made the cut.

Except the FLOC meeting was starting in less than five minutes. So I bolted and broke every traffic law to get to Immaculate Heart High.

♥ ♥ ♥

Out of my car, I clutched the cookie carrier to my chest and sprinted through Immaculate Heart's parking lot. Under the school's wrought-iron gates, through empty walkways, I ran, skidding to a stop at the sight of Ella guarding the entrance to Room 237. "I'm sorry I'm late."

"Fifteen minutes late to be exact." Ella sneered. "We're doing you this huge favor by being here. Over spring break, no less, and you *still* manage to screw up?" I had to give it to her. The Madeline impression was spot-on.

"I know. There's no excuse." For a split second, I forgot where I was and who I was talking to—and nearly blurted: *actually, I do have an excuse*. A dozen really good ones.

Ella's stomach growled. "Are those why you got held up? You were baking cookies for us?"

I nodded. A non-lie, technically.

"Well, in that case." She held out a palm. "Hand one over. I was stuck at this public beach doing cleanup all day. Community service always makes me so hungry."

I reined in an eye roll, snapped off the lid, and extended the platter. "How pissed is she that I wasn't here on time?"

"She's not pissed because she doesn't know." She took a cookie. "She's on her way though. You got lucky." Ella's words were a slap. A reminder that while Madeline could afford to break the rules, I couldn't.

Ella shooed me inside. "I can't eat with people watching. Plus, one of your little friends is already waiting." Ella smiled, flashing teeth so bleached they reminded me of the skull perched high on one of the shelves in AP Anatomy.

I wanted to take the cookie back, save it from being gnashed by those chompers. Instead, I brushed past her, pushed the door open, and walked in.

Exposed rock stretched up the walls. Antique chains dangled from vaulted ceilings. Glass orbs the size of balloons hung from them, swaying with the cold blasts of AC. The only thing that brought most of us together, inside this weird mix of Stark Tower conference room and executive boardroom, was our shared goal of making it into the Ivy Leagues. Some may have considered it a sad fact, but to me it was no different than the bonds in *The Avengers*. I walked to the long, exquisitely carved mahogany table where we planned each semester's networking, fundraising, and volunteer events.

Usually the table buzzed with type-A activity. Today though, it was only Torie, reading an issue of *Sports Illustrated*. Wait a minute. Where the hell was Devon?

I pulled out my phone to get an ETA. "Sorry about dragging you here during break." I slumped into the chair across from Torie. "I don't know why Madeline insisted on all of us meeting if she's the only one with the contacts to make the interview happen. FLOC protocol maybe?"

"No biggie. I was on campus for softball practice anyway." She cracked her knuckles and then her neck. "But protocol? Come on, Rubes. You know Madeline better than that."

Yes, I did know Madeline better than that. I clutched the cookie carrier tightly across my chest. "Right. She probably wants me to beg or something." The words fell out of my mouth, so cold they burned.

Torie's high ponytail swished with each headshake. "Madeline's a future politician. She wants an *audience* to watch you beg."

I blinked fast, as if waking up from a bad dream. How could I have been so oblivious? "Well, as long as I also get what I want, I really don't care who watches."

Only I did care. A lot.

Madeline kept undermining my attempts to prove I was more than the token brown member of the FLOC. She kept doubting me, instigating the rest of the FLOC to question my place here. All the old worries about my self-worth crept back in again. I glanced at the door, half-wishing she'd walk in already so we could get this over with.

"On the bright side, since it's spring break, Madeline's audience will only consist of Ella, me, and—"

"Surprise!" The door flew open.

"Devon?"

She stormed across the room. Tossed a handful of freshly dyed locks over her shoulder and angled her head into the light. "Well? Do you love it?"

I sprang from my chair to admire her new hair. Devon would've looked good with a dirty mop for hair. "Obvi. But why didn't you tell me about this makeover sooner?"

"I would've told you about it if you answered your phone

earlier." Her voice was full of teasing, but there was also an undercurrent of something else. "You were probably still too busy *academically purposing* with Ryden."

"His name is Ryan." I licked my lips. Before I swooned and spilled all the details, I changed the subject. "But that wasn't the reason I didn't pick up."

"Then what was?"

A pause for dramatic effect. "I was competing in Bake-Off!"

"Bake-Off?" Her voice rose an octave. "You really competed after all?"

I nodded. "That's why I was late."

"Rubi!" She threw her arms around my neck, pulled me in for a tight hug. "This is freaking amazing!"

The way she'd said it made me think competing hadn't only been the right choice, but also a brave one. I squeezed her back tighter.

Torie turned from the table. "High-five, buddy."

"Let me show you what I entered." I pulled Devon back to the table. She plopped down between Torie and me.

I slid the cookie carrier across the table. "Introducing: Malta Condensada Chocolate-Chip Cookies. Bake-Off should be posting who advanced to the next round any minute." Inside my chest, a million emotions buzzed. "Taste them and let me know what you think."

Devon's hands flew to the carrier. She snapped off the lid, handing Torie a cookie before taking one for herself. When they took their first bites, it was almost as if I stood at the judging table again.

Were the cookies transporting them somewhere? If so, where?

The door slammed and Madeline strode into the room. She

frowned at the sight of us, taking the chair Ella pulled out for herself.

"Emergency Future Leader of Orange County meeting number twenty-nine, the matter of Rubi Ramos, is now in session." Only after she cast her lackey a scowl did Ella hit the bejeweled gavel against the table.

"Will you two get off your high horse and tell Rubi when your aunt can interview her?" *Thank you, Devon!* "There's still time for us to get home in time for *Runway Fashion*."

"Ah, Devon." Madeline gave an exaggerated squint. "So it *is* you." She steepled her fingers under her chin. Turned her focus back to me. "Yes, about my aunt."

I wasn't surprised she waited for me to start begging. I was only surprised at how much it stung to put my failures on display like this.

Then again, better they were on display here than in the prep room. Anything to protect my parents from the truth.

"You mentioned she's on the board?"

Madeline licked her lips, her tongue flickered like a snake seeking out prey. "She most certainly is." She grabbed her phone, scrolled down the screen until she found what she was looking for. She turned the screen in my direction.

I hunched forward. Squinted across the length of the table, until the name on the contact card became clear: ADDISON TEAGUE.

Addison Teague wasn't simply on the admissions board. She was the dean of admissions! If she had the power to sign my waitlist letter, she had the power to sign my acceptance letter too. "Can you please set up a meeting for me?"

"Does the week after next work for you?"

I restrained myself from leaping out of the chair and breaking into a happy dance. "Yes. I'll make anytime work."

"Perfect." Madeline brought the phone back to her face. The light illuminated a broad smile growing to Joker-esque proportions.

The air went artic, sending a chill down my neck. Judging by the way Devon's and Torie's eyebrows knitted together, it wasn't because the AC suddenly blasted on.

The side of Devon's mouth barely moved as she whispered, "Why isn't she making you beg?"

The back of the chair dug into me with every slump deeper. Yeah, why wasn't she? Did she realize failing at something didn't necessarily make someone a failure? Had she suddenly changed her mind about me?

My instincts told me to take the help she was offering. Run before she could change her mind. "Can you contact her now and set it up?"

"Sure. I'll text her right now." She brought her elbows onto the table and cradled the phone between her fingers. Her nails tapped against the phone as she said, "Aunt Addie. Exclamation mark, exclamation mark. Can you meet with an acquaintance of mine from the Future Leaders of OC? Praying hands emoji. She's on Alma's waitlist. I think she would make a very *colorful* addition to the incoming class."

The word went through me like a meat cleaver. The word hadn't flown under everyone's radar either. Devon dug her nails into the arms of the chair. Torie's cleats scraped against the floor. Ella bit down on some giggles. Even the less-colorful faces of past members grinned from silver- and gold-framed photographs hanging around the room.

I, on the other hand, kept my face perfectly still.

Beggars could boil with rage. They couldn't shout with it though. They couldn't do anything but be grateful for the occasional scraps thrown their way.

I swallowed the massive lump in my throat, sent the emotions back into the darkest pit of my stomach. I sat up in my chair. "Thank you for doing this, Madeline."

Madeline lowered the phone, casually showed me her finger, a mere centimeter left of the send button. "Speaking of thanks." Her voice was so saccharine it made my teeth hurt. "Aunt Addie needs a thank-you gift, right, Ella?"

"Totally. I mean, she's *only* related to you by marriage. Whatever gift you get her needs to be huge." Her spiel seemed too rehearsed, a monologue Madeline had surely written for her.

"Rubi, you also agree, right? A gift, a nice one, would be the proper way to show my aunt thanks?" She flashed that pointy smile again. This time I thought of a great white shark.

A hunger spread across her face, and finally, it hit me.

Madeline had never intended for me to get on my hands and knees to beg. Hell, she probably didn't even care about flaunting my inadequacies anymore or making a public show of my inability to keep up with the rest of the FLOC.

I'd done that myself.

She'd simply sniffed out an opportunity to take something from me in return for her "help." "Madeline, what do you want?"

"Your captain's title."

Devon and Torie gasped at the same time I did. Was she freaking serious? After all the hours I'd spent helping Sister Bernadette whip up the team into the best debaters they could possibly be?

Devon swung her leather backpack on the table. Torie threw her gym bag on top of it. I pushed the cookie platter forward. All of our items blocked Madeline from view.

"You can't give her your title, Rubi," Devon whispered. "You earned it."

"Plus, you've made it to the championship. You deserve to go out as captain," Torie added.

Both of their arguments echoed my own thoughts, fanned the flames of my fury.

The title wasn't merely a title. It proclaimed that my thoughts and words were worth listening to. Even Madeline had to follow my lead. It was also the only thing Madeline's money couldn't buy. And now she wanted to take it from me?

Giving my title away was a step backward. It was also potentially dangerous.

If she was in the driver's seat at the tournament, she could very well bench me for most of the rounds. How bad would that look to Alma's admissions board?

Then again, without the interview, I doubted Alma would see me at all.

I buried my head in my hands. "Rubi, you can't be seriously considering this," Devon said. I peeked over our makeshift wall. Madeline sat patiently. Her irises blizzards of ice stinging me with the hard truth.

"I'm weaponless, Devon," I whispered. "Madeline marched into the room armed with the dean of admissions while I stumbled into an apparent Law and Debate coup with what? Cookies?"

"They are exceptional cookies though." The spark of our usual banter failed to make me feel any better.

"I don't have any option but to accept her terms."

Torie draped her arms around us, huddled us in even closer. "Are you sure you can't bypass Madeline altogether? You know, have your parents send Alma a charitable contribution?" Torie winked. "My parents donated"—another wink—"when my older brother got rejected from USC. You only got waitlisted. They'd only need to buy a room or two instead of an entire building."

"First of all, my parents can barely afford the house we live in let alone a few extra rooms or building at an Ivy." After Immaculate Heart's tuition and saving for Alma so I wouldn't have to take out loans, money at home was tight by Pelican Point standards. "And even if they could *donate*—"

A weight slammed down on my shoulders. The weight of all their "donations" over the years, everything they'd sacrificed so I could have what they never did. "I couldn't ask for one anyway."

"Why not?" Torie asked. "Lots of people do it. There's no shame in it if nobody finds out."

Devon's head swung to Torie. A shadow flicked across her eyes so quickly I probably imagined it.

"I couldn't ask them, because I already told them I got in."

Devon's jaw dropped while millions of questions swam across Torie's face.

"Holy crap, Rubi." She blinked and blinked, obviously in shock.

I swallowed hard, because wait—there was more. "I even told my dad I'm framing my acceptance letter as we speak."

They both sucked on their teeth, looking away in horror. When they were finally able to make eye contact with me again, they nodded, reluctantly understanding what needed to be done.

I pushed away Devon's backpack, Torie's gym bag, the cookie platter. Faced Madeline head-on.

"You know what?" Madeline said. "I'm feeling extra gracious today. I'll give you until the end of next week to keep conferring with the peanut gallery."

"Is this a joke?" Or worse, a trick? "Will the offer even stand then?"

"I'm a woman of my word. Obviously, it'll still stand." She grinned again.

I scoffed. Of course, she wanted to play with her food before eating it. If, in the end, I'd win Alma, game on. "Deal. End of next week."

"Great." She motioned to Ella to bang the gavel again. "This concludes the Future Leaders of Orange County meeting. Ladies, it's been a pleasure, as always."

Torie jumped out of her chair, the cleats of her softball shoes clacking as she stormed out. Devon tore her scowl away from Madeline long enough to make sure I was able to get up on my own. "I'm fine," I lied, waving her forward. Slinging my messenger bag over my shoulder, I reached across the table to retrieve the cookie carrier.

"Wait. I didn't even get to try your cookies. Ella said they were super yum." Depleted of the energy to scrounge up a level of pettiness to match hers, I shrugged, leaving the carrier on the table.

Madeline strutted over. She studied the cookies, scooped up the best-looking ones. I snapped the lid shut and headed to the door.

Devon and Torie waited there, holding it open. One foot was already on the other side of the threshold when Madeline's voice hooked me again.

"These are actually really good." I stayed frozen, taken aback by the sincerity dripping from her voice. "I love the flavors."

How could she love the flavors, but not the people that mixed them together? Not the places where these sugars and spices grew? She gave a satisfied moan. Wiped the corners of her mouth with her manicured claws. "I hate to admit it, but you have a real talent here. Ever consider working at your parents' bakery after graduation?"

I pressed the carrier into my chest like a shield, protecting myself against another reminder that I didn't belong here.

"Bakeries," I corrected through clenched teeth. Devon grabbed me by the elbow to yank me away. I shook her off, gestured for her and Torie to wait for me outside. "They have *two* bakeries."

"Whatever." Madeline crunched into a second cookie. "My point is, wouldn't it be much easier if you gave up all this rigmarole over Alma and go work for them?"

I clutched the carrier even tighter. Knuckles whitened around the edges. The tiny scars my mother had told me to hide bulged. The longer the moment stretched, the more it became obvious. I wasn't only protecting myself from Madeline, but also the forbidden possibility of following in my parents' footsteps. "No," I said, "it wouldn't."

Chapter 14

I stormed from the FLOC room as fast as I could. Scrambled off the paved walkways, onto the central courtyard's thick grass. The air carried notes of wet dirt, freshly cut grass, and something sweet.

The aromas of expertly tended flowers on the verge of blooming.

Devon and Torie sat cross-legged on the grass. Torie's hand rested on Devon's shoulder. The two huddled so close the sides of their foreheads touched while they watched something on Torie's phone.

Devon sprang to her feet when she heard me approach. "Rubi, you did it!"

"Yeah, I'll get the interview." I collapsed next to them. "It's not going to come cheap."

"I'm not talking about Alma. I'm talking about Bake-Off."

I snatched the phone away.

The names of the bakers chosen to compete in the next round lit up the screen.

Mine being one of them.

I leapt to my feet, broke out into a happy dance. The cookies jangled against the plastic like edible cheerleaders. "I made the cut! I'm going to the second round!"

"As if there was any doubt," Devon said.

The soft carpet of grass cushioned my body as I squished between them. "There were a million doubts, Dev." Freshly wait-listed by Alma, a part of me had worried Bake-Off wouldn't be any different.

I nibbled one of the last cookies. It tasted like success.

I handed Torie the phone back. She refused to take it. "Keep scrolling. You didn't even see the last-minute change to the next challenge."

"Or the Prize of a Lifetime," Devon said.

I scrolled past the list of bakers.

"For the Signature Challenge, contestants can now bring an assistant!" I squealed, digging my nails into Devon's arm. I popped the last piece into my mouth, and kept scrolling.

And there, in big letters, was the grand prize.

An all-expenses-paid summer seminar in international desserts and bread making. Part of the soon-to-be-revamped culinary arts program at Alma U.

"Alma's leveling up their culinary arts program!" I screamed into the phone.

There was no cause for the yelling. I mean, I'd applied to the pre-law program, after all. Whatever upgrades Alma was planning to make to the culinary program shouldn't matter. None of them fit into the Recipe.

A mouthful of cookie lodged in my throat. I leaned forward, choking.

Devon pounded my back like a true bestie. "Keep reading."

"'Seminars will be taught by master chefs. The winner gets to choose their destination. Paris, Tokyo, Istanbul.'" My voice rose with every city. "'Rome, London. Hong Kong.'"

Oh my god.

Havana.

"If I win Bake-Off"—I swallowed hard—"I get to go to Cuba for a summer."

It was a dangerous dream. Wanting to do the thing my parents did so I wouldn't have to, and doing it in the country they'd fled. Only I couldn't help myself. Baking was in my blood. It was one of the only ways I could connect to my Cuban heritage. Until now.

Now, if I won, I could connect to Cuba itself.

"You're so going to win," said Devon.

"Plus, it's affiliated with Alma, so maybe you won't even need Madeline's 'help.'" Torie made air quotes over the word. "Getting into the finals will make you stand out to the committee."

"And winning it? Now that will make you *really* stand out, Rubes."

If my lips weren't so tired from kissing Ryan, I would've smooched them both. "Yes." Two huge weights began to lift off my shoulders. "Oh my god, yes. I'm doing this."

Devon beamed. "I know your dad probably has first dibs on the assistant gig, so at the very least let me do your hair and makeup for the next challenge."

"Are you saying I look bad?" I grinned, barely able to keep the real story at bay.

"It doesn't look bad, it's just . . . The foundation looks—"

"Too colorful?" I asked, sparking fits of laughter.

"Madeline is the literal worst," Devon said.

"She is, and sadly, she'll probably be president one day. Which is why I need to bypass all her BS and trade the interview for another win."

Thanks to Bake-Off, maybe I could have my cake and eat it too.

I settled into the grass and licked my lips, practically tasting cookie dough and oceans again. "Also it's flour, not foundation."

Devon rolled her eyes but flashed those perfect teeth. "I'll tell you all about it when you come over later with that swimsuit you need me to model for you."

"Good." She pulled out her sketchbook. Drew me with an apocalyptic bun crowning my head. Dotted it (and my face) with what I assumed were dried specks of cookie dough. Tendrils of steam rose from them. If only she knew the steam was also rising from—

"We can practice some other looks too. I can't let you go into the next challenge looking like Marie Antoinette."

I flung a chocolate chip at her. She dodged it. Torie placed a hand on Devon's shoulder. "Hey, the woman did know her cake."

"Thank you, Torie!" I said, cracking up.

"Speaking of cake," Devon said. "Any clue about what you're going to make next?"

♥ ♥ ♥

The bakery's rhythm thrummed like a heartbeat, constant and steady. I wanted to lose myself to it, like always. Only for this shift, I couldn't. I needed to stay awake to the techniques and bakes taking place around me. Search for a bread idea to use in Bake-Off's next challenge.

Feeling more like a baker than a baker's daughter, I pulled the prep room doors wide open and walked through. Paused to breathe in the tang of yeast, the sweetness of sugar, and study the blur of hands weighing, cutting, wringing, pounding, shaping, and scoring balls of dough.

Some of the bakers' faces lifted, nodding as I weaved through the back of the prep room. A few calls of "Hola" and "¿Cómo estás?" came my way.

I so badly wanted to tell them I was good.

Tell them I was one step closer to Alma. To Cuba.

But I couldn't risk any of it getting back to my mother. So I shot back a "Hi" and "Bien, gracias," keeping Bake-Off to myself on the sprint to the break room.

I stuffed my messenger bag into the locker. The movements must've pushed on the edges of my phone because a beam of light shot from the bag.

I reached inside to turn it off, but not before Ryan's message flashed on the screen:

I can't stop thinking about earlier.

My lips curled at the memory of us kissing in his kitchen. The cloud of flour dancing around us as we did. I can't stop thinking about it either, I typed back.

A set of gray dots appeared on my screen. Same time tomorrow?

Yes. I was anxious the trig session would turn into making out. Or maybe anxious it wouldn't. I switched off the phone, startling at the sight of Fabiola standing right in front of me. "I'm not too young to die of a heart attack, you know."

"Well, somebody's in a better mood today," she said, probably in reference to the ginormous smile taking up most of my face.

"Really?" The tiny steps I'd made toward Alma made the lie feel less egregious now. Hell, they were slowly morphing into the truth. Then, of course, there was Bake-Off. And Ryan. "Actually, you're right. I'm in a way better mood today."

Fabiola tut-tutted as she swatted my shoulder. "Teenagers," she said in Spanish. "The less I know about your cute redhead, the better."

"Ain't that the truth."

She shook her head. "Anyway, tell your Apá to call me as soon as he gets back."

"As soon as he gets back? Where is he?"

"He left to deliver a wedding cake to the Montage. Okay, chica, me voy." At the doorway she turned back. "Don't forget to tell him to call me. There's a quote I need him to approve by tonight. I left it on his desk." Her eyebrows furrowed as she patted the back of her pants. "Never mind, I have it right here."

I plucked the yellow order slip from her hand. "I'll take it for you." I followed her out of the locker room, nearly smacking into Rafa. With a stern expression he pointed to the clock on the wall. I stuffed the order slip into my pocket, piled my mane into a topknot. "I'll take it to his office *after* my break."

Bent over the kneading table, I scraped the ball of dough out of a large bowl. Let it plop onto the table. The heels of my hands sank into it. The dough stuck to them like a second type of skin. I pushed it down and away from my body. Sprinkled a little more flour over the table and dough. Then folded the dough over and pushed down again. Repeated the process over and over.

The gluten strands are beginning to thicken.

I could tell by the way the dough was springing up. How all the imprints left by my palms were vanishing more quickly. I swallowed the sudden lump in my throat and kept kneading with the entire weight of my body.

Soon, the dough became smooth and silky.

After tucking an escaped curl behind my ear, I scraped the dough into a large glass bowl then covered it with a plastic liner to let it begin to proof. I walked through the heat and the noise of the central prep room, under the simple archway leading to a quieter section.

The pantry, I called it. Here, adjustable roll-out racks and shelves wrapped around the walls. Stacked with everything from large sacks of flour and sugar, to gallon-sized bins of gelatin powders and syrups. The proofing cabinets were also here. Rows of them, arranged in the middle of the room.

Inside of them, different breads and puff pastries rested and rose. I glimpsed through their glass doors until I found the proofing cabinet holding the bolillos.

Each rack was devoted to a tray of them, or bolillo dough in different stages of fermentation. I slid mine into the rack reserved for rising, pre-shaped loaves.

I stepped to the proofing cabinet to my left. The one reserved for the bakery's famous eight-strand, plaited sesame loaf.

Next to them, the cabinet of bolillos looked rustic. Which I liked. Obviously, the customers did too. Bolillos scored up there amongst the bakery's bestsellers.

I closed my eyes and suddenly I was back inside Bake-Off's tent, right next to Katherine's fancy star tower—reliving the judges' main criticisms.

How my Malta Condensadas looked too "simplistic." How the presentation was "disappointing." "Maybe too safe" for the competition.

Okay, so I need to keep the caliber of the taste high, but work on leveling up the design. Turning back to the proofing cabinets, I headed straight to the one filled with puff pastries.

Paper-thin layers of dough and butter curved to form dozens of crescent moons. In the rack above the croissants, raisins and cinnamon powder dusted swirls of creme pat. The creme was piped across the tops of round, spiraled dough. Raw, rising, and bursting with colors, Dad's take on the classic pain aux raisins looked more like edible sculptures than fancy cinnamon rolls.

The aesthetics of them were anything but simplistic, disappointing, or safe. "This is it!"

Because Dad was still out on delivery, Rafa would have to green-light me spending the rest of my shift at the French pastry station.

I hurried back, finding Rafa hunched over the bolillo table. With a heel of one palm over the other, he pushed into the dough, again and again, as if giving it CPR. He must've read my mind because he looked up.

With a grin he rarely shared, he said, "Dándole vida."

Giving it life.

It weirdly felt like a life lesson instead of a kneading technique.

His smile broadened wide enough for the light to catch on the gold cap behind his right canine. Showing off a grin that literally sparkled, I wondered if the bread had breathed life into him too.

He motioned to the bowl filled with freshly mixed dough. "Don Rafa, since I've known you, you've only worked with bolillos," I said in Spanish. Without tugging, I pulled the edge farthest away from me, up toward the rim, back down again before folding the dough in half. "Why only them?"

"Bolillo is traditional, it has no frills." *Like you*. "Como yo." I snorted with laughter.

"But that's not the only reason, Rubi." He made his fist into a claw and raked it inside the empty bowl to illustrate. "This was how we used to mix dough in Guatemala." He rolled his fingers on the sides of the bowl. "My aunt showed me how to twist it this way. Así the dough picks up every last bit of flour."

He looked at me, and I understood. "Nothing goes to waste this way." As soon as the words left my lips, something loosened inside of me. Little baking tips I'd picked up over the years rose to the surface. From Dad. From Rafa. From everyone else at the bakery. Even Johnny Oliver's from earlier.

Rafa nodded. "With all baking, I guess, but especially with bread, it's more than the ingredients or steps written on the page. It's about the people who taught you how to make it. Honorio knows this. He knows I know it. Por eso I like your Papi's bread recipes. I don't need to make anything else."

Suddenly, the notion of asking him to switch to another station seemed unnecessary. Silly even. I didn't want to show the judges something French or fancy, something Katherine would undoubtedly bake. And bake a million times better than I ever could.

I wanted to keep showing the judges who I was. Not who I'd assumed they wanted to see. And who was I if not an extension of my parents?

When the next ball of dough was shiny and springy, ready to begin its first rise, I glanced up at the round clock, then across the prep room.

Dad's office was still dark. As I stared into that darkness, an idea took root.

Chapter 15

I slipped through the doorway. Tuned in to a black-and-white movie on *Cinelatino*, the small TV on top of the filing cabinet barely cast enough light to illuminate his small office. Next to the cabinet, inventory binders and hardcover baking books, in both English and Spanish, stood a small bookcase.

My eyes darted between two books in particular. Johnny Oliver's and Madame Terese's.

I tiptoed toward them, halted in my tracks. Because of the Ban, I'd have to hide that I'd met them today. That they'd tasted my cookies. Liked them enough to send me to the next round.

So much for asking him to be my assistant.

Footsteps thudded outside the door. I froze. My hand flew to my back pocket, grabbing the cake quote. "Fabi told me to give this to you. I was just leaving it here."

From the other side of the door, Judith stared at me. If she suspected me of doing more than dropping off the order slip she didn't mention it. She simply nodded, then continued past the door, carrying a tray of chocolate cake sheets to the decorating room.

I plopped into Dad's chair. *Get a bread recipe and get out.*

Instead, I let myself settle into the massive chair and rub its leather arms, worn and torn by years of his presence.

Topped with stacks of paper and lists, his small desk wasn't too far off from mine at home. It felt natural to sit here. It also felt like a forbidden throne.

Get a recipe and get out. Dad was probably well on his way back already. Not to mention the bolillos in various stages of proofing. I couldn't leave them unattended. Or leave Rafa hanging.

I opened the desk's bottom right drawer. A steel document box lay inside. The key was already tucked into the keyhole. The sides of the box already unlatched. The book inside of it knew I was coming before I did.

The noises of the prep room faded away when I flipped open the box's top and picked up my great-grandmother's recipe book.

My fingers brushed over the tome's crimson cover. It seemed to pulsate under my touch. The gold filigree embossed on the binding and edges flashed in the TV's light as I opened the cover.

Abuela Carmen had filled yellowed page after yellowed page. Slanted lines of tiny print instructed how to make the recipes. Rough sketches illustrated the way they were supposed to look.

Dad had put his own twist on many of these recipes, like I had with the Malta Condensadas. Other recipes though, he'd taken straight from the book. Like the pastelitos de guayaba, croquetas de jamón, and banana rum custard tarts, all bakery staples.

I slowed down to study the recipes. There were some I'd never heard of.

Cazuela de plátanos? Cucuruchos de coco? I imagined my

great-grandmother writing these recipes. Pictured a tiny house in the Cuban countryside. Inside it, my dad learning how to make them.

Tracing my fingertips over her handwriting, I felt like I was discovering something new about who my family was. Who I was.

The possibility of baking some of these recipes in Cuba this summer—that wasn't a key opening the door to everything forbidden.

It was a battering ram to knock the whole thing down.

I flipped through the recipes until they came to an end. But Abuela Carmen had left plenty of pages blank. Enough for Dad to fill some in? Enough for me too?

Something warm poured into my heart. For the first time ever, the secret chamber felt full instead of crammed. I thumbed back through some classics.

Whoa. I knew this one. It was a seasonal item the bakery sold during the first week of January called Rosca de Reyes.

This "king's cake" was more of an enriched dough than an actual cake. Filled with cajeta, the Rosca's dough was first plaited then twisted into the shape of an oval ring before being topped with a variety of candied tropical fruits. The scope of the Rosca's colors and textures was matched only by the various baking skills it took to make.

I skimmed a finger over my great-grandmother's sketch. A replica of a bejeweled crown, ergo its name. Thoughts of crowns and royalty led to thoughts of winning.

This is the bread I have to make for Bake-Off's next challenge.

I pulled out my phone and snapped a picture of both the recipe and its corresponding sketch. The door creaked behind me. The switch flicked on, lighting the whole office.

I inched my head around to the doorway. The fluorescent lights made the confusion on his face shine brighter.

"Rubi?" Dad's jaw tightened as he walked to the desk. "What in the world are you doing?"

I stayed silent, fingers pressed across the edges of his grandmother's book. He glanced at the book and back at me, exhaling a sharp breath.

I willed him to remember our days at the beach making sand cakes. Sent him images of us huddled in the prep room's R&D corner. Of us baking at home before my mother instituted the Ban. The strips of mamey from the other night.

I shot memory after memory. Everything to reinforce the baking bonds built when I was little. But no, Jedi mind tricks weren't a real thing.

Which sucked, because my mouth watered with everything I wanted to tell him about Bake-Off. The glitz and glamour inside the tent. Fans going wild when the contestants revealed their bakes. Judges bilingual in baking *and* pastry.

There was no one in the world I wanted to share this new side of baking with more than him. Beneath all of it, there was another desire too:

To come clean to him about everything.

"Rubi, I asked you a question," he said in Spanish. His tone was clipped, a perfect copy of my mother's when she was pissed. When I didn't immediately answer, he switched to English, like that'd make it easier for me to understand. "What are you doing with this?" He pulled the book away and shut it.

The *snap* echoed down to the marrow of my bones, slapped me awake from any wishful thinking.

Now, even *he* thought this was the wrong book for me to be studying. No matter how desperate I'd been to tell him about Bake-Off, our baking bonds were too rusty to carry its weight.

And if I couldn't tell him about Bake-Off, there was no way I could tell him about Alma. Even less about a summer in Cuba.

I slumped deeper into his chair, back at square one with nowhere to go.

"Rubi?" His voice was as raw and brittle as his expression.

I couldn't look.

I stared at his desk. Fabiola's quote lay within arm's reach. I grabbed it, waved the yellow slip like a white flag. The only way to get out of this office unscathed.

"No, Rubi. Whatever that is, it can wait." So much for that plan. "What were you doing with my grandmother's recipe book?"

"I, um. I was—" My throat swelled shut, probably trying to stop me from spitting out another lie.

Another. Lie.

The only way to see Bake-Off through was to tell him another lie. I swallowed, hard.

He must've heard it because he took a step back, softened the edges of his voice as he spoke. "Look, I only want to know what's going on with you. Like I said the other night, you're acting strange. Even for you."

The attempt at a joke made me feel even worse about what I had to do. My lips flapped open, barely wide enough to let the lie through.

I had to do it. Oh, boy. I couldn't do it.

He arched a brow while he tapped the recipe book's spine. His hand moved down it, then over the worn cover, like he was inspecting it for damage. He lifted the book to his nose for a moment before lowering it down to his chest.

He kept it there. Brown eyes that had stared at me so intently, now looked light-years away.

Something flared in my stomach. It came from somewhere deep. Ancient even. And then, I knew.

The recipe book was more than an anthology of closely guarded family recipes. It was more than the only item he'd brought with him from Cuba. For him, this recipe book was family. It was Cuba.

He'd left it all so I could have it all. Giving him anything less than the truth, most of it anyhow, would be a discredit to those sacrifices.

"Dad." Heart and conscience clashed hard in my chest. "Today I competed in OC's Bake-Off. It's a new amateur baking competition. I found out about it from your baking magazine. I don't know if you noticed the missing page." Words flew from my lips at light speed, pausing all questions and concerns undoubtedly buzzing on his. "I know it wasn't the smartest idea to enter. But considering it's my last semester at Immaculate Heart, I figured no harm, no foul."

Harm and foul had found me. *After* I'd entered. Still, it'd be easier for him to digest it all if I parsed it out in small chunks. "Plus, I thought, how far could I possibly get in a baking competition anyway?" I forced an awkward laugh.

His eyelids narrowed. "How far *did* you get?"

"I made it to the second round." The rush of accomplishment hit me all over again. "That's why I was looking in your book. I wanted to make something Cuban. And what better source of inspiration than Abuela Carmen's book, right?"

If nothing else, it was nice to know I was still capable of telling my parents—er, my dad—the truth. But the truth didn't exactly set me free. In the silence that followed, I could almost hear the gears in his head turning. Swore I could make out the words forming on his lips: *You've had your fun but now it's time to bow out and focus on Alma.*

Time stretched forever, and then, without any warning, the recipe book thumped in front of me.

"Did you find what you were looking for?"

"What?" A light pulsing started at my temples. Dad grabbed

the back of the chair and swiveled it in his direction, leaving me extra dizzy.

"Did you find a recipe to use for the next challenge?" Wait. Were those dimples?

My jaw dropped. Words didn't come. The shock must've amused him because he smiled bigger, making crinkly lines appear all over his face.

I grabbed his hand and squeezed to make sure he was real. That this moment was real. "Wait, you're not going to make me quit?"

"The Ramoses aren't quitters, Rubi. By now, you should know that." He brought his hand to the back of his neck, kneaded it. "Look, I'm not going to lie to you. I'm disappointed you didn't tell me about this competition. But since we're being honest with each other, I have to say, I also understand why you didn't." He moved to the window, opened the blinds to let views of the prep room in. "Our relationship to baking is . . ."

"Complicated."

"Yes." He turned back to me. "You should've asked me to look at the book first. Not so much to get my permission, but to ask for my help in navigating it. None of Abuela Carmen's recipes are easy."

"La Rosca de Reyes especially."

"Ah, sí." He sat on the corner of the desk and opened the book, flipped through the pages until he found it. "La Rosca." He'd said it softly, through a wistful smile and eyelids closed tight.

Whether he was remembering the way his grandmother made it, or imagining the way I would, I couldn't tell.

He slid the book toward me. "Is this what you're going to make?" Excitement dripped from his voice, charging the entire office with raw electricity. Hints of approval too. Less detectable though was acceptance.

"Yes. But before I tell you about it, I want to tell you more about the competition."

The world's longest minute ticked past. Then another. When I thought he was going to tell me to put a lid on it, the corners of his lips curved with the tiniest hint of a smile.

"Okay, mija. Tell me."

Chapter 16

The summary I gave him about Bake-Off's logistics did little to quell his curiosity. He buffeted me with follow-up questions. The rapid-fire nature of them reminded me of a Law and Debate sudden death match. Only the topics were about baking this time, making it easier to pretend there was no difference between who I was and who I was supposed to be.

"Is Madame Terese as tough as she comes across in her pastry books?" He glanced at the bookshelf, pressed against the far wall.

"I haven't read them, but she's tough in a good way."

"Whose arms are more muscular, mine or Johnny Oliver's?"

"Tied, I think. It's hard to tell through all the tattoos. He's much taller than you though. Not a single gray hair either." Dad frowned. I laughed. After all these years, OC was finally beginning to rub off on him. "Oh, but his hands are grisly and battered. Like yours."

"So, he *is* a real baker then?"

Johnny Oliver's voice echoed in my head. *Powder puffs and soda spreads*. Perhaps the quote wouldn't make it into the top ten quotes of all time, but it deserved to crack the top one hundred.

"Dad, he's the real deal. You know he is. Otherwise, you wouldn't have spent money on his books."

He shrugged, moving on. "What about the rest of the contestants? And are most of them your age?" He pulled at his polo's collar as he paced the side of his desk. "Or mine?"

"I think I might be the youngest. A lot of them are around Fabiola's age, the rest are closer to yours or older. And I totally suspect there's a faker among us." Katherine's smug face and her spinning tower of stars played in my mind. "But the rest of them seem to be the real deal too."

"Wait." He stopped in his tracks and snapped back. "You haven't even told me what you made."

"Malta Condensada Chocolate-Chip Cookies."

"As in Malta Hatuey?"

I nodded.

"And the judges *liked* the taste of it?"

"Well, there wasn't any at the house so I used brown sugar and condensed milk as a substitute."

"Interesting. Interesting." He ran his hand through his curls, then snapped his fingers. "Oh, and there is some at the house. Only you probably missed it behind the jars of palm in the fridge."

I mumbled something in agreement, didn't clarify I hadn't been looking inside *our* fridge but Ryan's. His kitchen definitely didn't have any jars of palm hearts or bottles of Malta Hatuey. "Back to the cookies, Dad."

"Yes, back to the cookies." He walked behind the desk, braced his hands on the back of the chair I sat in. "Did the judges like them?" Hopefulness peeked through his voice.

I paused for a dramatic beat, a Law and Debate staple, looked him straight in the eye. "The judges didn't *like* my cookies, Dad. They *loved* them." His grin stretched from one corner of his face to the other. "Which means the judges loved your cookies too. I used your chocolate-chip recipe as a base."

The way his teeth flashed made the edible pearls on Katherine's cookies seem dull in comparison. I settled back into the chair, basked in the glow of recognized achievement.

Yes! We were back to being baking BFFs. I grabbed his hand. "Bake-Off feels special. I really want you to come to the next challenge and see it for yourself. They're letting the contestants bring an assistant for it." My shoulders vibrated with excitement. "Will you be mine?"

A small gasp broke from his lips. He squeezed my hand, then kissed it. An unspoken promise that he would. "The prizes? What about the prizes?"

"An international, all-expenses-paid summer seminar!"

"Fantastic. Plus, since it's during the summer, it won't disrupt your classes in the fall."

I cleared my throat, brushed a curl from my cheek. "Yeah, if I win, it won't disrupt anything at all."

"Where would you go? Maybe the Boss could give me some time off and I can go visit you." He winked at me. "Only fair if I'm going to help you win it."

"Um." I chewed the inside of my cheek. Oh boy, here goes nothing. "You know, lots of baking and pastry capitals around the world."

"Paris, London?" I nodded. He kept going. "I've always wanted to see Milan—"

"Not Milan, Dad. There is Rome though."

"Where else?" He rubbed his hands together.

I glanced down at Abuela Carmen's recipe, her sketch for the Rosca de Reyes. My fingers trembled against the corner of a withered page. "Havana."

As soon as the word left my mouth, a giant black hole materialized inside the tiny office, sucking up all the air. All the excitement drained out of him, and he turned away from me—but not before I caught a glimpse of his face.

I'd always assumed they'd left their lives' hardships on the shores of the island. But the ghosts followed them across land and sea. There they were; etched in the lines of his face, streaked in the premature gray on his temples, in the way his mouth shuttered tightly.

Fleeing Cuba had scarred him as much as it had my mother. Because her scars were visible, it was easier to forget he bore them too.

"Rubi—"

He didn't have to finish. I knew.

I also knew I owed him the rest of the story. Most of it anyhow.

"You know how Alma's got a culinary program?" My voice trembled, hope evaporating from it fast. "Well, they're revamping it. These international seminars are going to be a part of it."

"Look, I'm happy you're competing in this Bake-Off thing, and I'm relieved that it's part of Alma. I really am." He bowed his head, reached across the desk, and closed Abuela Carmen's book. "The Boss will probably kill me for telling you this, but . . ." He rubbed his temples. "The possibility of—" He shook his head, as if in disbelief at what he'd almost said.

"The possibility of what?" Knowing Cuba outside its food? Baking my own recipes? Enrolling in the culinary program? I needed answers!

Without supplying any, he turned to the door and pushed it all the way open. Bakers moved back and forth. Traces of whatever pastries they carried wafted into the office. I wanted the world to stop, force Dad to answer the question.

But the world carried on, business as usual. As much as he'd briefly enjoyed some parts of our pit stop, he was apparently ready to get back to work.

He extended a hand to me, closed his calloused fingers over mine. I flashed to Johnny Oliver's similarly rough ones, before Dad pulled me out of his chair and lifted me onto my feet.

"I know Alma accepted you already, but can competing in Bake-Off put your acceptance in jeopardy? The other night you said something about colleges being able to revoke acceptances if grades slip."

"Alma isn't going to revoke my acceptance." Alma couldn't revoke an acceptance it hadn't made. But I couldn't tell him I'd lied about Alma. Not after doubling down on it. "I won't let anything happen to Alma because of Bake-Off." I'd said it forcefully, as much for his benefit as for my own. "If anything, it'll help."

"Help with what? You're not thinking about switching majors, are you?"

So it was true. No matter how many times he'd let me bend the Ban, the conviction in his voice . . . in his face . . . was crystal clear. The Ban was unbreakable. And becoming my accomplice in Bake-Off was the maximum radius he'd let me bend it.

In my silence, his forehead wrinkled. Disappointment and worry swam between the lines. If I didn't say anything soon, his jaw would stay clenched forever.

"Of course not. I don't know why I said that."

I didn't know why I'd momentarily forgotten there was One Recipe to Rule Them All. Or held out hope that maybe he had.

"Good. I trust you, Rubi. You're doing this for fun only." He motioned to the recipe book. "You don't need this anymore, do you?"

I shook my head. "I took pictures of the recipe. Don't worry, I didn't use a flash."

He set it on the desk and reached for Fabiola's quote. "Flash photography is the least of my worries." He collapsed into the chair, shuffling between all the new orders. I wanted to believe he'd been talking about business worries, not daughter worries.

"For the record, you *are* okay with me competing in Bake-Off, right?"

"Have your spring break fun, but make sure Alma always comes first." He stopped shuffling the papers. "Deal?"

I nodded, on the verge of breaking into the second happy dance of the day. "So, Dad? About the assistant thing for the next challenge . . ."

He lifted the stack of papers. "Not a good idea after all, mija. Too much work." His voice a stilted staccato. "Sorry, Rubi. Can't."

"I get it." His conscience wouldn't let him help me win a trip to the island they'd fled. I braced the side of my head against the doorway. I never should've put him in that position. How ignorant it was of me to have even asked.

"Ask Devon." The smile on his face started to crumple.

"I will." My voice didn't drip with disappointment. Or ooze excitement at Devon subbing in. The only thing that betrayed the dozens of emotions washing over me were these damn beads of sweat. I wiped my hairline. "And Dad? About telling the Boss any of this—"

"What happens in the prep room, stays in the prep room." A little glint flickered in his eyes, and a small smile began to tug at the corners of his lips.

"Great minds think alike." I winked.

This got me a little laugh at least. "Now run along." He waved me off. "I have inventory and orders. Smoke's probably coming out of Rafa's ears because you were due back at the bolillo station two minutes ago. See? I am capable of paying attention to the details as much as the Boss. Close the door please, not all the way."

On the other side of the door, I broke out into the dance. Yes, my arms swung a little slacker now that Dad had bowed out of being my assistant. But as I walked past the ovens, they enveloped me with warmth.

I was going to Bake-Off's second round. With my great-grandmother's Rosca de Reyes. For now, it was more than enough.

Chapter 17

The next morning, Ryan and I sat next to each other, cross-legged and hunkered over the coffee table for our second tutoring session. We sat close. So close that each time one of us shifted, an elbow or knee brushed against the other's.

It wasn't totally accidental on my part. Made me wonder if it wasn't accidental on his either. I bit into the pencil to hide a grin.

Focus. I took the pencil out of my mouth and forced myself to work through the rest of the problem. "Okay, so, *a* represents the length of one of the diagonals, and *b* represents the length of the other," I said.

Ryan nodded. "Yeah. Now plug the values into the formula."

The tip of the pencil scratched against the lined notebook paper as I wrote out the formula: A = 1/2(a)(b). I plugged in the values for *a* and *b*.

"Good, now work it out."

Trig was sticking now that I viewed the formulas like recipes to follow. Converted sines and tangents into angles of various pastries before figuring out how to slice them up, piece parts back together, or make them whole. "Ten *m* squared?" I cleared my throat, sitting taller. "I mean, ten *m* squared."

Ryan tilted his head, an uneven smile tugging at his lips. "Huh. Let's check to make sure you got it right." He leaned over to check my work. Maybe it was just my overactive imagination, but I swore leftover sun radiated from his skin. "Nice."

"So nice." I shook my head and sharpened my pencil, thrilled Alma's pieces were continuing to click into place. If I got the rest of the problems right, then maybe I wouldn't need to do another set of problems tonight. I'd use the extra time to practice making the Rosca dough instead.

"You're really getting the hang of this," Ryan said.

"Well, like I said before, you're a really good tutor."

I thought of all the other things he was really good at too. The faster we got through this lesson, the faster we could get to practicing some of those things. I scooted closer to him.

He grinned. "Don't you mean a really good . . ." He pressed his face to the side of mine like he was going to let me in on a secret. Hot breath skimmed my ear when he whispered, *"Boyftu?"*

My entire body stiffened. Whatever desire I'd had to flirt, and more, vanished. Embarrassment swooped in to take its place, followed by confusion. The only way Ryan could even know the word existed was if he'd been inside the tent.

"Were you at Bake-Off?"

"It definitely felt like I was there. Bake-Off's cameras are way better than Surfline's."

"Cameras?" The word sprouted goose bumps across my arms. The tent's delights intoxicated my senses, yes. But not so much that I forgot to check for any dangers lurking inside of it. "I didn't see any cameras. Are you sure you weren't there? Because aside from the list of finalists, which I read and reread like a million times yesterday, there wasn't anything new posted on the website."

"There was this morning." *Blink before your eyeballs dry out permanently.* "A link to their YouTube channel."

Damn it. They had a channel now?

"It wasn't supposed to be this big reality-show type of competition," I said, mostly to myself. Still, with the challenges going live, no wonder it was morphing into one.

"I don't think it is. I mean they didn't have full episodes or anything. Only had a few clips and snippets. They're pretty short too."

I sighed and slumped against the couch behind us. All the info had probably been there in Bake-Off's entry form all along. Tucked away at the bottom of the page in light gray, super-fine print that nobody ever read. Except future lawyers. Future lawyers always read the fine print.

I'm a future lawyer!

What the hell was wrong with me? The weight of a new worry pressed my body deeper into the couch.

How many other people had watched these clips Ryan mentioned? And by other people, I meant my mother. Had she watched any of them? Considering her exceptionally good mood earlier, a mood she'd been in since "Alma accepted me," chances were she hadn't, but still.

"How many clips was I in?"

"Only one."

One was good. None would've been better. Because all it would take was a customer's passing comment or a forward into my mother's inbox, and adios Bake-Off.

"Hey." His voice grew soft. He angled back into the couch, propped his head on the cushion so his eyes were level with mine. "I only checked the site after you told me the cookies pulled you through to the second round. I swear I wasn't watching in a stalkerish way. I mean, I *did* help you make the Malta Condensadas." His Spanish accent was surprisingly good. He'd obviously paid attention to the way I'd pronounced it. "If anything," he continued, "I was watching in more of an invested boyftu way."

I cupped my hands over my face. "Oh my god." I groaned into them. "I can't believe I said that."

Ryan's hand latched onto my left wrist. In spite of my mortification, I let him peel it away. Slowly, I summoned the courage to look at him. Sunlight fell on his hair, sparking it with every shade of a California wildfire.

All at once, an AP Biology lecture rose to the surface. Pines, sequoias, and chaparral shrubs needed heat for their cones to open. Fires were natural, and necessary, for certain plants to give up their seeds. The key ingredient to forests renewing.

"Don't be embarrassed." He ran a thumb across the top of my hand. "The clips were awesome. You were awesome." All the warm and fuzzies I'd felt in the tent, stirred again thanks to his soft touch. "I needed to see it."

"What do you mean?"

He scratched the back of his head. "You kicking so much ass low-key inspired me to put a deposit on the surf trip I told you about."

"Really?" My chest swelled.

"You don't think that's weird?"

"No, I don't think it's weird at all."

"Well then, see? If I needed to see it, maybe everyone needs to see it."

"Not everyone." I glanced away from him. The afterimage of his face, open and ready, like a plot of land safe for me to plant my seeds, flashed behind my eyelids. "I mean not my mother." Breathe, just breathe. "She'd kill me if she found out about this.

My dad too, because he knows I'm competing and promised to keep it secret. I've turned him into an accomplice now."

"I thought your parents were bakers?"

"They are." My stare veered to the small nicks on the back of my hand. I couldn't see them without imagining my mother's much bigger, much deeper ones. "You know how your dad didn't want you to go on your surf trip to Indonesia? Well, my mother doesn't want me baking. She wants more for me."

"First off, I'm still working on the whole telling him I'm going part."

"Ryan! You have to tell him!"

"The lady doth protest too much?"

I full-on snorted, but hey, dude had a point.

"And secondly, what do *you* want for you?"

I nestled into the crook of his arm to take cover from his question. "It's not that simple, Opri-Wan."

"We're officially still on the clock, Rubi. Which means you have to answer every question. I'm not letting you off the hook just because it's off topic."

"Fine." My nostrils flared. "I'll give you all the bends and twists in the equation and you can see if there's a right answer."

I told him about my parents' sacrifices and expectations.

How despite it all there was this longing for baking.

And an ache to know Cuba. So deeply calcified in my bones I never knew it was there until the summer seminar pulled it to the surface.

But then there were also the inevitable payoffs if I continued checking off all the right boxes. The sweet satisfaction of proving Madeline and the haters on the admissions board wrong.

The even sweeter satisfaction of proving everyone in the prep room right. Que sí se puede. *Yes, we can.*

Ryan's eyes widened with each element of the equation. Never once did they harden with judgement. Devon had been right about secrets. They must be part of teen DNA because never once did he look away. "Here's the worst part." I braced myself for the cherry on top. "I told everyone *I already had*."

"What do you mean?"

I brought my legs to my chest, wrapped my arms around my knees. My head hung heavy between them. Then I told him about the Lie. "Now that you know everything, Opri-Wan, what's the right answer?"

The moment of silence stretched for an eternity. Oh no, he's going to make a run for the beach, isn't he?

Except he didn't.

He didn't even shift his knee away from mine. "Damn. I was hoping you had one. That way, I could copy and paste it on my parents." Ryan scratched at a callus, as if trying to unpeel it from his finger. "Because while I put the deposit down for Indo, I also may have also told Pops I'd do the internship."

My eyebrows shot up. "And let me guess. They both take place at the same time?"

He sucked air through his perfect teeth, nodding.

I tucked a curl behind my ear. Looked at him, mirroring back the empathy he'd always shown me. I wanted to tell him everything would be okay. Then again, I didn't want to dish out platitudes. They had this habit of never turning out to be true.

I shifted my face to the table, to the small corner free of books and binders. Ryan's reflection floated on its shiny surface, his face glazed with worries I deeply felt. The rest of him looked especially tan today. So much so he resembled a bronze statue more than a flesh-and-blood boyftu. I rolled my head into my knees again and cracked up. *Not again*.

"What's so funny?" Ryan laughed. "You needing a costume

ASAP to conceal your secret baking identity? Or us apparently needing clones this summer?"

"Nope. But I like where you're going."

"Then what?"

"Oh, just something I thought of." The rogue curl escaped from behind my ear again. Ryan caught my hand before I tucked it back.

"What? Tell me." His low voice skimmed my ear.

"It's nothing you haven't heard before."

The reddish flecks in his green eyes smoldered. "Tell me again anyway." His hand moved down the side of my neck. Cupping my chin, he angled closer. His face stopped mere inches from mine. "I want to hear you say it."

"How about I show you instead?" Before the last word had fully left my mouth, I pressed my lips to his.

Chapter 18

The timer went off on my phone. I leaned across my desk to peek out the window. The moon shone silver against the inky sky. In the distance, lights drifted down PCH like blooms of jellyfish floating in a current.

My parents were probably caught in the traffic. It was well past nine and their cars were still not parked in the driveway.

I shut my Law and Debate binder, crossed my room, and turned off the lights.

They never came into my room when the lights were off. Sleep was as healing for the mind as the Boss's big pot of caldo was for the body.

Tiptoeing into my closet, the lights switched on automatically, illuminating two rows of clothes. Checkered skirts, polos, and woolen suits for school and debate matches on the right. Bakery uniforms, cutoffs, printed tees, and tanks on the left.

I lunged over the pile of pj's on the floor. Headed to the back of the closet, past the shoe rack to the built-in dresser.

I slid its top drawer open. Two buttered bowls covered with Saran Wrap lay inside it. Through the plastic linings, the balls of Rosca dough glistened. More importantly, in the time it'd taken to outline the pros and cons of a ban on books, both had doubled in size.

"Perfect." I rubbed my palms together. "Now let's see which method works best."

I lifted one of the balls, easing it onto a cutting board I'd placed on top of the dresser. I dipped my hands into a small bag of flour, then formed a hole inside the center of the dough. When the hole was big enough, I stretched the sides gently to form a ring.

Then I covered it with the wrap. Placed it in the second drawer down for a second rise.

I was in the middle of rolling the second ball of dough when I heard it.

Three knocks on the closet's door. The turning of the knob. A creak of the door opening. My mother's voice from the other side of it.

"Rubi? Are you decent?"

Panicked, I leapt over the mound of pj's. Pressed my cold body against the door before she barged through. "Mamá, don't come in! I'm—" *Think, brain, think*. "I'm half-naked."

A full-on laugh. "Nothing I haven't seen before, niña."

"Ma!"

Giggles tapered into a sigh. "Look, I only wanted to come in and tell you again how proud I am of you. Jeez, ¿es un crimen?"

No, but lying to her for the hundredth time sure was. Baking in her house was too. My heart pounded into overdrive.

"I also wanted to tell you, I'm sorry." *She* was sorry? "I haven't taken you out to celebrate Alma like we should. The new bakery is taking so much time. Faulty oven. Driving to and from Santa Ana every day." The weariness in her voice was palpable. "On the bright side." She drumrolled the door, pitch flying all over the place when she said, "Papi told me about you framing the letter!" Did the floor suddenly turn into batter? Or was that sinking feeling just me?

"Ohhh, and I ordered us matching Alma cardigans!"

The log of dough went slick in my hands. Gravity sagged the middle, slumping my shoulders with it. "Wow, Mamá." I wanted to kiss debate practice for teaching me how to force words through a throat swelling shut. "That's great."

"I promise we'll get lunch or dinner this week." She paused. An exhale. "Next week at the latest, okay, mija?"

I swallowed hard. Braced my forehead against the sturdiness of the door. "I can't wait."

A light thump sounded on the other side. Maybe she leaned against it too.

"Te quiero." Her voice came out soft, excited. Vulnerability vibrating through the door.

I pressed a palm on the wood. "I love you too." At the very least, this part of my performance was true.

When she left, I told myself to be smart. Swap the dough for books and get a good night's rest.

Instead, I fixed the log as best I could and kept practicing.

♥ ♥ ♥

The tent's size had doubled. The crowd inside of it tripled. People chitchatted around the faux islands. Clinking glasses filled with mimosas and rosé. Snatching milk chocolate petit fours from passing servers. I tugged Devon's sleeve and said, "Madame Terese's recipe, I think." She plucked one from a platter and popped it into her mouth. She moaned, licking her fingers. "And here I thought her outfits were going to be the pièce de résistance."

I took one for myself. My face did the same gymnastics hers did a second ago. More probably, because I was here. In the tent.

Competing again, and hopefully one step closer to Alma—all sans Madeline's "help."

One step closer to Cuba too.

I could've stood there, awestruck by it all, but the Rosca de Reyes wasn't going to bake itself. I grabbed Devon by the elbow and led her through the tent. Artificial grass crunched under our shoes. She'd insisted I swap my sandals for wedge (and glittery) sneakers. Because she was my assistant for the day, I indulged her.

With Abuela Carmen's sketch as a base, my improved math skills, and Devon's expertise for beautification, the Rosca's presentation could be light-years ahead of the Malta Condensadas'.

Suddenly, I found myself striding through the tent like I was born in these shoes. Heads turned in my direction. People clustered closer to one another. Whispered. Nodded at me. Eyes tracked me all the way to the platform leading to the judging table.

"People totally know who you are," Devon squealed into my ear. "Omg, Rubes. You're a fan favorite."

My chest swelled with pride. No, this wasn't a dream. I was actually being noticed for baking.

Noticed for baking.

My stomach dropped. So did my head. I yanked Devon to the side of the tent. "Dev, I can't have all these people recognizing me." How could I have forgotten about the cameras—again? With the competition going live, they'd probably stream the entire bake online this time. "The Boss will kill me if she sees this, remember?"

"Bakers, judging will take place in five minutes!" Summer Rae's voice boomed over the speakers. Some bakers downed their drinks. Others sprang forward. I remained frozen.

To Bake-Off or to Take Off?

I couldn't keep avoiding the question for fear of picking the wrong answer. It struck me then: all my life I'd been so afraid of picking the wrong answers I'd hardly ever asked myself the right questions.

To Bake-Off or Take Off? That'd always been the right question.

"I need a disguise."

Devon tore the baseball cap off her head, shoved it into my hands.

"Los Angeles Angels of Anaheim," I read, tracing the cap's raised embroidery with a thumb. "This doesn't even make sense, Dev. How can a team be named after two different cities? From two very different counties no less?"

"It makes perfect sense. Put it on."

I slipped the cap on. The curved, oversized bill bathed my face in shadows. "What's up with you wearing all these caps all of a sudden?"

She shrugged, sidestepping my question. "No time for that now, Rubes." She grabbed a handful of my curls and tucked them under the cap. I stuffed more in. "Okay, my turn." She slipped off her hair tie, shaking out newly black tresses. Tossed some in front of her shoulders, curtaining her face with them. "What do you think?"

"Beautifully unrecognizable." The Boss hadn't seen Devon's new look yet. This could totally work.

Keeping our faces low, we linked fingers and sprinted forward. Clipboard Lady only had one page of names this time. She checked the box next to mine, waved us up the platform with a huge smile matching ours.

Two rows of workstations ran down the stage, ten on each side of the tent. Behind them, the huge refrigerators were there, dominating the back of the stage like before. Only now, three normal-sized ones sat between them too.

In the back corners were two massive cabinets. Every inch of their shelves was packed with bowls, pans, and molds. Hundreds of containers of ingredients.

Dizzy from the sight of it all, Devon had to drag me to my workstation.

Atop a gold place card holder, there was my name, printed in bold cursive.

"As Torie would say, *Get your head in the game, Rubes.*"

I shook my hands as if that would sling off the extra nerves. "You're right." I shot Devon an uneven smile, letting my fingers drift over the food timer, KitchenAid mixer, oven knobs, and stovetop to familiarize myself with the equipment. Sounds of the other bakers and their assistants doing the same floated around us. "Head's back in the game."

Good thing too because the lights dimmed, and Summer Rae's voice boomed from every corner of the tent. "From fifty contestants to twenty, we've begun to separate the wheat from the chaff. Today, our judges will find the ten *rising* stars heading to the semifinals." My pulse beat hard against my temples. "Bakers, are you ready?"

Spotlights fell onto the giant fridges. The doors sprang open. Summer Rae and the judges leapt out of them.

Cheers erupted throughout the tent.

My palms stung from how hard I clapped. If I didn't stop woohoo-ing and yay-ing, my voice would be hoarse. Even worse—gone—for next week's debate practice.

I kept cheering.

"Rubes, this is wild. Like closing Fashion Week wild."

Even if I didn't know what that meant exactly, I did understand. I turned to face the crowd. If Dad couldn't be on the stage with me, at the very least I wanted him shoulder to shoulder with all these shouting faces. Squished inside this crowd who appreciated, respected, and loved baking as much as he did.

A flash of pink tweed and blond hair cut through the crowd. Katherine snarled something to the Clipboard Lady, ran up the platform, and took the empty station in front of us.

She scoped out the rest of the bakers. When she got to me, she took in my linen pants and blouse. "Well, you sure clean up nicely."

Some sort of backhanded compliment? "Thanks," I said through clenched teeth.

"Not sure if the hat goes with the rest of your look." Nope, just backhand.

"The hat goes with anything," Devon said. A true ride-or-die.

"Plus, I can't take it off," I snapped. At that Katherine raised her brows. "What I meant to say is, it's my lucky hat."

"I see." She smirked. "In that case leave it on, sweetie. Today you'll need all the luck you can get." She spun to her station.

"Madeline four-point-oh much?" Devon said.

I swallowed my fury, packed it into the deep pit in my stomach where the rest of the bottled-up anger dwelled. There was no time to unleash it on Madeline 4.0. Not when the judges made their way down the makeshift aisle between the stations. A camera crew trailed them. Summer Rae strutted several feet ahead, mic in hand.

"Bakers, it's dough-time." She and the judges settled behind the judging table. "For this Signature Challenge, you must put your own spin on a cake or bread recipe that'll make the judges' dreams *crumb* true."

Devon looped an arm around my shoulders. "She's epic."

"Wait until you hear the judges."

"Everything you need will be found on the shelves or in the fridges. You were also allowed to bring specialty ingredients to make *whisk-ier* creations or to use as decorations. As well as a non-baker pal to assist you however you wish. You will have three hours for this challenge." She sucked in a mouthful of air. "On your mark. Get set. DOUGH IT!"

Ovens thrummed on. Bakers barked orders. Shoes pounded from one end of the stage to the other. I tied the provided apron around my waist, dropped to my knees, and turned the oven's knob to 375 degrees. Burners sparked to life. I cracked the door open a half inch. Small waves of growing heat rushed out. They rolled up my arms, through my skin. I basked in the warmth of it—of this.

Clanging the door shut, I rose onto my feet. "Dev, let's dough it."

I covered the ball of dough and put it in the station's drawer to let it proof. "He's coming," Devon said, looking up from her sketch pad.

Johnny Oliver, arms crossed, stood at the base of my workstation. The camera crew trailed a few feet behind him. "How long are you going to let it proof?"

"For the first proof on this, I'd typically do one and a half hours." I kept my chin down, away from the cameras. "But it's so hot in here, I think I can get away with just one. Then thirty minutes for the second proof after I shape it."

Every single voice on the stage rose and fell, swimming around us. Except Johnny Oliver's. His mouth remained clamped shut. I tilted my face up an inch in case there was some indication of what he was thinking.

Nope.

My stomach began to knot.

"And your assistant? How will she be helping?"

"*She* will be doing design and decoration." At least Devon had the good sense to keep her face lower than her voice.

"She will also be doing the dishes." I whacked her with a dishrag.

Devon's head swung up, towel in hand to smack me right back. But she got a peek at the cameras and glanced back down to her sketch. Brought some locks of fading black hair over her face for good measure. "Yes, boss."

He nodded and moved on to the next baker. But I was pretty sure he smiled before he left.

"Bakers, you have two and a half hours remaining," Summer Rae said from the judging table. Pans clattered into sinks. Fridges slammed shut. Grunts and groans escaped lips, mine included. Katherine did none of those things, turning on a mini fan instead to cool her cake sponges.

How was she doing this all so fast and without an assistant? I hadn't finished any of the tasks it took to complete the Rosca. And there were so many left.

"Devon, where are you?" I muttered, glancing toward the back of the tent.

There she was, plucking the last candied and fresh lemons and oranges from glass bowls. She sprinted back, citrus clutched close to her chest, dodging bakers like she was on a football field. With moves like that, she really *had* been spending more time watching sports with Torie. Hell, she was probably playing them now too.

"Whew." Devon dabbed her forehead, spilling the goods onto the island. Everything else I'd brought with me. Goat milk for the cajeta. Dried papaya and guava paste for the decorations. A single black bean.

"Thanks, Dev. Seriously, you're the best. Now let's start shaping these into your designs."

When we popped off Tupperware lids, Katherine's handheld fan must've swiveled in our direction, because the scents of the citrus peels and tropical fruits funneled straight up my nose. Kicking off my shoes, I dug my toes into the blades of artificial grass. Whiffs of tropical fruits made it easy to imagine I was dipping my feet into the hot sands of a Cuban beach instead.

If I won, I wouldn't need to imagine it.

♥ ♥ ♥

Devon and I stood side by side. "Can you cut these guava strips into wave designs with one of your fashion design ruler thingies?"

"You mean my French curve ruler?" She held up the plastic squiggly thing.

"That contraption is actually perfectly suited to cut designs of all radii." *Look at me talking math*. Devon shook her head, cracking up. "When you're done with those, can you start on shaping the lemons into suns?"

"Aye-aye, captain." She rolled a piece of guava between her fingers. "I don't think cutting fruit patterns will be so different from cutting leather ones."

As she cut fruit, I molded palm trees and surfboards from colored sugar paste. Whittled Mickey Mouse heads from candied pineapples.

"Damn, Rubes. Ryan must be a really good tutor because your cutouts are beyond symmetrical."

I piled the decorations onto small plates. A new appreciation and respect for tangents, triangles, and slopes rushed over me. "Yeah, he's an awesome tutor." I picked up a candied lemon peel and bit into it. The weirdly delicious combination of sweet and tart reminded me of another odd but good duo—sunscreen and seawater. "I guess his lessons are rubbing off on me."

"Just as long as they're the only thing rubbing off on you right now."

Behind us, a throat cleared. We spun back. Madame Terese stood there, lit by the glow of the camera crew.

Devon cracked up. I choked on the lemon. And as Madame Terese turned on patent leather boots, a huge smile swept across her face.

"Devon!" I gasped for breath. "She totally heard."

"Like I said, people know who you are here. Even the judges." She slapped me a couple times on the back. "Now, while you remember how to chew, go grab some almonds. I don't know if it'll mesh with your recipe or not, but something oval on the top will bring all of these shapes together."

"And add crunch! Great idea."

I hustled to one of the shelves. Halfway there, a baker stumbled into the aisle. Bangs hung low over his right eyebrow. The top of his teal V-neck, loose and plungey, showed off a sweaty chest, heaving incredibly fast. "My creme pat. Have you seen it?" I shook my head. "Are you sure? Maybe you took it by accident?"

"Um, I didn't even make cake."

He brushed past me, stopped Hipster Granny who made her way up the aisle. "Did you steal my creme pat?"

I looked around the tent—like *really* looked. The bakers who'd chosen to make cakes paced at the fridges. So did their assistants. High-pitched commands came from all over. Hands scraped on linen aprons. Whisks furiously clanked against the edges of bowls. Oven doors slammed. Mixers whirred.

With so many people baking so many things, had he misplaced his custard? Had someone taken it by accident? Hipster Granny and Summer Rae led the crying baker back to his station, promising him no one had taken it on purpose.

But what if someone had?

I shook away the thought. Either way, the competition was firing up. And frankly, not all of the bakers were withstanding the heat. Like the mustachioed baker one workstation over. NICO, his name card read. "Mr. Oliver, I got this move from your advance kneading techniques." Johnny Oliver stood at the edge of the station, arms crossed, tight-lipped as always. "The SSF," Nico continued. He stretched the dough about two feet wide, swung it over his head like a lasso. Slapped it onto the table before folding it. "Stretch. Slap. Fold."

He demonstrated the steps again, but on the next swing forward, the dough escaped his grip.

It flew ahead, a parabolic path headed straight for the purple-and-blue-haired baker at the workstation in front of his.

The dough bull's-eyed the back of her head with a *thump.* She yelped. From the impact, yes. But probably even more at how her glasses popped off her face and plunged smack-dab into the bowl of melted chocolate she'd been stirring.

Gasps broke from every corner of the tent. Summer Rae and Nico rushed to her side. "Sorry, I'm so sorry." His chin—and the tips of his mustache—twitching.

The baker fished out her glasses with a ladle, wiped the lenses with the hem of a cat-print apron. Picking up his dough, she handed it back to him and said, "It's o-k-k-kay, mistakes h-h-happen."

Applause filled the tent. "Folks, another example of when

things go *a-rye* in the kitchen." Summer Rae draped an arm over a sniffling Nico. "It's best not to hold a *fudge*."

My fingers flew over glass containers. I searched through aluminum tins, silicone bags, and cartons. Almonds, where are you? My shoulders caved. Okay, maybe I could just sprinkle some sea salt flakes over the wave patterns. Make them glitter the way they did in real life, plus add a tiny crunch to those bites.

"Bakers! You have one hour remaining."

I wiped my sweaty palms on my shirt, grabbed the container of sea salt. Something about the container rooted me in place. I flipped the lid open.

The grains were too fine. The scent too sweet. I grabbed a pinch between my fingers and licked it.

Sugar—not salt—melted over my tongue.

I edged back to the shelf, to the exact spot where I'd grabbed it. Coarse flakes of salt glittered through the glass sides of a container labeled SUGAR.

My stomach turned into Jell-O. "Someone switched these labels," I muttered.

Hipster Granny—who stood a few feet away, grabbing some last-minute ingredients of her own—turned toward me. "What was that, dear?"

I showed her the two containers. "Sydney, I think someone swapped these on purpose. I mean I didn't see it happen, but . . ." My gut twisted, knowing that it was true.

I peeled off the sticker labels and fixed them. Only sheer will kept me from running back to Devon and figuring out who'd reached for sabotage.

Sydney blotted her forehead with a silk hankie. "Goodness,

you saved me! I don't think I would've noticed until it was too late."

"So much for us not holding a *fudge,* because this is totally *fudged* up."

That earned me a chuckle. "It is. But no harm, no foul, right?"

I flinched hard at her words. I'd applied the same reasoning to enter this competition. Now, the sentiment rang hollow. Selfish even.

"Did you find what you were looking for?"

"Nope." My arms hung limp at my side. "All out of almonds."

"This is your lucky day. I have loads of extra ones. Follow me."

Chapter 19

Everything depended on the Rosca rising the way it was supposed to. Otherwise, it'd be too late to make anything else. "Here goes nothing." With a flick of the wrist, I whipped off the cloth.

"Whoa," Devon said. "It's, like, doubled."

Exhaling, I threw my head up to the tent's ceiling. The rows of lights made my vision blur. Or maybe it wasn't the lights. Maybe it was the Rosca.

Even though it was supposed to be for this competition—for Alma—in that moment, the bake felt like it was also for Abuela Carmen . . . for the rest of my family tucked away between the covers of worn recipe books and fading memories too.

Because there, within layers of bread and slices of tropical fruit, the curves of this ring connected me to an island, and people, I thought I'd never meet.

The more I baked Abuela Carmen's recipes the more I would know them. The more I baked my own . . . the more I would know me.

I blinked hard and fast to keep the tears back. The tent

had already witnessed more than enough waterworks for the day.

Devon and I were halfway done arranging the sugar paste and fruit decorations on the Rosca when she tugged my blouse. She coughed loudly. So loud, I wondered if she was doing it to get the passing camera crew's attention.

Attention was gotten, all right. She waved them over. "Dev, what are you doing?"

She pressed a small Tupperware into my hands. Through the translucent blue lid, a small mound of candied cherries sparkled inside. My chest filled with emotion. "Devon, did you make these for me?"

"No." She paused. The camera crew scooched closer. "Read the note on the lid."

I took off the lid and turned it over. A highlighter-yellow Post-it Note was stuck to the front. Red ink. The small scratchy letters could only be Dad's handwriting:

Last-minute delivery, mija. Sorry I couldn't come to watch. Call me when you get out and remember: shine bright like a Rubi.

I brought the note to my heart. Tears welled up so fast no amount of blinking kept them back this time.

♥ ♥ ♥

"Time! Bakers, please bring your bakes to the judging table."

"You got this," Devon said. I nodded, dropped my chin, and pulled the cap over my forehead. Abuela Carmen's Rosca de Reyes needed to take center stage, not me.

Under the tent's spotlights, the Rosca's oval edges shimmered with egg wash and a dusting of sugar. The kaleidoscope of candied fruits blinked against the lights, creating a halo of warm light hovering over the Rosca. Easing it onto the judging table, I smiled at the sight of it.

Smile crumpled when Katherine set her bake right next to mine.

Rising from a mint-green, porcelain platter, her cake was an edible 3D replica of Bake-Off's tent. White fondant covered the long sides of it and the sloped roof panels—which she'd dotted with silver, bite-sized pearls.

The short sides of the cake she'd left bare. Most likely to show off the six layers of sponge sandwiched between layers of white and orange ganache. All of it somehow projected even more beautifully onto the sides of the tent.

Great. So she'd managed to nab one of the semifinal spots before the judging had even started. Her chest puffed out like she knew it too.

Cold seeped through me. The notion of not making the semifinals froze me to the core. I'd barely studied debate all weekend. I didn't want to go back to Madeline to ask for help again. Much less for Cuba's shores to recede from my grasp.

My palms went sweaty. Weirdly, I longed for Law and Debate's tall lecterns. My fingers twitched for their angled, shelved tops that kept note cards from slipping. Perfectly constructed to conceal shaky hands too.

The judging table here was the exact opposite. Flat and low with nowhere for my hands to hide. I swung my arms behind my back. Twined my fingers together to shield them from the judges.

One of my fingertips grazed the small nicks and raised spots on the back of my other hand. I trailed a thumb over them, as if reading a new type of Braille etched into my skin.

Shine bright like a Rubi, Dad's voice echoed.

I closed my eyes, pretended that the sweat pinpricking the back of my neck was a spray of the Caribbean Ocean. The heat in the tent—hugs of relatives long gone, but not lost. Relief flooded me. Then all the reasons why I needed to stand here right now.

Ready or not, I opened my eyes and let go of my hands.

Katherine leaned over. "It's magical, isn't it?" She breathed from the side of her mouth, gesturing to her tent cake.

"The roof panel." I observed more closely. "You used square sheets?"

"Obviously," she scoffed.

"You should've cut them into right angles before assembling them. It would've given you a steeper roof. Then your design wouldn't have needed this." I pointed to the inch-wide line of royal icing she'd used to cover an exposed strip of sponge. "Personally, I think it would've looked neater without it." Katherine shot me an icy glare. "Trig, right?" I shrugged, smiling wide, thinking of Ryan. "Who knew math could come in so handy?"

I didn't know if this exchange was what Dad meant by *shine bright like a Rubi*. All I knew was when dealing with witches, sometimes it was better to cut sharp like steel.

Katherine kept her face steady as the judges studied her cake. "The idea is exceptionnelle," Madame Terese said. Obtuse angled roof or not, even I had to admit the idea was good. At Madame Terese's comments, Katherine exhaled an infinitesimal sigh.

Summer Rae brought her face inches from the cake. "The pearls add so much elegance."

"Thank you." Katherine leaned forward like she was about to let Summer Rae and the judges in on a secret. She touched the strand of pearls clasped around her neck. "I wanted to put a little piece of my family in this bake."

The pearls weren't a family heirloom, rather limited-edition Chanel. Devon had bought the same exact necklace. Last week. At South Coast Plaza. While most of the crowd ate up her story, I turned back to our station. Devon pretended to gag. Under the safety of the baseball cap's lid, I mouthed, *I know.*

By now, I should've known nowhere in the tent was safe. Johnny Oliver tipped his head at me. The corners of his mouth curled.

Wait.

Did he see through this calculated attempt to win brownie points? Her loading up on peacocking but skimping on passion? He clapped his hands and rubbed them together. The baking tattoos danced. "Let's dig in."

Katherine handed Johnny Oliver a cake knife. "Please, Johnny O, I'd be honored if you'd cut it."

Riiiiiiight.

Johnny Oliver took the silver handle, its engraved design as ornate as her bake. The knife cut through all the layers smoothly. Katherine handed him a porcelain plate and a fork. Instead of lifting a piece of cake to his mouth, Johnny Oliver scratched each layer of sponge with the fork. "How many cake tins did you use?"

"Three."

"And all three were placed on the same shelf in the oven?"

"Come now, Johnny O." She chuckled. "The ovens here aren't big enough for that." A smattering of laughter rippled through the tent.

Johnny Oliver lowered the fork. "The reason I ask is because different shelves mean different cook times." He paused to let it sink in. "Rotation for an even foundation."

Ah! So that's why Dad had insisted on purchasing the most

expensive rotating rack ovens for the bakery. And why the Boss hadn't fought him on it. "Absent rotation, a general rule of thumb is for a browner bottom, like a pie crust, lower rack. Browner top, upper rack. Your layers of sponge are baked. Sadly though, because you didn't fit them on the same shelf, or rotate the tins, the layers aren't even."

Pink spots broke out over Katherine's cheeks. Johnny Oliver passed the plate of cake to Madame Terese without even tasting it. She lifted a small mouthful of cake to her cherry-glossed lips.

"The fondant is great. I get a nutty taste. Is that walnut coming through?"

"And pistachio."

"I could've done with even more pistachio actually. Iranian pistachios pack an even greater punch of flavor. They also give a richer color."

Iranian pistachios! I couldn't wait to tell Dad.

"I'll keep all of your tips in mind for next time." In spite of her false bravado, Katherine's voice trembled. This time for real.

I turned to Devon again and winked, ecstatic they'd seen through Katherine's facade. When I glanced back at her bake though, something bitter slid down my throat. It took massive cojones to always strive to be the best. Thanks to the waitlist, I knew firsthand how much it massively sucked to fall short of it. As much as I wanted to ignore it, I couldn't help but feel (a little) sorry for her.

"Now on to our youngest contestant. If it is still *you* under the hat," Summer Rae said. I nodded. Laughter and applause floated across the tent.

"Well, what do we have here?" Johnny Oliver asked.

"A Rosca de Reyes." I kept my head down. Angled to avoid the cameras, but not so low that I couldn't make eye contact with the judges. "It's a Latinx version of a Louisiana king cake." I turned to Madame Terese. "Or a galette des rois like it's called in France."

Perfectly arched brows rose higher, probably impressed with my pronunciation. Now, if I could also impress them with my bake.

"The design of your bake is magnifique," Madame Terese said. "The symmetry of the various slices of fruit is impeccable and très jolie." She paused, her forefinger circling the oval shape of the Rosca. "I do wish, however, that you had focused on making the loaf as symmetrical as everything on top of it."

My heart thumped. Or maybe it was the sound of math boomeranging back to kick me in the butt.

"Overall, the look of your bake is very tempting. I can definitely still see a resemblance to a crown." Laughter flashed in her eyes. "Or an heirloom necklace."

Considering Madame Terese was French, she probably knew her macarons as well as her Coco Chanel. I bit down a smile, taking a deeper look at the bake.

The Rosca *did* look like a necklace. A real heirloom. Abuela Carmen hadn't been able to pass down a house or a pearls. The only thing she'd left behind were memories Dad had already forgotten—or tried to. And these recipes.

"Let's have a taste." Light bounced off Johnny Oliver's black hair when he shifted around the Rosca. "Utensils?"

Oh no. Utensils! In my rush to the judging table, I'd forgotten to bring a bread knife and plates. Was I really going to have to ask the International Pastry Diva to rip into my Rosca with manicured hands?

Wow. Okay, she tore off a piece like she meant business. So did Johnny Oliver. "You know, I really appreciate a baker who knows bread is meant to be broken by people you share it with."

Madame Terese's lipstick glimmered. "Absolument."

They couldn't have said anything that rang more true. Yes, I'd failed the utensil part of the challenge. But when their gazes connected with mine, I think they picked up on the fact that I (fingers crossed) had understood the assignment.

Clings and *clanks* jangled across the judging table. All the bakers with bread recipes rushed to hide their utensils.

Johnny Oliver examined the inside of the Rosca closely. Poked a finger inside the dough. "Baked all the way through." My shoulders relaxed. "The layer of caramel—"

"Cajeta," I corrected. "I used a layer of cajeta." The judges exchanged amused looks with each other, then inched closer with newfound interest.

"The layer of cajeta looks even," he continued. They lifted the Rosca to their mouths.

"Wait." I held up a hand to stop them from eating. "As you probably know, tradition calls for a lucky charm to be baked into the Rosca's dough. Whoever finds it becomes a king for the day. Originally, the lucky charm was an unbaked bean. Now it can be anything from a plastic doll to a crown. I wanted to keep it old-school, per my Abuela Carmen's recipe, so I went for a black bean. The type used in Cuban cuisine." I took a deep breath and continued. "As a future lawyer, I need to warn you of any potential choking hazards before tasting it."

Future lawyer?

Abuela Carmen?

Cuban cuisine?

I'd just revealed bits and pieces of my identity the red cap was supposed to keep under wraps. "I'm going to stop talking now, so you can actually, you know, taste it."

The tent erupted with laughter. I never would've guessed my monologue would be rewarded with so much of it. "Are you sure?" the judges asked in unison, sparking more laughs. Including my own. "Because you can tell us more about your bake if you want," Johnny Oliver said.

I loved the way they held the door open for me to keep talking about the Rosca.

Squaring my shoulders, I lifted them a little bit higher. I wanted to tell them that by using her recipe, Abuela Carmen wasn't a stranger anymore, and that now I knew a little bit more about Cuba too. But I didn't.

"If I told you more we'd be here for hours." Some of the bakers cracked up. Others nodded in agreement. "But right now, all I want is for you to taste it."

So they did. Through closed eyes the judges sampled the Rosca de Reyes.

"You've transported me to Old Havana with all these tropical fruits," Madame Terese said. My heart raced with excitement. She ripped off another piece. One topped with waves of guava and Mickey Mouse ears molded from sugar paste. "Each fruit, whether tangy or sweet, gives a slightly different flavor to each bite." She chewed again, slowly. "Making it very easy to justify eating the entire bake."

A feeling of warmth enveloped me. Abuela Carmen's arms wrapping around me. "Speaking of the different fruits," Johnny Oliver said. "Can you please explain your decision to bake the fruits on the outside of the loaf versus inside of it?"

"I wanted to stay as close to my great-grandmother's recipe as possible. I think she understood putting the fruits inside would've added extra moisture to the dough. The layer of cajeta already adds plenty, so adding even more via the fruits . . ."

The judges grinned. Yes!

"Would make it easier for the dough to lose the brioche-like quality the Rosca calls for. Plus, I like the idea of the dough and the fruits complementing each other but still being able to stand out on their own."

"And the idea of one single bean smothered underneath it all—"

"Not smothered." I interrupted Johnny Oliver. "Protected. Protected underneath it all, on the brink of being discovered."

Johnny Oliver nodded as if he not only understood, but agreed with my baking choices. He extended a closed fist across the table. My breath caught in my throat. Two in a row?! "Folks, give it up for the first fist bump of the day," Summer Rae said. Cheers exploded from every corner of the tent.

I reached out a shaky fist to make contact with his. We bumped. As I brought my hand back to my side, he grabbed it.

Was he going to give me a handshake too? Instead, he turned my hand upward. "Even though I found it in my piece of Rosca, I think it is safe to say that you, young baker, are the real king for the day."

Even though it was just a black bean landing in the middle of my palm, it felt like a boulder cracking every wall of my heart's secret chamber. When the crowd roared, the walls came crashing down.

I made zero attempts to pick up the rubble.

Chapter 20

Monday meant the end of spring break. Evidence of it was written all over Immaculate Heart's library. Scents of floral and citrus body mists mingled with the rise and fall of whispers and clacking keyboards. Morning sun poured through the oversized windows, spilled onto the dark wood of the communal study tables already jammed with overachievers.

A pang for the prep room gnawed at my stomach. So did anticipation for the judging table. And there, in the middle of the library, a rush of electric tingles went through me.

I was a Bake-Off semifinalist!

I pressed the messenger bag into my chest. Braced my galloping heart against the toughness of the cake mold. A squeal escaped me, causing an entire row of students to swivel around chairs and *shush* me.

As much as I wanted to celebrate, they had a point. This week needed to be all about school.

Stepping out from the rows of bookcases, I saw that only one individual workstation was free. I sprinted to the far end of the room to claim it. My messenger bag landed on its polished surface with a *thump*.

Plopping into the chair, I felt my phone stabbing the side of my butt. Before I could plug it into the workstation's socket, a notification from Dad flashed on the screen.

Finally, he'd responded to the link I'd texted him. A Bake-Off clip showing Johnny Oliver giving me the fist bump for the Rosca de Reyes.

I haven't watched it yet, but will soon.

He'd made time to come watch every single one of my Law and Debate matches. I'd assumed he'd be equally eager to see me in action at Bake-Off's judging table. Especially since I'd made his grandmother's recipe. Topped with the literal cherries he'd given me.

Shine bright like a Rubi.

His advice welled up in me the way it did the first time around. How should I implement it at the next challenge?

I left something else in your bag this morning.

PS But don't forget our deal. Alma comes first.

Probably not the best time to tell him putting Bake-Off first also weirdly meant putting Alma first, so. I sent back three tan thumbs-up emojis instead, and reached for my bag.

Shoving the textbooks and debate binder aside, I searched for whatever treats he'd stashed inside. Only they weren't treats this time. Sandwiched between AP book covers, two titles stood out from the rest.

Johnny Oliver's *Dough Boy* and Madame Terese's *The Art of Patisserie*.

I spread the cookbooks over the workspace. Cracked open *Dough Boy* first. The pages released different scents on the flip through. Freshly baked bread and spices. Dad's old-school cologne. His handwriting was scribbled all over this too. Annotating recipes. Adding footnotes. Sketches in the margins.

Exactly like in most of my textbooks. Law and Debate's binder especially.

I cracked it open and turned to a fresh page. *Possible Bakes to Practice for the Mystery Challenge,* I wrote at the top of it. I'd nearly rolled out of bed last night when I discovered every single Trig quiz this semester had come straight from the extra problem sets in the back of the textbook. If luck was on my side, maybe the Mystery Challenge would prove to be something similar. The key to nailing a technique or particular bake could very well be hidden between the covers of these recipe books.

I thumbed back to the cookbook's table of contents. Dad had underlined some of the recipes. Great minds think alike? I laughed, jotting some of them down.

Chocolate-Hazelnut Streusel. Parmesan Churros. S'mores Bomboloni. "What's an Elisenlebkuchen?"

I grabbed the phone to google it. It vibrated in my palms before the results loaded on the screen.

Have you figured out what you're going to bake next? Ryan texted.

Do you have ESP? I grinned. Literally working on it RIGHT NOW. Anything you think I should practice?

Nope. You'll figure it all out. You always do.

IDK about that, but I'll have some ideas ready before our next SESSION. I chewed my lips and sank deeper into the chair, trying hard not to swoon and melt right off the seat.

"The Law and Debate tournament is *two* weeks away!" a voice whisper-shouted, and I practically fell out of the chair at Madeline lording over the workstation. She peeked inside my binder. "And you're wasting time outlining '*Possible Bakes to Practice for the Mystery Challenge*'?!" She snorted. "Please tell me you're not competing in an unsanctioned extracurricular right now."

"It may not be sanctioned through the FLOC, but it's sanctioned through Alma."

Her eyebrows went up. "Ah, yes. My aunt mentioned some dingy little cook-off." She twirled some platinum locks between red manicured claws. "Something about an upgrade to the culinary arts program."

"What did she say?" I angled forward, momentarily forgetting how much we despised each other. "Is the major still going to be impacted?"

"I wasn't really listening. Culinary arts. Eww." Okay, I remembered how much we despised each other. "Why do you care? I thought you applied to their pre-law program?"

"I did." My throat suddenly dried up. "But you know what they say, any press is good press."

"Ah, I get it." She paused, probably letting the wheels in her head grind at full speed. "You think winning this local pie-eating festival will get you on Alma's radar, so you can therefore decline my offer of help?" She licked her lips. "Two birds one stone, eh?"

"You forgot the kill part."

Despite her full-on cackling, she refused to be sidetracked. "I was beginning to wonder why you haven't called." She craned her long neck toward my phone. "So, besides this ill-advised plan of yours—which I won't even get into—you're also involved in 'sessions,' whatever *that* means, with someone named"—she squinted at the screen—"'Ryan/BOYFTU'?" The grin broadened into a smirk. "Wait, is he your boyfriend or something?"

Or something.

"Huh . . . How you got yourself into this waitlist pickle is all starting to make sense. You don't know how to pick a lane, Rubi-with-an-i. Much less how to stick with it."

The overhead lights bounced off of her body, outlining her head with an icy halo. Madeline Crowley, Patron Saint of Bitchiness.

She smacked her lips. "Looks like Law and Debate will have a new captain before the tourney after all, don't you think?" She drummed her fingers on the top of the workstation. If she was waiting for a retort, I refused to give her one. "Offer's still on the table."

I held on to everything I'd earned. Everything she wanted to take away from me. Silence was the only thing she deserved.

After what felt like an eternal standoff, she flipped some hair over her shoulder. "Fine. Save it for today's practice, amiga. Trust me, you'll need all the breath you can get."

I glared at her until she disappeared around a bookshelf. I slumped against the chair, and the wood felt suddenly stiff. The words Madeline had spit at me began to sting.

Because there, strewn across my workstation, were two cookbooks. No trig. No debate. No homework of any kind. Ugh, I hated when the devil had a point.

I closed *Dough Boy*. Turned the page in the binder. Kept flipping until the possible bakes didn't seep through the page. Time for unfinished Law and Debate topics. Fun.

Overhead lights poured bright onto the stage. I rushed down the dark aisles of the school's auditorium. The AC hissed from the vents. I wrapped my arms around my shoulders, warded off chills as I stepped onto the creaky floorboards.

Pausing at the foot of the stage, I turned back and stared deep into the gallery. Zeroed in on the spot where my parents always sat, watched.

If we did well at the tourney next week—

I shook my head. No, if *I* led the team to victory next week, I'd land on Alma's radar. Probably more than winning Bake-Off could.

Dad's text flashed in my mind. *PS But don't forget our deal. Alma comes first.*

Fine. I'd devote the rest of the day to Alma. Its pre-law program, not culinary arts.

This was the last practice debate before the tournament, and I intended to master debate the hell out it.

Master debate. I cracked up at how different it'd sounded in the bakery's parking lot with Ryan.

It had been so warm and bright that day. Ryan's house was always like that. So was the prep room. Inside Bake-Off's tent . . .

Focus.

I walked past the two podiums at the foot of the stage and took a seat at the rectangular table behind them.

The team began to trickle in. Scraps of conversations that'd filled the hallways all day now carried across the auditorium.

Recaps of spring breaks and spring breakups. Snippets of college acceptance stories. Not a single peep about rejections. Even as we exchanged hellos and head nods, I didn't chime in with any of my (mis)adventures during the break.

Then again, not all of my misadventures had resulted in something horrible. Some of them had resulted in white tents and tall surfers.

Sister Bernadette's clogs pounded from backstage. They stomped in brusquely, wiping out all discussions at the table. Cut through all the commotion in my head.

She marched through the curtains. The black-and-white cloth of her habit swished behind her, beat in the cold air like wings of a bird of prey. Madeline followed a half step behind, took a seat at the other end of the table. She stooped forward and, ugh. There's that smirk again.

I shifted in my seat. Turned my attention to Sister Bernadette's war march instead.

Arms folded behind her back, she paced between the podiums. "The word 'trophy' comes from the Greek word 'tropaion.' A monument built to commemorate the destruction of foes." She halted, midstep.

"This team has made it to the tournament three years in a row, only to fall short." She stared through us rather than at us. "I need not remind you how soul crushing destruction feels."

"No, ma'am!" we chanted in unison.

"Decades later, the Romans decided to tweak the Greek formula. Instead of building monuments in distant battlefields to ward off future foes, why not make the monuments smaller, they asked." She clicked her clogs together, turned, and resumed her march. "Make them portable. Fashion them from indestructible and precious materials to show off to their people."

I squeezed my eyelids shut, imagined her wearing a war general's outfit instead of a habit. It wouldn't make her more intimidating, only more badass. More like herself.

"And thus, the trophy was born. Irrefutable proof of being the best. Impressing those you need to impress most. Procuring respect, prestige, and, more importantly, favors."

I glanced sidelong at my team; some nodded, others rubbed their palms. Madeline craned forward again, tapped her patent leather ballet flats. I ignored her; Sister Bernadette's speech was making me too hungry to focus on Madeline's nonsense. My stomach rumbled, starved for victory, for the trophy out of reach these past three years.

My stomach grumbled again, flooding my mouth with phantom sugariness. It was impossible for me to think about this trophy without thinking about the other one.

"But perhaps most importantly, the Romans figured out trophies held an even greater power. The power of inspiration. Inspiration to win for the first time. Inspiration for a whole new crop of people to join your cause."

I sat up taller in my chair. If I won Bake-Off and brought home physical proof of the victory back to my mother, perhaps the trophy would show her baking wasn't just a means to an end. A victory could show her baking could be more.

"So." She clapped her hands together and turned to us. "Who wants to win this trophy? For this team and all teams after you?"

The team's claps thundered in the empty auditorium. I clapped until my palms felt sore, until I was the last one clapping.

Chapter 21

"Before we get started." Madeline rose from the chair. "I'd like to make a few announcements pertinent to the tournament."

Sister Bernadette's clogs screeched to a halt. She turned her head back slowly. "How pertinent?"

"I have it on good authority the tournament will be moved from UCI to Alma."

Alma? This had to be a good sign.

"This authority of yours, how good is it?" Sister Bernadette asked.

"Good enough to guarantee notifications of the location change will be sent tonight at six."

Sister Bernadette took a few steps in Madeline's direction, habit whipping around her ankles. "In conferring with this authority, did you happen to stumble across anything else?"

Madeline's canines pressed against her lips. "They confirmed your theories about this year's questions, Sister Bernadette. The majority of the questions will in fact revolve around global politics. There will be those random curveballs in the preliminary rounds to keep us on our toes, obviously. Pop culture, sports. Those sorts of things."

Pop culture. Sports. As captain, I should've been brushing up on those topics, but hadn't. I pulled my binder closer, jotted the info down. Underlined it twice.

"And this authority, they wouldn't have happened to give you some examples, right?" The round lenses of her glasses fogged up. "Not the actual questions, of course."

"Of course not actual questions. Only a few *examples*." The team giggled, started nudging each other in the ribs. Madeline reached for her briefcase, a black and shiny thing covered with the scales of some poor reptile. She pulled out a large manila envelope. "Which I happen to have right here."

The floorboards vibrated as Sister Bernadette charged from the podiums. She snatched the envelope from Madeline's hands. Tore it open with her teeth.

Eyeballs darted across the page. "This list is very similar to the one my own sources provided me last night." She pushed her glasses up the bridge of her nose. "I will combine the two lists and email these *examples* to all of you tonight. No eating, sleeping, or anything else before researching the topics and preparing arguments for each side." She fanned herself with the envelope. "I know you are all sick of me harping on this, but knowledge is power. Excellent job, Madeline. You have our many thanks."

The teammates closest to Madeline patted her shoulders. High-fived her. She, of course, ate it all up. As much as I wanted to wipe the self-satisfied grin off her face, I couldn't.

I couldn't deny connections were as powerful as knowledge and hard work. Maybe even more so. And once again, she was probably wishing I'd come crawling back, beg her to be the beneficiary of the connections she had and I needed.

Ha! As if I'd let that ever happen again.

"Now, team, anything else before we get started?" Sister Bernadette asked.

Madeline edged forward on her seat, tilted herself in my direction. Her smile wasn't as big as it'd been a second ago, but something about it grated my nerves.

"It'd be a good idea to use some of those examples today for practice. Start with some of the sports ones and work our way up?"

Groans broke out. Shoes shuffled underneath the table. I did both.

"Any objection to this suggestion, captain?" Sister Bernadette asked.

"Yeah, *captain*?" Madeline scoffed.

I rolled my eyes at her. "No objection here, *vice-captain*."

Carolina and Nina *oohed*. Nat shout-whispered, "Girl fight!"

"Team!" Sister Bernadette swatted the side of the podium with the envelope. "We have a mock debate to get through. How can you expect me to send you to the front lines of the last battle if you're too busy bickering or engaging in buffoonery among yourselves?" She massaged her temples. Okay, maybe Sister Bernie had a point. "From this second on, I expect *everyone* to start acting like a captain. Capisce?"

"Capisce," we all mumbled.

"Since the matter's settled: Madeline, Rubi. You're up."

Great.

"This will be a two-minute match with simultaneous rebuttals," Sister Bernadette said. Madeline straightened her spine, flicked platinum locks over her shoulders. Under the lights, her hair flashed like a curtain of diamonds. The image of Dad's note came to me.

Shine bright like a Rubi.

Diamonds were so overrated.

"We will start with the sports question Madeline provided," Sister Bernadette said. Madeline jutted her chin at me.

I placed my hands over the edges of the podium. Gripped the edges. The nicks and raised lines shifted over my skin.

Proof that whatever her evil master plan was, I could withstand its heat. I'd been raised in a kitchen, after all. The prep room had taught me improvisation. I carried the skill into this auditorium, into matches. Maybe this was the main reason why I was captain of the team instead of her. So even if I was underprepared for this battle, at least I was ready for the war.

I pushed back my shoulders.

"Resolved: golf is a sport. Rubi, you will be arguing the affirmative." Sister Bernadette reached into her habit and pulled out a kitchen timer. The same timer at every station in Bake-Off's tent. "Your time begins now."

"A sport is typically defined as a physical activity," I said. "Involving skills and specific sets of reci—"

I bit the side of my cheek before the rest of the word came out.

Judging by the way every single tip of those pointy teeth flashed, yup, Madeline definitely knew what the word was. She licked her lips—probably picking up on the scent of blood—and now she wanted more.

I shook my head to reset it. Cleared my throat and said, "Involving skills and a specific set of rules. Golf meets the definition of the word 'sport.'"

"Golf better suits the definition of a *hobby*, an activity done for personal amusement," Madeline said. "A pastime performed outside one's actual day-to-day duties. Regardless of any competitive nature, they rarely yield anything other than temporary diversion." Her tone dripped with insinuations that got under my skin, made it prickle all over.

"Like with many other sports, golf requires coordinated muscle movements of the hands, wrists, arms, and core. These movements must be sustained for long periods of time." I paused. Exactly *like baking*. "Longer even than most sports. Not to mention that the swings have to remain consistent to produce uniform results throughout the long day."

Again, like baking.

I tightened my grip on the podium, anchored myself to keep from floating off to Bake-Off's tent again.

"Unlike most sports, *golf* can be performed by people who are"—her voice broke off, for dramatic effect—"not fit. If these unfit people can engage in the activity"—Madeline's glare veered to my hands, squeezed tight over the podium—"which even my opponent concedes is mostly manual, it lacks the overall athleticism to be considered a *real* sport."

The twinkle in Madeline's eyes confirmed it.

We weren't actually debating golf anymore.

The twinkle turned into a dare.

I nodded, dare accepted. "*Golf* requires hours of practice and skill to achieve a certain level of excellence."

"So does eyebrow tweezing or playing video games. Both clearly not sports."

"It's in the Olympics."

"Only since 2016. A decision the Olympic Committee made to appease this PC culture we're living in rather than on its merits."

"You want to talk about merits?" *That's it*. For four years Madeline had shaken the soda can of my emotions—no—an entire vending machine's worth of them. All the bottled-up hurt and anger fizzed up my throat. Not even Sister Bernadette's ringing timer could stop me.

"Golf is respected and beloved. Its roots date back nearly eight hundred years." My voice boomed off the auditorium's walls.

"Just because it is old, allegedly respected, or beloved, doesn't mean it isn't a waste of precious time."

"Time," Sister Bernadette yelled.

"It *isn't* a waste of time, Madeline." The microphone sizzled with my breath.

"Really? Tell that to King James the Second, who banned it in 1457 when Scotland was under attack by the British. Instead of preparing for battle, people were off playing golf." She spoke slowly and clearly, like she was giving me a chance to spot the trapdoors hidden under every word. "Distracted by a silly game to the point of defeat. Sound familiar, captain?"

"Girls, enough!" Sister Bernadette huffed as she stomped toward us.

But I couldn't stop myself from defending baking. Or Bake-Off specifically. "If I'm distracted by anything, Madeline, it's you. The hours I've devoted to Bake-Off are nothing compared to all the time and energy I've wasted playing your twisted games. As a FLOC member, you were supposed to help me."

"As a Future Leader of Orange County, you weren't supposed to screw up."

Her words struck, and yet. Mine kept coming. I couldn't stop them if I wanted to.

Not this time. Not ever again.

"Well, it's a good thing I did, so you could use it to your advantage. And when you saw that I had a plan to sidestep yours, you came up with this, right? Try to get me to crack in front of the team—"

I turned back to them. So many mouths hung open I'd definitely need a crane to lift them up again.

"Get me to crack in front of Sister Bernadette? So you can take my title? Why? Because you were sick of waiting for me to serve it to you on a platinum platter?" Awareness streamed through my fingers. So did anger so hot it'd probably leave singed palm prints on the podium. "Or, let me guess, try to get me kicked off the team altogether because of how 'unfit' I am to lead it?" I flung her own words back at her. "'Rubi's too sensitive. Too emotional. Too spicy. Must be that Latinx temperament'?"

I ground my teeth, stood even straighter at the podium. If I was going down, I'd do it in a blaze of glory. And burn Madeline to the ground in the process.

"Well guess what, 'amiga.' Those are all the reasons why Sister Bernadette made me captain in the first place. Not you."

The hollow of her neck deepened, pinkie twitching against the podium. Infinitesimal signs she wasn't as indestructible as she thought she was. She wasn't as indestructible as I'd thought her to be.

I tightened my knuckles over the podium. The sprinkling of scars on the backs of them were made even more noticeable against my skin. As were my veins, pumping hard with everything I'd ever wanted to say to her.

Almost everything.

I slipped a hand into my pocket. I rolled the Rosca's black bean between my fingertips. "You've tried your best to bury me." I gave the hard edges of the bean a squeeze.

Madeline had overlooked the fact that beans were seeds. Seeds only knew how to do one thing. Grow.

I brought my hand back to the podium. I spread my fingers wide, put my scars on full display. "I'm not ashamed about living on the other side of the hill. Or coming from a family of bakers. I don't regret competing in Bake-Off. The only thing I regret is trying to prove to you I *am* FLOC material." I pushed up my sleeves. "When the only person I ever needed to prove it to was, well, me."

The team howled with cheers. For a split second, I was in the prep room again, then inside Bake-Off's tent. The team kept cheering until Madeline shot eye daggers and Sister Bernadette stormed up the floorboards. She gave a single clap as if to bring this debate to a close.

When she moved past me our eyes locked, and I knew. The single clap was meant for me. *It's about time,* her steely expression said.

Yes, I nodded. It was.

"Team, I think we can all use a fifteen-minute break," Sister Bernadette said. "Except you, Madeline. You stay put." She turned to me. "Rubi, I will speak to you after."

My stomach tightened. The shoulder claps from Carolina and Nina's high-fives made it relax a bit. The rest of the team whispered accolades the second we reached the bottom of the steps, out of Madeline's earshot, and into the safety of the auditorium's empty darkness.

Only the auditorium wasn't safe. It certainly wasn't empty either. Even in the shadows, the questions swirling across her face were crystal clear.

My body went cold. Somehow, I managed to choke out, "Mother, I can explain."

Chapter 22

Except which part of the outburst should I explain first? Not that she looked in the mood for any explanations, to be honest. Clacking heels echoed up the aisles. The extra-large mocha I drank before practice sloshed around my gut in my scramble to keep up with her. "Mamá, wait!"

The set of double doors flew open, then slammed shut. She kept fleeing, fast and furious, away from me.

Outside, the late morning was warm and cloudlessly sunny. Too postcard-picture perfect for the conversation we were about to have. I brought a hand to my face, shielded my eyes against the brightness.

My vision adjusted. There she stood, at the edge of the courtyard.

Purple jacaranda petals swirled down in the breeze, mixed with the smaller white blooms drifting from the dogwoods. She brought a sleeve to her face and brushed something away.

The possibility of her wiping away tears, not petals, made it hard to breathe. I approached slowly. "I'm sorry you had to see that." *I'm sorry, I'm sorry.*

"I'm not."

I inched forward. Carefully, as though treading the surface of a cupcake not fully baked through.

"I stopped by to surprise you." She turned to face me. The sight of the Alma cardigan wrapped around her shoulders crushed my heart until it broke. "Take you to lunch to celebrate Alma, like we'd planned, remember?" I swallowed. *Oh, I remembered.* "Both of us have been so much busier than usual." She frowned. "Now I have some idea of what's been occupying all your free time. ¿Qué es Bake-Off?"

All those jagged little heart pieces sank to my stomach. All the confidence I'd felt at the podium earlier, hell, even the judging table days before, leaked out of me. Even the sugar rush of the coffee, gone.

Nothing remained but the worry that once the cat was out of the bag, she'd say to lock it back up. Force me to throw away the key forever.

She held my gaze, waiting for an answer. As scared as I was to give it to her, a part of me hoped telling her the truth about Bake-Off would at least cancel out the guilt over lying about Alma.

"It's a local baking competition." Nope. All the emotions were still there.

"¿Por qué, Rubi?" Her voice was edged with confusion and frustration. "Why did you do it?"

The breeze picked up. Made another swirl of leaves drop soundlessly at our feet. Blown off the branches, the petals, so vibrant with life, would wither up and die on this grass.

I opened my palm and caught one before it fell. Let it float off my hand and keep flying for a little bit longer. "Because I wanted to have a last hurrah for baking."

A dozen emotions washed over her face. Not one of them good.

I was afraid to tell her the rest of it. To tell her it started that way, but it certainly wasn't where it stopped. I was afraid to tell her Bake-Off was making me dig deeper into my longing to bake. And it led all the way back to a place she once called home.

Instead, my attention turned to the falling leaves. Some flew straight to the ground. Others danced down in spirals. A few rode the breeze the way I imagined Ryan rode waves. Fearlessly and for as long as they could before physics and gravity took hold. Before they crashed onto the shore in a million little droplets and the ocean dragged them back whole.

"But each time I moved closer and closer to the finale—" My shoulders tensed; somehow I whipped up every last bit of courage inside of me. "The last hurrah turned into something else."

She paused. "What did it turn into?"

"Hope." My throat went dry. "Hope if I won, you'd look at baking differently."

She made a noise, something between a scoff and a sob, and shook her head. "For your sake or mine?"

For both of ours, I wanted to say but didn't. I was too busy cringing about how I'd handled nearly every single situation since getting Alma's waitlist letter.

My intentions had been good.

The ways I'd gone about to solve said situations, not so much.

"I thought so." She shook her head, making her way to the bricked flower bed doubling as a courtyard bench and sitting down.

Spring blooms cupped lean and bushy stalks. A brown spray of sparrows flew over them, landed on a stone statue of a holy mother cradling a sacred child. Vines wound up the base, shackled the mother's feet. The tips of the child's fingers, chipped. Weathered by SoCal sun and reshaped by Santa Ana winds.

Even when I came and sat next to her, her gaze stayed locked on the statue. "I was born on an island that stripped me of my family and my dreams, Rubi." A white dogwood bloom landed on her black trousers. "This country gave a family back to me, but my dreams . . ." She lifted the flower from her pants. The scars on her hands moved as she squeezed the flower's delicate petals. The flower disappeared into her palm. She opened it, letting the crumpled petals fall onto the ground. "I gave them up for you. So you could become everything I couldn't."

Once upon a time, the thought of being an avatar for someone's stolen dreams, of being both the investment and the return on it, inspired me.

Now it only infuriated me.

My shoulders collapsed under the weight of her sacrifices and the immense pressure of paying off the debt I still owed. The combined heaviness crushed down on the hurt, the guilt, curdled them both into righteous indignation that threatened to blow. "Just as long as I became a lawyer or a doctor, right? And we all know about me and math."

My mother winced. Her fingers tightened over her pants. Skin pulled taut or not, her scars were always visible.

For so long I'd looked at her scars as irrefutable proof of her superpowers. But I blinked, and the burns, ragged edges, divots, they turned into something different. They became the other things they always were.

Wounds . . . and heartache . . . her lack of power.

All the effort it took for her to be able to stitch herself together.

Untold stories too painful to ever express with words.

It was no wonder she kept her past locked up tighter than a vault. No wonder one of her favorite mantras was pa'lante.

She was hyperfocused on the future. I was never brave enough to ask about the past. Baking had been one way for me to link the two.

A stronger breeze came through the courtyard. The feathery

stalks of the marigolds behind us rustled. Heads of orange and gold flowers clashed with each other. My mother scooted closer to where I sat. She cupped my hand inside both of hers.

Our pulses beat against each other. After a while, I couldn't tell them apart. "If I'm against this baking competition, it isn't because I'm ashamed of baking. I'm not," she said, breaking the silence in Spanish. "It's a part of us."

"It's a part of me."

"Maybe." Her voice shook, her face softened.

I slid closer to her. Inched closer to the possibility of her understanding, accepting even, my need to see Bake-Off through. To win the summer seminar in Havana.

"But Rubi, I'm your mother. I'm never going to stop wanting more for you." Her fingers threaded through mine. She blinked to keep the tears at bay. "I'm sorry if sometimes it comes off as me wanting more from you. If I pushed you hard it was only because I know you're capable of great things." She cracked a brief smile. "Like giving it to the bruja in there."

Her words surprised a laugh out of me. My mother laughed too. "She had it coming," I said.

"She did." My mother gave my hand another squeeze, which I returned. We went back and forth like that, wringing out all the nervousness and tension between us. Finally, her fingers relaxed around mine. "It was long overdue, mija."

"Trust me, if I hadn't needed her for the waitlist—" I pressed my lips together.

My mother's spine went straight. "What waitlist?" The air grew thick. My palm got sweaty. Hers turned to stone before she tore it away. "Rubi, what waitlist? Why are you talking about a waitlist if you already got into Alma?"

She kept staring at me, waiting.

No matter how deep I dug to find the right combo of words

to make this less awful, I couldn't. Not without finally telling the whole truth and nothing but the truth.

"No, Ma," I whispered. "I didn't."

She drew in a sharp breath. Every single line on her face deepened. "What are you talking about?" She'd asked it slowly. Like she was trying to stop the caldo of emotions from bubbling—exploding—over.

"I lied about Alma." I fought the urge to look away. "I got waitlisted, not in."

The bite was gone from her espresso-brown eyes. Now, she just looked bitten. "I told you baking would distract you from school. The shifts at the bakery. Now this competition." A snort and a head shake. "No wonder you kept all of this from me. Y mira, you got waitlisted because of it."

"Not true. Alma waitlisted me *before* I even competed in Bake-Off."

"You already lied, Rubi." She rose so fast she nearly knocked a loose brick off the makeshift bench. "You expect me to believe you now?"

"Believe what you want, Ma, but it's the truth. Bake-Off didn't make Alma question anything about me." The last two Bake-Off challenges. Baking with Ryan. Every shift in the prep room. Even my blowup on the podium. All of it coursed through my veins. I was grateful for it. It forced me to keep going, keep hitting on all the things that mattered but we never talked about.

"It was Bake-Off that made *me* question everything."

She staggered back. Red stained her corded neck, spilling onto her cheeks. "So, what now? You're going to throw Alma away?"

"I'm not throwing Alma away. The debate is at Alma. Plus, Bake-Off's part of Alma's culinary program now. If I win both, I'm as good as in."

"'As good as in' isn't the same as in," she snapped.

"It will be if I stick to the plan."

After a long pause, she nodded. "Sí. I know all about plans." She turned to walk away, though not before opening her large purse. She set a matching Alma cardigan next to me. "Do the right thing, Rubi." Her face darkened, shadowed by something worse than anger or disappointment.

Disbelief. Her eyes swam in dark currents of it.

After everything she'd worked to achieve, her dreams were in danger of being stolen all over again.

Only this time, by me.

Chapter 23

Sister Bernadette stood at the entrance to the auditorium. Sunlight bounced off of her glasses. The glare made it impossible for me to get any hints about whether she planned on ushering me in or out of practice. I stopped a few feet from her.

She closed the gap between us, the habit's black cloth rustling with every step forward. "Do I really have to remind you to eat something? You look terribly hypoglycemic." At the mention of food, I was back on the brink of tears. "I can't have the team captain fainting halfway through practice."

I heard nothing after the word "captain." "After everything that happened in there . . . you still think I should be captain?"

"I don't condone the way you two acted up there. Although I must confess, it was slightly amusing." Sister Bernadette tapped her chin. "Frankly, it also proved if you can destroy Madeline the way you did, you can destroy anybody."

"My mother would wholeheartedly agree." It slipped out without me meaning it to. The dam keeping all the tears behind my eyelids finally broke. They rolled down my cheeks, hot and fast. Each time I wiped one rivulet away with the Alma cardigan, two more rushed out to take its place.

"Yes, Madeline alluded as much. Something about a predicament with Alma? She also mentioned something about cavorting with a boy. A so-called 'foodie call'?" she said, using air quotes.

I squealed a single bark of laughter before I could think better of myself. "Ryan's not my foodie call. He's my math tutor. And possible boyfriend."

"Pragmatic." Her voice dripped with approval. "She also mentioned a baking competition." I nodded, sniffled back a runny nose. "It sounds like you have a lot on your plate right now."

"Thanksgiving-sized portions," I said, wanting to kindle her pun with a joke of my own. But any levity I'd hoped to spark was smothered by replaying all the things she'd just listed. All the things she hadn't. And despite my best intentions, all the screwed-up ways I'd handled both.

I couldn't meet Sister Bernadette's gaze so I covered my face with the cardigan. The Alma logo above the pocket scratched my nose. And apparently sent a knife through my gut too. "I'm sorry about hijacking practice like that." Tears began to spill. "I'm sorry I haven't been prepping for debate as much as I should."

"We can talk about it later." She patted my arm. "Right now, just let it all out."

So I did. The tears flowed and flowed, with no signs of stopping. "I don't know where all this is coming from."

Except of course I knew. Which only made them pour harder. "Great, besides earthquakes and wildfires"—I hiccupped—"California has to deal with floods now too."

"On account of the droughts, perhaps a flood is exactly what Pelican Point needs."

My breath steadied. Tears slowed. Sister Bernadette took her hand from my shoulder and dipped it into the middle layers of her black habit. She pushed something waxy into my hands. *A dessert envelope?*

I unfolded the top of it. What? A half-eaten pastelito de queso y guayaba?

Crumbs from the glazed top of the puff pastry were stuck between layers of the guava and cream cheese–filled center. The golden crumbs only enhanced the guava paste's reddish-pink glow. A hue almost matching the color of the candied cherries I'd used to decorate the Rosca.

Shine bright like a Rubi, Dad's voice echoed again.

I stuffed the pastry into my mouth, desperate to embody his words, desperate to have them reawaken my shine. The buttery layers of puff pastry flaked, then dissolved in my mouth . . . dissolving some of the leftover acid from the blowouts with Madeline and my mother with it. Cream cheese melted over my tongue. A tiny burst of orange blossom popped through the guava.

"This pastelito's as good as my dad's recipe." My body relaxed. "Wait, is this from his bakery?"

"If you mean Rubi's Bakery, then yes."

Hearing the official name of the bakery out loud gave me pause, because, well, it could never be mine. I cleared my throat and said, "If I knew you were a customer there, I would've hooked you up with a discount."

"Discount, shmiscount. They're worth every penny. Now." She motioned to the last bit of pastelito in my hand. Popping it into my mouth, I chewed.

A familiar sweetness warmed my mouth. As it went down, my throat constricted with more loss. When my mother had said *Do the right thing,* its only translation was: give up Bake-Off now, it will help make giving up baking later easier.

"Ready to finish this, captain?" Sister Bernadette asked.

Wiping my mouth, I nodded. "Ready." As far as everything else, no. I wasn't ready to finish. Not even close.

Chapter 24

After practice, I headed to Devon's for advice. I found her out back, splayed out on a teal float in the middle of the pool. Her head was turned away, with a kombucha in one hand and her phone in the other. To my recently more seasoned ears, her rushed and honeyed tones sounded like flirting.

Only if she was flirting, why hadn't she told me she'd met someone to flirt with?

I kicked off my flip-flops and plopped onto the pool's edge. Thick, low clouds blocked out the sky but not the heat. I rolled up my pants and dipped my calves into the water, welcoming its coolness.

I started kicking, hoping the splashes would get Devon's attention.

Her head craned over the angled headrest. Once our eyes locked, we smiled the way BFFs did after a few days of not hanging out.

Then her smile slid off her face a bit. "Hey, Rubi's here." Her voice went back to normal. Deeper, more stilted than normal actually. "Uh-huh. Yep. Going to tell her right now. Call you back later."

She rolled off the float and landed in the water with a soft splash. Her long limbs swished under the water before pushing through its surface. Brushed wet locks from her face to take a long look at me. "What the hell happened, Rubes?"

"You go first." Devon just blinked and blinked though. Was the pool water really that chlorinated? "On the phone, like a second ago, you said you're going to tell me something?"

"Oh, yeah." She tilted her head back, dipping her hair into the water. The black had faded to a chestnut brown. I kinda admired the dye's willpower to cling to her tresses for as long as it did. "We'll get to it in a minute."

"Okay," I said, slowly. "Well, who were you on the phone—"

She flicked some water at me. "The water feels so good. Don't you want to go swimming? It might make you feel better."

"You're giving me emotional whiplash, Devon." I squeezed my temples; she cracked up laughing. "And as much as I would love to go swimming. I can't stay long enough for a dip."

"Why not?"

"I'm pretty sure a pool party of two violates the rules of my being grounded, so. I need to get home before the Boss busts me." Again.

"You? Grounded?" Her mouth hung open. "How did that happen?"

A lump formed in my throat. "She knows."

She sucked a mouthful of air through her teeth. "What does she know, exactly?"

Rivulets of pool water ran down Devon's face, foreshadowing the tears soon to be running down mine when I told her everything. She hoisted herself out of the pool, settled next to me. Waited patiently for the recap.

I started from the beginning.

♥ ♥ ♥

Freshman year, my mother bought me my first suit. Shoes clicked down the hallway. I pulled my head up from one of the many AP books spread around me, craned my neck to the hallway. Expected to see Devon dropping in unannounced, like always.

Shadows swallowed most of her. The outline of pants came into focus first, then a blazer. At the sight of my mother stepping into the kitchen instead, I braced myself against the chair.

"Mamá. ¿Está todo bien?" I asked, careful to keep the quiver out of my voice. All the worst-case scenarios responsible for yanking my mother out of work during business hours piled on top of the other.

Dad had gotten hurt at the bakery.

One of the ovens blew out again, and the Boss hadn't been able to find someone to fix it.

They couldn't afford my tuition anymore.

They couldn't afford the mortgage.

She crossed the kitchen and placed her hand on the back of my chair. Surveying the books and notes strewn across the kitchen table, she patted my shoulder. "Todo está bien." She pulled a garment bag from behind her. "I wanted to come home and give you this. For your first debate match."

The chair scraped against the floor when I leapt from it. I threw my arms around her neck. "Gracias." She buried her face in my mass of curls, pulled me closer. "Come on." I untangled myself from her arms. "Let's see how it fits."

She held me in place for a second. Inhaled deeply. Whether she was catching her breath after a long day or testing the air to make sure I hadn't broken the Ban, I couldn't tell. After a moment, her face relaxed. "Okay. Pa'lante."

The gray suit washed out the bronzy skin I'd inherited from my Afro-Cuban father. Clashed too with the dark curls. "I love it." Deep down, a part of me did.

Like when I tipped my head toward the mirror, at just the right angle, the gray shone a steel-silver reminiscent of Frodo's mithril shirt or Aragorn's suit of armor. Perfecto. This suit was designed to help me during battles after all. Ones where I'd wield logic and words as my shield and sword.

The color also matched the steel of a dough-scraper knife.

Like that, it started to grow on me.

Though I still wasn't sure about the suit's fit. I brushed a hand down the long sleeve. Fingers hit the price tag. Before I could see what she'd paid for it, my mother tore the tag off and stashed it in her pocket.

"Mamá! Now you won't be able to return it if it doesn't fit."

"I'll worry about the cost. You worry about the debate." She patted the blazer's bulky shoulder pads. "We'll make it fit."

"You don't think they're too big?"

"No, not at all. I really like them." They bordered my head the way a frame did a painting. Considering the suit was meant to showcase my brains though, it was no wonder she did.

Our smiles met in the mirror. Hers was so big it brought out rarely seen dimples.

She played with my curls, pulled a handful up into a half pony. "Ooh, I know the perfect thing to pull this all together." She charged across the room, plucked the pearl necklace from the jewelry dish on the nightstand. Her quinceañera gift to me. And clasped it around my neck.

We hadn't spent time like this since school had started. It felt good.

More than good. Evocative of the BA era.

Before everything revolved around Alma. I wanted to stretch this time out as long as possible. But like with so many other things in Pelican Point, time wasn't a luxury my mother could easily afford.

She drew a small box of safety pins from her pocket. Kneeling on the floor behind me, she cuffed the overflowing pant legs. "We'll have to get it tailored professionally, of course. This is just for us to get a sneak peek of the final result." She rose to her feet. "Brazos."

I stuck my arms out zombie-style for her inspection. The sleeves were wide and long, swallowing my arms and hands whole. She ran her hands down the sleeves, probably deciding to try to fix the width issue first.

I kept my focus on her hands as they moved around the fabric.

"This looks better," she said. "Now the length." She tugged up the cuff, exposing the back of my hand. Her hand shuddered against mine.

She rubbed the biggest scar with her thumb. At first, I thought she'd done it as a symbol of recognition.

Until she rubbed harder, like she was trying her hardest to erase the mark from my skin. "You said working at the bakery would help with Alma."

"It is going to help with Alma." I didn't add it was also a loophole around the Ban. And I sure as hell didn't say anything about wishing for her to—one day—lift it.

Judging by the way she wrinkled her nose, that day would never come. "Honestly, Rubi, I'm counting the days until Alma accepts you." Her gaze sharpened. "Until you never have to step foot in the bakery again."

She rubbed my hand harder, offended by the nerve of my scar for holding its ground.

It burned, raw.

"You're hurting me." I tore my hand away. Stuffed it into the pants' pocket. In the mirror, through misty vision, the suit morphed again, from suit of armor to steel bridge.

A bridge leading from my parents' Cuban past into my American future. The only way to vindicate their sacrifices was by crossing it.

"We'll keep the sleeves long." Her voice grew distant. "I've got to get back to work."

Because she was my mother, because it was the only way to keep the before-Alma-consumed-everything version of us kindled somewhere in the universe, I told her it was a good idea.

It was best to keep my scars hidden.

♥ ♥ ♥

It'd been so long ago, the memory should've rotted. Instead, it'd rooted itself around my heart's innermost chambers. Over the years the vines had climbed up the cement and mortar. Until everything came crumbling down that day inside Bake-Off's tent.

"I've been keeping so many things from so many people. I don't want you to think I was keeping this one from you too or whatever." I hung my head low, rubbed the back of my hand. "If anything, I was probably trying to keep it from myself."

"I get it." Devon studied me quietly. "All of it is super heavy, Rubes. Your mom's expectations. Yours." She kicked her feet under the water. "Other people's."

We sat side by side, staring at our legs. The pool water both magnified and distorted them. *Things are closer than they appear.* Everything except how to convince my parents that winning Bake-Off didn't also mean letting go of the Recipe for Success.

Devon broke the silence. "Are you considering *not* competing in the semifinals? Is that what your mom said she wants you to do?"

"I mean, my mother didn't come out and say it." She didn't have to. "But it was abundantly clear she wants me to quit."

"Right." She paused before taking a shaky breath. "But what do *you* want to do?"

"I want to make the right choice." I winced, tasting my mother's words inside my own.

"Is there even a choice to make?"

"Of course there's a choice, Devon." My hands itched to sink into another ball of dough, to rake through Ryan's hair, to sift through Cuban sand. "There's always a choice."

"No." Devon kicked her legs through the water. The top of the pool shimmered with waves. Right when I thought she'd generate a tsunami, she stopped. "Not always."

Devon stood. A few rays of sun pierced through the blanket of gray clouds. "Sometimes you don't choose something." Her voice trembled with a conviction I'd never heard from her before. Where was all this coming from? "Sometimes things kinda choose you."

Her eyes got shiny. Wet actually—and not from the chlorine. She scratched her stomach, hard, like she was trying to get out something that was gnawing deep inside of her.

"Devon . . . you're not talking about Bake-Off anymore, are you?"

"No." She glanced down to her brightly painted toes, then back at me. "I'm talking about being queer."

"You're queer?" Millions of memories recalibrated to the weight and lens of this new info. When they settled, I nodded. "You're queer."

"That's what I wanted to tell you." Her long legs trembled as she lowered back down to the pool's edge and sat next to me. "Does it freak you out?"

I twined my fingers through hers. "No. Does it freak you out?"

She shrugged, managing to look blasé and nervous at the

same time. She swished her legs through the water again. Only this time, she shivered. "They say you can't get used to the water if you keep jumping in and out of it."

"So jump in," I said. "I'll jump in with you."

Slowly, the corners of her mouth curled into a smile. She let go of my hand and dove in.

The sun started to burn through the clouds. Rays of it fell in bright stripes across the pool's surface. Long shadows did too, cast by the palm trees lining the pool.

Devon's long strokes made the water ripple. Shades of blue strobed bright.

She broke through the surface, lifted herself onto the float. "My parents are cool with it by the way," she said, panting.

"That's awesome. To have parents who accept you for who you are, it's . . ." As ecstatic and relieved as I was about Dev's parents, my throat tightened. "It's everything."

"Yeah, I know," she said, from the other end of the pool. "Is it enough though? I mean I want to come back here after college. Yes, we're in California. But OC *isn't* San Francisco. Not even close. And I want to design bathing suits. What if some models or buyers here . . ." She frowned, hesitating. "What if some people . . ."

"Ignorant people." Firsthand, I knew how many of them were still around. The twin dragons of expectation and prejudice were ones I had to battle with every single day of my life.

I wanted to hug her and tell her sometimes, a lot of times, they would swallow us whole. The world worked that way.

But even the fiercest of dragons could be slain. The tightness in my throat softened.

The strain on Devon's face didn't. I wanted to reach out and hug her. On account of standing at the pool's edge, I couldn't.

Screw it.

I jumped in.

A hard slap of water, then chlorine rushed up my nose, burning. Khaki pants and cotton polo weighed me down. The water buoyed me. I paddled and kicked until my head bumped into the float.

Devon's hand clasped around my arm and hoisted me up. "Rubi! I can't believe you did that!"

I heaved onto the float, rolled onto my back. My vision blurred from the mixture of soggy curls, the sting of chemicals, and suddenly bright sun.

"I told you I'd jump in with you. Plus, you said it yourself, Dev. You can't get used to the water if you keep jumping out of it."

"But you were never in!"

"Says you." I spit out pool water.

The float wobbled until it adjusted to our combined weights. Adjusted to find balance in this brave new world, now spinning on entirely different axes for both of us. "The seams of your tighty whiteys are totally showing through your pants now."

"They're tighty yellowies, FYI. Maybe you can use this as inspo for your summer collection."

Devon roared with laughter and so did I. She let go of the side of the float to lie down next to me.

I squeezed her hand and she squeezed back.

We stayed that way for a while, hands clasped, drawing warmth and comfort from our togetherness. I curled into her side, opened my lips to ask her who she'd been on the phone with.

Torie's name popped into my head before I spoke. "Jeez," I said. "Who the hell would've predicted both of us would've ended up with jocks?"

Devon blushed and we both cracked up again.

When she was finally able to breathe again, she said, "I know, right?"

We lapsed into silence. "Hey, Dev?" The ocean roared in the distance. "How long have you known?"

"Always . . . Recently . . . I'm still figuring everything out."

A new set of waves rolled in. They barreled high and fast from the horizon, hungry to break onto the shore. I rolled my head to her shoulder. "Makes two of us."

Chapter 25

Are we still on for tutoring tomorrow?

The screen glowed with Ryan's text. I pushed away the trig problem. It didn't feel right to keep getting tutored without trying to give him one lesson back: If you don't tell your dad you booked the surf trip, I reasonably foresee it blowing up in your face.

A set of gray bubbles appeared on his end. In his face too, I added. The bubbles disappeared. I learned it the hard way today. I'll fill you in after I finish studying.

His response came shortly after: Okay, but am I still escorting you to the semifinals this weekend?

I slumped against the chair. Now it was Ryan I pushed away and math I tugged closer. Strange times. Hunched over my desk, I worked all afternoon. Each problem had a specific formula to untangle it. Exactly the way recipes did for bakes.

Only with math there was no leeway for experimentation. Maybe it was a good thing, because sticking to the right formula yielded one single answer. I powered through. Solving these problems was a preferable alternative to figuring out my own.

Three knocks sounded at my door. In slow motion, I glanced over my shoulder.

Dad's face poked through the crack in the door. He nudged it open. "¿Puedo entrar?"

I'd braced myself for a loud and angry voice. Not a broken and crumbly one. I looked down into my binder. "Of course you can come in."

He crossed my room and sat on the far corner of the bed. Beams of setting sun streamed in through the slanted blinds, striped his face with reddish-orange light. I fidgeted in the chair, still too chicken to face him. "I'm guessing the Boss told you everything."

"Was it everything, coño? I'm not sure anymore."

Ouch. As much as I wanted to mitigate nearly a month of wrong decisions with all the semesters of right ones, I couldn't. Over the past few weeks, I'd omitted huge chunks of the truth. Or straight up lied about it.

For so long I'd feared I was the fraud in the FLOC, but I didn't see how I was becoming the fraud in my family. And by doing that I'd hurt the people who really mattered.

I couldn't keep hurting them. It wasn't the type of person my parents raised me to be. It wasn't the person *I* wanted to be. So, if there was a way to make things better with him right now, I sure as hell needed to try.

I glanced back at the phone. "Ryan. I didn't tell you guys about Ryan." The air in the room thickened. I flicked my eyes to the window. Through the space between the wooden blinds, dark waves were swallowing the sun whole. "When Alma waitlisted me, they gave me these prompts to work on. One of them was to raise my GPA. I'm getting my Trig grade up to do it."

Dad scratched the side of his neck. "And Ryan is your tutor?"

"He started out as my math tutor. I mean he still is my tutor. But now . . ." I shifted in the chair again, face flaming. "I think he's also—"

He put a hand up. "I get the picture. Once upon a time, I was your age too, you know." His Adam's apple bobbed furiously. "Wait. He *is* your age, right?"

"Dad!" I covered my face with my hands, peeking through my fingers. "Yes. We're in the same grade. He goes to Lazarus, our brother school."

His sigh mimicked the squall of a Santa Ana wind.

"Before you get too relieved . . ." I wanted to get into the layers of why I'd lied about Alma. Part of me wished my mother could be here too to hear it. "Remember in the prep room, when you overhead me gushing on the phone with Devon?" He nodded. My pulse hammered in my ears and my stomach knotted. "I was telling her I got into Bake-Off. Not Alma."

A memory flitted across his face. The lines on it deepened.

"You told everyone the 'good news,' and the entire prep room started clapping . . . like I was the physical embodiment of the American Dream . . ." I swallowed the lump in my throat and continued. "Then the Boss was there . . ." Tears teetered on my eyelids but didn't spill out. "I'd never seen her so happy. I didn't want to take it away from her. Or you. Or everyone else there." I lifted my face to meet his. "I screwed up. I'm sorry, but I screwed up."

His shoulders relaxed, sighing long and slow.

"I honestly thought I'd be able to fix everything without you knowing. I didn't want you worrying about the waitlist."

"Our job description involves worry."

"But you already have so much to worry about, I didn't want to pile this on top of it too. I lied to protect you." I unclenched my jaw. "Except I also lied to protect myself."

We sat there for a moment, long enough for our raspy breathing to sync up. "In your office, when I told you about Bake-Off . . . I almost told you everything then. But I knew if I did, you'd tell me to forget about it. And I *really* wanted to keep competing." I braced myself against the chair. "I still do. I want to win."

"You want to go do the program in Havana."

"I do."

"Rubi, I have no family there. Your mother has no family there." He paused as if to let the implication stick. "The government there . . ." He trailed off.

The silence lasted forever. The distance between us felt treacherous again, like the ocean separating Cuba and the US.

"Look, I'm not going to tell you I'm not furious, because I am. I'm not going to tell you I'm not hurt, because I am." I blinked back tears, willed my heart not to break for the millionth time in twenty-four hours. "But I'm also not going to tell you I don't understand."

I blinked at him. "You're not?"

He rose from the edge of the bed without answering. Walked to the nightstand and picked up the framed picture.

The sepia-colored photo captured the first day we'd moved to Pelican Point from Santa Ana. In it, Dad and I were at Matteo Beach. Big smiles stretched our faces wide. To the casual observer the streak under my hand was probably a blur of light. In reality, it was a tendril of sand falling from my clenched fist into the cake mold Dad held.

The sight of my tiny fist extended out toward his, made me think of Johnny Oliver and his signature move. Before I spiraled further into Bake-Off, Dad spoke. "Sand cakes." He chuckled. "The Boss thought we were using it because I'd forgotten the sand-castle molds at home. We left them at home on purpose. Grabbed these instead, to build sand cakes."

I held onto the top of the chair and leaned forward. "You remember?"

"Of course I do. Do you remember saying, 'Papá, why isn't the bakery at the beach? You could get all the flour, sugar, and spices for free.'"

I nodded and closed my eyes. For a second, I felt the damp texture of the sand inside my palm. I split my fingers a little, letting the imaginary grains spill down in a rainbow of colors. "How could I ever forget? I never got rid of the mold, by the way." I patted the messenger bag slung on the back of the chair. "I have it right here."

At last we'd hit on our baking origin story. I stared at him to keep talking, knowing by doing so I treaded on dangerous ground. Talks of beginnings often led to talks of endings. And I wasn't ready to face Bake-Off's end. Not until I won.

"I know the Boss wouldn't ever go back," I said. "But would you?"

He didn't answer. He simply glanced at my bag. Back at the photo. "I had a picture similar to this of me and my mother. Abuela Carmen was in it too." His voice was barely loud enough for me to hear it. He tracked a finger along the tops of waves, the outline of my body, of his. "I had to leave it behind."

I only noticed the corner of the island when he tapped it. After all these years, I'd never spotted it. Only it'd been there all along, looming behind low-hanging clouds. "Catalina," I said.

"Yes. Catalina." His voice brimmed with longing. I knew then. He wasn't touching this island, but trying to feel the one he used to call home.

"Dad, you never answered. Do you ever want to go back?"

He closed his eyes as if to ponder it. Or maybe to remember the last time he'd spent the day on a Cuban beach with his mother and Abuela Carmen.

"No." His jaw clenched. "I don't think I would." He hung his head. "The Cuba of my childhood doesn't exist anymore, kiddo. Coño, it was changing by the minute when I was there." Maybe that's part of the reason why he never talked about it. He didn't want to dole out recipes knowing some of the ingredients were long gone. He put the photo back on the nightstand, next to the small jewelry dish.

The skin of the black bean glinted against the iridescent strand of pearls, clasps of a gold charm bracelet, and diamond studs. He picked the bean up, rolling it between his fingers.

"It's from Bake-Off." No more half-truths. "I put it in Abuela Carmen's Rosca de Reyes."

"I know. I watched the clip. You were great."

My mouth flapped open. "You watched?"

"Of course I watched. And rewatched. Abuela Carmen would've been very proud of you. So proud." His voiced was tinged with unmistakable pride. Maybe, despite all the messed-up ways I'd gone about competing, he was glad I had.

If that's what you mean, then why can't you say it?

I stared at him, waited for his approval, for a push in the direction opposite the one the Boss thought best.

Except his lips remained sealed. No push into the semifinals. Only silence. With each passing second, the possibility of finishing Bake-Off began to feel less like the dense seed between his fingers and more like the blur of sand in the photo. Grainy and slipping away no matter how hard I tried to hold onto it.

I heard the words before I realized I'd spoken them. "Will I still be a baker if I drop out of Bake-Off?" *Or if I stopped baking?*

Dad swung his head toward mine. He reached over and pulled me out of the chair, folding me into his arms. "Oh, Rubi. Of course you'll still be a baker. No one can take that away from you. Look at me, I'm still Cuban even if I'm not in Cuba. You're still Cuban even if you never end up going. Is that why you decided to do this competition? To prove you're a baker? To prove you're Cuban enough?"

"One of the reasons," I mumbled into his armpit. I was grateful my face was there, making it impossible to elaborate further. He hugged me tighter. Maybe he was beginning to forgive me.

After a few more seconds, he let go and moved back to the nightstand. He dropped the bean back into the jewelry dish like it was the most natural place for it to be.

"I need to get back to work to close the bakery. But first, I need to stop by the Santa Ana one and talk to the Boss."

"Tell her we talked everything out?"

"We talked most things out. We still need to figure out whether it's a good idea for you to keep your weekend shifts. Or wait until after you hear back from Alma." My face must've been full of disappointment because he said, "Don't worry. This will blow over in a few days."

"Or a few centuries."

"Your mother has survived worse. She will survive this too."

I looked up at him. "Only if I quit Bake-Off. But I'm not going to. I have to see this through."

He hugged me again. The smells of the prep room lingered in the fabric's fibers. Both dulling and highlighting the sad truth: my days at the bakery were numbered. He walked across the room, stopped at the door, and glanced back.

I waited for him to say that sticking it out was the right thing to do.

Only he didn't. He didn't say anything at all.

Chapter 26

"All of the bakers standing here have taken culinary risks. Several of your bakes have even moved the judges, myself"—Summer Rae turned to wave at the crowd, thicker than ever—"and the fans to *tiers*."

The tent exploded with applause. The heat inside it grew more airless, suffocating. Or maybe it was just me, still reeling from yesterday. I rose onto my tiptoes. Swept my eyes over the throng of people. Searched for Dad, nowhere in sight.

"Sadly, I suspect there will be more tears for today's Batter Royale, as only five of you will be advancing to Bake-Off's finale."

I put my fingers over the knob. The second Summer Rae gave the green light, I'd turn the oven on. If my hands stopped trembling, that is.

Yes, I'd betrayed my mother by being here. But wouldn't it be betraying myself if I didn't show up? And what did it matter if I tampered with the Recipe for Success? Couldn't this be exactly like a math problem? As long as Alma accepted me, in the end, it didn't really matter how I got there.

Still, if all this was true, why couldn't I make my stomach

stop churning? Or shake the sense that something about the stage was different today?

The workstations were here. Five of them lining each side this time. I waved to Sydney behind one of them. The purple-and-blue-haired baker was there too. So was the tall guy with glasses and a sweater vest. Nico with his perfectly coifed mustache. And ugh, Katherine.

There were bakers I hadn't seen before too. One with long, dark hair, wearing a lab coat instead of an apron. DR. AHMADI was embroidered above her breast pocket. Another one with blonde French braids. Her name card read JUNO. One hand hovered over the oven's knob, the other gripping her wheelchair's joystick.

The huge stage fridges, wedged between the regular-sized ones, were here too. Same with the shelves. Wait. I did a double-take. They were all empty! What the f—

"The judges have seen what you can do, but now it's time to see if you can bake it like they make it. For today's Mystery Challenge, the judges want you to make one dozen s'mores."

Katherine gave a smug grin. Some of the other bakers dabbed sweat off their brows. My fingers twitched against the knob while I waited for the curveball.

"But these aren't any s'mores." Of course not. "Your s'mores must feature a graham cracker base and top, ganache, marshmallows, nuts of some kind, all elegantly coated in tempered chocolate. A SoCal and Parisian mash-up to make all of Johnny's and Madame Terese's culinary dreams come true!" The audience clapped, oohing and aahing. "All of the ingredients for the bake will be found in your ovens, along with a few extras that may"—she winked—"or may not be useful."

The nervousness in my stomach frothed at full speed.

"You have two and a half hours. Judges, any words of advice?"

"Keep your cool," Johnny Oliver said.

"Keep everything else cool," Madame Terese added.

"Bakers. On you mark. Get set. DOUGH IT!"

I dropped to my knees and opened the oven. I unwrapped the palm tree–print fabric covering the wicker basket. I set each packet, container, egg, and bottle across the top of the station.

Several groans broke out on the stage, a few smatterings of *You've got to be joking.* In the chaos of utensils clanking against counters, ovens thrumming on, and eggshells cracking, I realized what everyone around me already had.

There wasn't a nut, grain, stick, or drop of extra ingredients.

There was only one shot at making these s'mores. Considering my recent history at first shots, today needed to be the exception to the rule. "Here goes nothing."

I added the milk mixture to the flour mixture, stirred them with the KitchenAid until the dough began to form. I pinched an end, attempted to pull it up.

Only the dough was too wet. Too sticky. Better suited for trapping my parents' past and my future in the middle than it was for sandwiching marshmallows. Great.

All around me, the other bakers were in various stages of each step. Instead of moving pa'lante, I was clearly falling behind. I added a little more flour to my dough and tried to keep up.

Too many bodies were pressed inside the tent. Ten ovens thrummed at 300 degrees. Every single stovetop burned. Sweat plastered curls to my forehead. I wiped them away with a hand towel.

Of course it slipped. Landing right in the middle of the

saucepan simmering with heavy cream. Behind me, someone sucked air through their teeth. A camera guy. He must've captured the fail in all of its high-def glory, hence the cringing. Kill me now.

"Bakers, you have two hours remaining."

Get your head in the game, Devon's voice yelled in my brain. "I'm trying to," I muttered back.

I plucked out the towel and held it over the saucepan. Half of the cubes of caramel clung to it. Even worse, nearly all of the chocolate had congealed onto the cotton fibers.

Gasps rippled through the crowd. More when I chucked the towel into the trash. Rummaging through the remaining ingredients, I found a bag of white-chocolate chips.

One last shot at the ganache. The pressure building in my chest dialed up to a hundred.

"Bakers, that's two hours on your s'mores." Make that a thousand.

The lights in the tent suddenly blinked brighter. The lights of the camera crew, moving up and down the makeshift aisle, grew brighter too. And brightest of all, the white-hot intensity of Johnny Oliver's and Madame Terese's stares.

She paused at my station. Glanced at the trash, the stovetop, then finally at me. I mopped the sweat mustache glistening above my lips. Tossed white chocolate into the saucepan. "Using white chocolate and caramel–infused ganache, n'est-ce pas?"

"Um. I. Yes. Exactly?" I hated the way my voice rose, how it came out sounding like a question.

"Chocolat blanc is trickier to work with . . ." My shoulders caved. I'd never worked with white chocolate before. "But it tends to work better in high humidity and heat, like we have today."

Thank god. I'd thought it was just me.

"You and Katherine are the only ones using this type of chocolate for the ganache. Good work. Carry on."

Hope crept back in. I clung to it for dear life and stirred.

My bowl of ganache wasn't in the fridge. Neither was my ball of dough. Whether by accident—or sabotage—one of the bakers had taken them out of the fridge, left them both on the counter right next to it.

My heart pounded into high gear as I peeled back the Saran Wrap covering the dough. I poked a finger in.

"No, no, no." If the dough clung to my finger like this, it was still too sticky to roll out before baking. And as I lifted the bowl of ganache—*gasp*—it'd reverted back to its liquid form again too.

I shoved them back into the fridge. Opened the freezer above to poke my head inside it. Took deep breaths of icy cold air.

I'd held Bake-Off too close to my chest. Focused too much on all the things I'd gain by winning, not enough on all the things I'd lose if I didn't.

I pressed my palms against the fridge. Sure, the ganache and dough were probably already hardening. Everything else, though, was melting through my fingers.

Every time a gasp rang out, my eyes flicked to the sides of the tent. Shaky hands piping unevenly were projecting all over them. Ganache dripped down fingers. Marshmallow creme dampened sleeves.

To be honest, most of these projections were of my ganache trickling down my fingers. Sweeping over the sides of my graham crackers. My marshmallow creme refusing to stay in place.

The entire tray looked less like half-assembled s'mores and more like melty icebergs floating on tectonic plates made of graham crackers. To top it off, the camera crew hovered close, as if waiting to capture the moment of impact. With my apron, I wiped away the sweat beading my hairline.

Keep your cool, Johnny Oliver's voice echoed. "And keep everything else cool," I whispered, repeating Madame Terese's.

Between my meltdown and my s'mores literally melting, I couldn't afford to go down without a fight. Not after everything. Not with so much on the line.

I set the piping bag aside. Grabbed the tray and ran to the fridges. Chilling the s'mores could still save them.

Sydney stood next to one of them, spine straight as if guarding it. "Any room for mine?" I asked.

"Of course, sweetie. I'll watch out for yours too if you need. Someone took out my ganache."

"Mine too! And my dough!" Blood rushed to my face, anger boiling under my cheeks. "So we *do* have a Lando Calrissian in the tent."

"It appears so." She fixed her gaze on the baker with wire-rimmed glasses wearing the argyle sweater vest. DEXTER PHAM, according to the name holder on the edge of his station.

"Him?!" My voice carried down the stage. Some of the bakers glanced up from their bakes, Dexter included. I shot him the frostiest look possible and mouthed, *We're watching.* He dropped his eyes first, then his spatula, disappearing behind his workstation to fetch it.

Ha! Let the weasel squirm. "I can't believe it. He looks like a thirty-year-old grandpa, not a saboteur." A snort so loud my head almost exploded. I was half-expecting the traitor to be Katherine.

"Looks can be deceiving."

"So can first-gen daughters," I mumbled.

"What was that, dear?"

I tucked a wayward curl behind my ear. "Um. I was wondering, should we rat him out?"

She shook her head slowly. "Snitches get stitches, sweetie."

I cracked up despite myself. My rage cooled to a simmer. "Do you have any other pearls of wisdom you can share?"

"It looks like you're already doing it."

"Doing what?"

"Following your bliss."

"Ah," I said with a laugh-snort. "Well, according to a great Cuban philosopher I know, following one's bliss only leads to blisters."

Hipster Granny smiled. "Then you must find bliss in your blisters."

I brushed a handful of curls from my eyes, feeling as if a fog was lifting and I could finally see more clearly.

For forever I'd thought duty and passion were like oil and water. And never the twain shall mix.

But maybe they didn't need to be mixed; maybe it was better to fold them over one another, like layers of a croissant or the rings of a Rosca. Maybe they could even be the same thing.

"I'll keep it in mind." I motioned to the fridge. "As I finish this bake."

She opened the refrigerator door for me. At the sight of the slightly more hardened s'mores, I pressed my sweaty palms to my chest. "Thank you," I said. "See you at the judging table."

"See you at the finale." She winked.

For the sake of Alma, of Cuba—of me—I hoped she was right.

"Bakers, your time is up. Please place your bakes behind the placeholder with your name."

I took a sidelong glance at the bakes being set across the table. Katherine's and Sydney's s'mores were the only ones that looked good enough to eat. Good enough to make the finale.

Argyle-traitor-guy's looked like a dozen mounds of dog poop.

Everyone else's fell somewhere in the middle. Actually, mine fell closer to the wrong side of the middle. The churning in my stomach increased by a hundred.

"Let's start here, shall we?" Madame Terese said, gesturing to my tray.

"Do we have to?" Laughter ripped through the tent, and more importantly from the judges' lips.

Johnny picked up one of my s'mores, scrutinized it from all angles. "The shape of the crackers are all very symmetrical, but the coating has major issues. You mixed the chocolate with the—" He glanced at me. "What types of nuts did you use?"

"Chopped hazelnuts. I wanted to go for a Ferrero Rocher look and taste." I cast Madame Terese a drowning look. Except she was too busy examining the outsides to save me again.

"Creative, but by doing that, you compromised the nice, shiny chocolate-tempered coat we wanted," she said.

"Exactly." Johnny Oliver scratched at a huge piece of hazelnut, sticking out way higher than the rest of the nuts. "They don't look as neat as they could."

I nodded, the flaws they pointed out now beyond obvious. "Yep. I shouldn't have put my nuts all over the place."

The tent exploded with laughter again. Johnny Oliver's face turned bright red. Madame Terese leaned into Summer Rae's ear, whispered something that made them both double over in a riot of giggles.

I would've laughed too, if I wasn't trying so hard to keep from crying. A snap went through me, quick and sharp. If I screwed up the outside of the s'mores by not following the relatively simple chocolate tempering recipe, what other "recipe" had I screwed up by tampering?

Johnny Oliver cleared his throat. "Um, let's see what these look like inside?" He picked up a knife. It went through the s'more smoothly, hit on the aluminum tray with a *clank*. "Beautiful crack."

The tent roared again. Johnny Oliver's cheeks flared crimson. Even the outlines of tattoos shifted as his muscles tensed.

"The heat in the kitchen isn't just affecting the bakers today, am I right, folks?" Summer Rae said.

The waves of cheers and laughter buoyed me.

Until Johnny Oliver split my s'more in half.

Blobs of ganache and marshmallow oozed out. "Definitely timing issues here. Neither layer had enough time to set."

I threw eye daggers at Dexter and his argyle sweater. He kept his gaze forward, glasses slipping down his nose. My anger rose, but at least it kept the sinking feeling at bay.

The judges took bites of the bake. "The graham cracker could've used an extra minute in the oven too."

"The chocolat blanc ganache is delicious," Madame Terese said. "So is the flavor of the marshmallow. But neither is quite ready, are they?"

I shook my head; my feet sank into the carpet of artificial grass.

The judges moved on.

I kept staring at my tray. The chocolate coating began to melt. The weight of the unevenly chopped hazelnuts only made the s'mores topple even faster. The top layer of graham crackers slid off. The marshmallow creme collapsed into the ganache . . . on top of . . . me.

Collapsing over everything I hoped to get out of this competition.

Sabotage aside, I should've stuck to the recipe. No deviations. No tampering with things tested and true.

My vision blurred with tears. I blinked them back and refocused on my bake.

So many ingredients pooled together in a sticky mess on the tray. Somewhere in the middle of it was my future. It sank so fast, I could no longer see it. No longer reach it.

No matter how hard I'd tried to keep hold, it was gone.

Chapter 27

Cold air rushed through the crack in the window, making my teeth chatter even from underneath the covers. I drew my knees together and curled myself into a small ball. Flicked away all of today's missed calls and notifications from the screen. Tried to do the same for the fresh texts still streaming in.

Devon: PICK UP!
Torie: This competition's a marathon, not a sprint.
Ryan: Don't lose hope.

I would've turned the phone off if it wasn't for what Summer Rae had said after the judging.

The list of the bakers going to the finale would be up tonight. So I refreshed. Nothing. Refreshed again. Nada.

I let go of the phone. Wrapped my arms tighter, made myself even smaller.

I swore I felt the email hit my inbox before the phone buzzed against the pillow. With a shaky hand, I reached for the glowing screen. Swallowed hard at my inbox:

Bake-Off: Finalists + Huge Announcement

I tapped the email.

Each line slammed me deeper and deeper into the mattress.

Jamming all those baking fans into the tent has become a huge whisk . . . This change in location will do everyone good . . . Alma U is providing state-of-the-art baking stations to help the winner rise to the top . . .

Of course Bake-Off had chosen Alma's new auditorium for the site of the last challenge. Of course the last challenge was now set for next Saturday.

Of course it'd start at almost the same time as the debate tournament.

My breath hitched too fast, my throat constricted too tight to laugh at the irony of it.

Even if I could laugh, I wouldn't. Not with Dad's voice drifting up the hallway. Followed by my mother's. Not when a set of footsteps stomped down one corner. Or when the hallway light blinked out of existence. And a door slammed at the far end of it.

I pulled the covers over my head. Pressed the phone to my heart, as if to keep the last shreds of it from breaking. When I peeled the screen away and scrolled down the list of bakers—Katherine, Sydney, Nico, Dexter, and Juno—it broke anyway.

I refreshed the screen. The names stabbed like a knife. Katherine. Sydney. Nico. Dexter. Juno. There had to be one missing.

Mine.

But no amount of frantic refreshing materialized it.

The covers pressed down on me. The air beneath them turned sour and thick. My eyes filled with tears. They spilled hot down the sides of my face. I didn't even bother wiping them away. The pillow dampened, then swelled with lost hopes for Bake-Off. Cuba. Alma.

The blow of it sent cracked pieces of my heart crashing to the bottom of my chest. Jagged edges mixed with crumbled remains of the walls once guarding my heart's secret chamber. I sifted through the rubble, picked up the pieces.

Only those cut deeply too.

After hours of twisting in bed, trying to reposition myself in a world filled with all this loss, I remembered the crap cherry to top the crappiest of days.

Madeline. I croaked out a single bark of laughter that burned the back of my throat raw. I had to call Madeline.

The phone trilled so long I thought she was sending me to voicemail. Until—"Why are you calling me? It's late."

My throat went Death Valley dry.

In the silence, her reptilian brain must've connected the dots. "Oh, I get it. Plan B didn't quite work out the way you wanted?"

"Up in flames." Drowned in ganache was more like it, but still. "Does your offer still stand?" Time flattened, seconds ticking forever. "If you want me to beg, I'll do it." What was losing my dignity when I'd already lost Bake-Off? When I was on the verge of losing Alma too? "Madeline, say something. Please."

"Yes, the offer still stands." My fingers loosened their grip on the edges of the phone. "Your title in exchange for a meeting with my aunt."

"But I get to stay on as co-captain."

"Vice-captain."

I looked up at the ceiling. A way out of this mess wasn't hidden somewhere in the gathering shadows there. "Fine, but I get to participate in the final rounds."

"I get to go last though."

"Of course, Madeline." I gritted my teeth. "Best's always saved for last."

"Done. I'm glad you're finally coming around to my way of thinking." On her end of the phone, I heard nails clacking on keys. Something swished through the air. Almost immediately, a chime. "Tomorrow at two P.M. Can you fit it between your shifts at the bakery?"

Considering I was probably now banned from those shifts too, I sank deeper into the mattress. "Yes," I mumbled. "Fits perfectly."

Three raps on the door. "Come in." I peeked over the covers.

Dad craned his head through a crack in the door. The light from the hallway fell on his curls and shoulders. It cast enough light on his face for me to see the sad truth.

"Hey, kiddo, I saw the website. Are you okay?"

The loss of Bake-Off pressed down on my chest again. So did losing the seminar in Havana. And the blowup with my mother. The icing on the cake was handing over my Law and Debate title. All of it made it suddenly very hard to breathe.

"Yeah, Dad, I'm fine." Scratchy voice told otherwise.

He stepped into my room, paused at the foot of the bed. "It's okay not to be fine, you know?"

I snorted. "Whatever you say. And who knows? Maybe it's better this way. The Boss gets what she wants; I go back to being the perfect Cuban-American daughter. The living embodiment of the American Dream." A hollow laugh flew from my lips.

Maybe getting eliminated *was* for the best. I should probably quit baking altogether while I was at it. Stop searching for my roots in ingredients. Stop looking for family members in old recipe books. Stop longing to set foot on shores I didn't know.

If I wasn't already lying down, I would have. Because constantly navigating between worlds was exhausting. Every single bone in my body ached from the weight of living between hyphens.

So, maybe it really was time for me to let go.

I threw off the covers. Bent over the side of the bed to yank the mold from my messenger bag. "Here." I extended it out to him. "I don't need it anymore."

"Rubi . . ."

"It's yours." I couldn't have the mold in my bag anymore. Or have it lurking under my bed like a monster. "Just take it." He stood, unblinking. "Please, Dad. Take it." My voice broke, and finally, he grabbed it.

My palms went cold. Well, that's it. The end of an era. But at least it's all over. No more lying. No more back and forth. I wanted to finally be able to breathe again.

I tugged the covers over my head. Curled my toes inside fuzzy socks. "Sorry I got you in trouble with the Boss."

"Don't worry about her. Just get some rest."

His slippers dragged over the rug, over the floors. The door creaked and he broke his stride. "Rubi, no matter what you do or don't do, you'll always be a baker. Okay?"

I sniffled back tears as quietly as I could. "'Night, Dad."

When he left, I drew the covers down. Stared at the ceiling while his words replayed loudly in my head.

He was probably right. I'd probably still be a baker even long after I quit . . . but would I still be me?

Chapter 28

A hostess led me through the Grill's main dining area. My heels clicked on the restaurant's stone floor, kept tempo with my pounding heart. I glanced around at the ladies who lunched, the men in dark suits. At the very least, I was appropriately dressed for this interview.

I shuddered, and not from the ocean breeze hitting me when I stepped onto the outdoor terrace.

"Right over here." The hostess gestured to a table overlooking the sea.

She pulled out my chair. I sank into it, took slow breaths when she said she'd let Addison Teague know I was here the moment she arrived.

I opened my messenger bag. There was so much extra room with the mold gone. A jolt of longing surfaced from deep inside. I pushed it down and reached for the index cards to shuffle them quickly. Refreshing myself on Alma's history, my academic one, and why Alma and I were a great fit.

The breeze blew one of the cards from my hands. I leaned over the side of the chair to pick it up.

That's when a pair of black pumps strutted toward the table.

I sat up.

There, dressed in a pink blouse and wide-legged trousers, holding a black leather briefcase against her hip, stood Addison Teague. Alma's dean of admissions.

"Rubi Ramos?" The voice was rich and raspy, with a faint British lilt.

"Ms. Teague." I stood to greet her, curbing the instinct to curtsey. "I'm so happy to meet you." Terrified, nervous, and hopeful too. She probably felt all those things anyway through my sweaty handshake.

She gave my hand one more pump, then waved me down. "Please, dear, sit, sit." The sunlight made her rings flash and her bracelets sparkle. They were even more bejeweled than the Rosca. Triple that of Thanos's Infinity Gauntlet. Just as powerful too. It'd only take one snap of her diamond-encrusted finger and I'd go from waitlisted to *in*.

"Thank you for taking the time to meet and discuss my future at Alma." My voice quivered. The confidence I'd felt in Bake-Off's tent had to still be there somewhere, buried deep under the weight of this interview.

"Of course. Anything for a fellow Future Leader of Orange County member and good friend of Madeline's."

Good friend of Madeline's? And without even a hint of sarcasm? What new game was she playing at? My throat dried up. I reached for the glass cup only to discover it was empty.

"One glass of Perrier-Jouët for me and a Perrier for my guest, please," Addison said to a passing waiter. She studied me across the table with a probing intensity not unlike Johnny Oliver. I fought the urge to look away. "Pardon me for taking the liberty and ordering for you, but you look a little frazzled, dear."

"Did the hair give it away?" I grabbed a handful of curls,

shoving as many as I could behind my ears. "I swear my hair acts like a mood ring sometimes."

Addison threw her head back and gave a throaty laugh. "Madeline was right. You are a wit."

She'd probably said "twit." If not, what parallel universe had I stepped into? The waiter came back with our drinks. I took one sip, then another. Tiny bubbles fizzed on my lips. So did the salty air. God, I missed kissing Ryan.

The breeze whipped a mass of curls across my face, forcing me to focus. "So, about Alma." I twisted the rogue curls into a bun.

"No," Addison said. "Don't tie it back. It looks wild and free. Stunning. Keep it loose."

"You think so? I feel like people are staring at it." At me.

Addison followed my gaze over her shoulder. The two women sitting at the table behind ours stopped whispering, shot their attention down to their overpriced salads.

Addison turned back, shrugged, and took a swig of her champagne. "Let them stare. As a Future Leader of Orange County, you need to be comfortable standing out."

"Future Leader of Orange County" was not "Future Alma alum." I didn't have to spend too much time holding my face still, hiding my disappointment over her choice of words, because one of the lookie-loos materialized at our table.

Smiling from ear to ear she said, "So sorry to interrupt. But can I get a picture with you?"

"Um . . ." I glanced around, convinced she must've been talking to someone else. No reason on earth she'd want a picture with me.

"You are Rubi Ramos, aren't you?"

The other woman rushed in right next to her. "The baker who made the Rosca?"

My heart stopped. They knew who I was because of my baking? "Yes. I'm—"

"I told you it was her!" A squeal so loud it garnered a few looks from people at nearby tables.

"We tried to meet you after the judging but couldn't find you anywhere."

"You were amazing."

A wave of heat radiated throughout my body, making me feel as if I'd been transported back inside the tent. It was definitely a little disorienting. But if I was being completely honest with myself, totally freaking awesome too.

I took my attention back to the ladies and Addison.

Addison leaned forward, cracking a tiny smile at the exchange. "Thank you," I said. "It was amazing to get the chance to bake my great-grandmother's recipe."

"The way the judges talked about your bake—"

"How it looked like a piece of heirloom jewelry—"

"How you were the real royalty of the day." She tipped her face up to the sky.

The other one pressed her hands to her chest. "So touching."

Her friend nodded. "So powerful."

Whoa. I was right. Baking could be something more than celebratory calories. Or the financial means to a collegiate end. Baking mattered. These women were proof of that.

Tears welled. I willed them away. Devon was too far away to come and redo my makeup now.

"Sorry again for the intrusion, but my sister and I totally wanted you to win."

"The feeling was mutual." I cleared my throat. "Let's take the photo before your salads get too soggy." They crouched down and snapped a selfie, the three of us sporting mile-long grins. They waved on their walk back to their table.

"Sorry about the interruption, Ms. Teague." Nice confidence boost though.

"Don't apologize. In fact, it was exactly the type of information I needed."

I blinked. "It was?"

Addison lifted her briefcase and thumbed through the pocket folders, stopping at the file with my name printed on its tab. Slipping a folder out, she shuffled through some of the pages inside of it.

"Yes." Her manicured finger trailed the lines of one page in particular. "Your personal essay told us everything easily gleaned from your CV and academic records." She narrowed her eyes. "Only nothing about it felt, well, *personal* in conveying why you're Alma material."

My eyes narrowed right back. What more than my academic accomplishments did she need to prove I was a good fit?

"I see you work part-time at a bakery that shares your name. Can you tell me a little about it? Do you own it? Are you one of these teenage entrepreneurs giving all us old codgers a run for our money?"

"Hardly. It belongs to my parents." I paused, stared into my lap.

"What is it, dear?"

"I mean, technically they own it. But the bakery has always been a financial means to a—er, my—better future. Maybe that's why they named it after me." A Montblanc pen materialized in her hand, flashing silver with every word.

Actually, she jotted more words than I'd said. I kept going, knowing she'd be able to keep up.

"As far as me working there, between their work schedules and my school schedule, my shifts on some weekends are pretty much the only way to spend time together." Addison's smile broadened. The pen sparkled against the sun.

"They recently opened a second location in Santa Ana."

"Serving the community there," she said, mostly to herself. "Fantastic. Are you working in the Santa Ana one now?"

"I stayed at the Costa Mesa location to work with my dad. My mother's request. It's closer to home and school."

"What a shame. It would've been great to reconnect with your roots that way." The Latinx population in downtown Santa Ana was mostly Mexican and Central American. We weren't a monolith. I didn't correct her assumption. "However, your mum's a smart lady. The 405 is, if anything, a beast during rush hour."

"She's a very smart lady." The puzzle pieces slowly started to click into place. "She's always been the brains behind the bakery—er, *bakeries*. That's why many moons ago, Dad and I nicknamed her the Boss."

Addison smiled at that, so big this time, she unleashed a dimple. "Dad, on the other hand, he's always been the baker."

"Baking. How lovely."

It grated on me how she'd skipped over my mother's accomplishments. Dad's too. I clasped my hands across my lap. Kneaded the frustration from my fingers. The tiny nicks and dots of the baking scars bulged white against my tan skin.

Baking was demanding, physical work. Done hours before the sun came up.

As much as I loved baking, it was not "lovely."

One of the very reasons why my mother insisted on a white-collar future for me.

"Perhaps we can talk about that." Addison angled forward. Her pen hovered hungrily over a fresh page.

The last puzzle pieces clicked together in my head so loudly I was surprised the entire restaurant hadn't heard it.

She didn't want me to tell her all the attributes I shared with the incoming class, the hand-selected type A's worthy enough to grace the domed buildings and pristine gardens of Alma U. She wanted me to tell her about all the differences.

She wanted to know how much I'd scaled to get this far. If she should extend her bejeweled hand and give me one last pull up.

Blood rushed to my face. I reached for the glass of water. Hoped Addison didn't hear how many ice cubes I crushed with my teeth. The chips of ice hurt going down my throat. They pooled in the pit of my stomach. Stung with cold shards of truth.

I'd done so much of the work. Done so much of it right, and still, it wasn't enough.

My shoulders slumped, ashamed at needing her help. But frankly, I was more grateful for the way she licked her lips, eager to give it.

Every noise on the terrace sounded like Alma's doors creaking open. Images of the prep room swept over me. Of the day everyone in it exploded with cheers thinking I'd already busted them wide open.

They'd cheered me on, only it was more than that. Because if I could get into an Ivy, their sons and daughters could too. All this time they'd thought they now had someone like them on the other side of the door, holding it open. Making sure it stayed that way.

The warring emotions vanished. Newfound clarity about Alma U swooped in to take its place.

I wanted Alma more than ever. There was no bottom to how much I wanted it.

Not just for my sake, or my parents'. But because one day, I wanted to be the person sitting where Addison sat, perched atop the highest peak in all of Pelican Point, across from a person who, like me, needed a hand on the way up.

Only I'd know they weren't reaching.

They were climbing.

It was a difference I knew, and Addison couldn't. Despite all of her best intentions, she'd never know.

So, I fed into Addison's game. It was the only way for me to someday change it.

I took my gaze across the terrace, searched for the perfect thing to say about baking and Bake-Off. Without clouds to pepper the sky or waves to froth the sea, it was hard to tell where one ended and the other began. And there, in the distance, Catalina. The closest island I'd get to this summer.

"Oh? Admiring the game, dear?" She angled her head to keep studying me. "So besides baking, is golf another one of your hobbies?" The pen resumed scribbling notes. "Is that how you get that stunning glow?"

"Ms. Teague!" I forced my laugh to sound organic. "The glow is not golf related, it's Afro-Cuban related." She nodded more vigorously as she wrote *Afro-Cuban* on the page. Exactly like I knew she would. "I'm only familiar with the courses because we've delivered so many cakes here. This is actually the first time I've been here as a guest. Or even come in through the front door." I paused to make sure she got it all down. "Every penny my parents make gets invested into my education. Every spare penny gets reinvested into the bakeries. They can't afford golf lessons too."

Every word I'd spoken was true, and yet. I took a swig of water because my mouth felt dirty.

Addison's curved into a grin. "We offer golf as an elective, you know. You'd love it."

Alma's door swung open. The breeze hit my face with onshore wind as if to prove it. "Oh, I don't know if I'd be any good at it."

"You don't have to be good at something to enjoy it."

The Rosca and the Malta Condensadas hadn't come out perfectly symmetrical. Or perfect by any means. Still. I'd loved making them. The judges had enjoyed eating them. And if the sisters who'd stopped at our table were any indication, the fans had enjoyed my bakes too.

Turning to Addison, I lifted my chin. With a boldness I only dared show off in debate tournaments, I said, "Very true, Ms. Teague. And very wise. Perhaps when I get to Alma . . ."

I paused, giving her room to correct my implication. My heart nearly leapt out of my chest when none came. "I'll take golf as an elective."

She pressed her torso into the table. "Speaking of electives, this baking competition those gals mentioned. It wouldn't happen to be Bake-Off, would it?"

I nearly choked on an ice cube before nodding.

"I recently met the dean of the new culinary program. They couldn't stop raving about how much fun they were having with it."

"It was some of the best fun I've ever had." I couldn't help but sound wistful. And even though Bake-Off's ship had long sailed, curiosity got the best of me. "Did they say anything about the contestants?"

She smiled and asked, "Why don't you tell me about your experience with it instead."

For a few minutes, I told her about the competition and what I'd baked. She listened with genuine interest, flipping over the page to continue taking notes.

I pressed my lips to keep from laughing at the irony. Breaking the Ban could ultimately be the very thing that saved Alma. I parted them to keep gushing, only to be interrupted by twin squeals of glee coming from behind us.

The two sisters barreled forward again. "Dexter Pham . . ." one of them panted.

"The guy with glasses and the sweater vests," the other finished.

My head darted between them.

"He got eliminated from the finale right now."

"There was footage of him sabotaging bakes."

"They just announced who's taking his place!"

All my blood rushed to my heart. I yanked my phone out of my bag. So many texts from Devon, Ryan, and Torie.

And there, on Bake-Off's website, my name, at last.

"You're going to Bake-Off's finale," both sisters shrieked.

"Waiter, another round of drinks, please." Addison grabbed my already shaky hand to shake it some more. "Congratulations, my dear. Do well at the Law and Debate tournament next weekend and you'll be going lots of places."

Addison had practically dropped Alma off on my doorstep. All I could feel though was how hard Bake-Off knocked at the door.

Chapter 29

The wind battered my topknot. A few curls writhed free and blew across my face. The scent of shampoo and conditioner funneled to my nose.

All other aromas, gone.

Not surprising considering it'd been days since I'd been in the prep room. Baked anything. Or even looked at Bake-Off's YouTube channel.

I ignored the way my stomach ached as I raked up my hair and jammed it back into the hair tie from where it'd escaped. Leaning forward on the teal railings, I looked down the pier.

With spring break over, Matteo Beach's pier was less crowded. Only a few joggers zipped by. A handful of yoga moms and imported nannies pushed strollers. Against the plethora of black polyester and the backdrop of the teal-blue sea, Ryan's burgundy-and-tan school uniform stood out. But not as boldly as the red flash of his hair.

The ache in my stomach began to melt. At least our relationship had survived last week's fallout unscathed.

I intended to keep it that way.

Not wasting a single minute, I wrapped my arms over his shoulders. Ryan's arms went around my waist. I rose on tiptoes, bypassed the hug, and went straight for his lips.

"You sure have an awesome way of saying hello." He laughed, then kissed me back harder.

I took note of the firmness and the warmth of it. The solidness of his body. The way his hand trailed up my back to the nape of my neck. How his thumb brushed at the loose curls there, as if daring them to break free.

He brought his face to my ear. "Although, I hope I'm the only person you greet that way. By the way . . ." His voice lowered, like he was letting me in on a secret. "I really like the way you look in your uniform."

"I like the way you look in yours too." I tried to match the width of his smile but didn't quite succeed.

"Uh-oh, what's wrong? You want to start with the bad news first?"

Waves slapped at the columns under the pier, infusing the already thick air with even more salt. I lay a cheek to his chest.

His heart beat loud and steady. I imagined a large, wooden clock. "On second thought, it's going to take a lot longer than the time we have left for off-campus lunch. Let's skip the bad and only talk about the good, deal?"

I untangled myself from his long limbs, but he reeled me back in and squeezed super tight. "Ryan!" Now it was my turn to laugh. He eased his grip a little. "Okay, fine, I'll tell you but, please, let's start with the good news."

He pressed his forehead against mine. Green eyes hunting for everything I hid deep inside my brown ones. I held his gaze, unblinking. Finally, he said, "Deal."

"You go first."

He lifted his chin. "I got into USD."

I threw my arms around his neck. "Oh my god, Ryan! This is so amazing!"

"It is," he said, laugh-choking. I loosened my hold. The breeze stirred his hair, blew mists of salt water off the tops of waves behind him. "The surf there's awesome. And . . ."

"And what?"

"San Diego's only an hour away from Pelican Point." Red splotches blossomed across his cheeks. "Which means it's only an hour away from Alma."

"In other words . . ." I wiggled my eyebrows. "We can still have our cake and eat it too?"

"Cookies. You had me at cookies, not cake, remember?" That blush crept down his neck. I nodded; my brown skin hid the way my own body was flaming now.

"So yeah, we can keep on having as many cookies as we want." His lips curled. "I mean, if you still want to keep having them, that is."

Yes. Sí. I wished I knew more languages so I could say it in those too. "Of course I still want to keep having them."

"Awesome." A huge grin. "We can even have them without trig lessons this time."

"About that." I led him to the cement bench beside us. Picked up my messenger bag from the bench top. Paused, still unaccustomed to how light it felt without the cake mold. "This is my good news." I pulled out the Trig folder. What lay inside of it brought warmth back into my fingers. I handed him the folder. "Open it."

Zeroing in on the grade marked on the top of the page, his eyes lit up. "An A minus! Rubi!" He lifted me off my toes and spun me around.

"It's more than amazing." With the A minus on the Trig midterm, I'd finally entered the top 5 percent of my class. Alma's door swung a little more open. Pressure lifted off my shoulders, made room for my chest to swell with pride. "I would've never thought crushing math was possible."

Ryan put me back down. "Let alone it'd come so handy in baking, right? You're going to kill it in the finale."

I buried my face into his shoulder to escape his stare. What I couldn't escape was his scent.

Ocean water lingered on his skin. A hand went to his hair. The sea lived there too. In the salt-stiffened tousles crowning his head.

Ryan wore the ocean like a second skin. Exactly like I used to with doughs and flours. I pulled away. "You went surfing this morning?"

"I go surfing most mornings."

Surfing was as much a part of him as his easy confidence and infectious excitability. As integral to his DNA as the genes coding for autumn-red hair, cilantro-green irises. Constellations of freckles sprayed across his skin.

The thought of Ryan not surfing, of not smelling or tasting like anything but salt and sun, was unimaginable to me. He probably thought the same about me. Not tasting the rush of sugar on my lips. No more globs of dough on the hems of my shirts. Or hair. Which was exactly why I hadn't told him yet.

A shot in the finals was the way to have my cake and eat it too. And wasn't that what I dreamed of? To get into Alma *and* compete in Bake-Off? Here it was all coming together . . .

Weeks ago, the sweetness of it all made my mouth water.

Now, it gave me toothaches. Truth was, one new recipe couldn't change the entirety of the Ramos Recipe Book. One new variable plugged into an age-old equation couldn't change the answer to my family problem.

"I can't kill it in the finale." A sharp and sudden knife cut to my belly. "I'm quitting Bake-Off."

Ryan's eyes widened. I stepped away from him. Put distance between me and my most recent confession. Between me and a baking future that had never really belonged to me in the first place.

I sank onto the bench. Ryan followed.

The marine layer had thickened. Blocked a view of Catalina Island, in the distance. Did Florida's sun and wind clear it faster than here? If I was sitting on a bench in Key West right now, would I be able to see Cuba?

"Why?" Ryan asked. "You were kicking major ass."

"Uh, hello? I only got back in because of a technicality."

"No. You got back in because that dude messed you up."

I snorted. "No, Ryan. *I* messed up." Every chance I got. I shoved my fists into my pockets. "I need to confess something else. Remember the payment deal we made way back when?"

"Tutoring for cookies?" His eyebrows rose.

I nodded. "I might've had ulterior baking motives." Deep breath. "Like at first when I wasn't sure if I'd compete in Bake-Off, I figured baking for you could be the next best thing." I offered him a weak smile. He didn't return it. I wanted to stop. Except stopping wasn't an option on my truth tour. "But then, when I was more sure I wanted to do it, I might've, sort of wanted to study at your place so I could use your kitchen."

"Ouch." He slumped against the bench, blinking slowly. "So, you were using me for my stomach? For my kitchen?"

Damn, it sounded so much worse when he said it like that. I bit my lip. "Maybe a little, and only in the beginning."

At that, he laughed. "All's fair in love and baking, I guess."

All right. Let's not get sidetracked by the L word. "No, Ryan, it's not. But I kept acting like it was. I convinced myself Bake-Off would actually make my application stand out. Tampering with all these recipes in the tent." My throat thickened. "It, like, gave me a false license to tamper with the only recipe that matters in my life."

"And who crafted this so-called recipe?" The corners of his mouth curled into the tiniest of frowns. "You or your parents?"

I crossed my arms against my chest. A makeshift apron to guard against his probing at things better left alone. "Does it matter?"

"Yes, it absolutely matters."

"My parents sacrificed everything for my future. And I repay them by what?" I snapped, voice cracking all over the place. "Lying to them? Disappointing them? All so I can go and do this thing that's a hundred percent about me instead of this dream we've all worked so hard to make come true."

"We. You keep saying 'we.' What do *you* want?"

The ocean roared. Waves crashed on top of each other, slamming on the sides of the pier.

"I want to do the right thing." Yes, it was true. My jaw clenched though, holding back other truths buzzing on the tip of my tongue.

"Again, for you or your parents?"

His questions were like oil jumping out of the pan, sticking to my skin before searing it. "Ryan, stop. Staying in the competition isn't as easy as you think."

"Maybe it isn't easy. But it's simple. You know it is."

Simple? There was nothing simple about honoring my parents' expectations without getting crushed by the weight of them. I scooted away from him. "Since math's under control, I think you can cool it with all the Opri-Wan quotes. I don't need a guru or Jedi training. What I need now is for you to support this decision."

"Supporting you doesn't mean I have to agree with you." He ran a hand through his hair. "And for the record, I wasn't quoting some mindless platitude. I was quoting Johnny Oliver and Madame Terese and *you.*"

I opened and closed my lips. All rebuttals vanished as images of the Malta Condensadas and the Rosca came to me as vividly as the day I presented them.

The simplicity of the ingredients and the difficulty of getting the bake right had not only grabbed the judges' attention, they'd taken me all the way to the finale.

A dozen seagulls hovered overhead. Wings flapped hard. The wind fought back harder. Kept the family of gulls from going anywhere, especially pa'lante.

"This is my future and my family we're talking about, Ryan. I'm not going to rely on cookie or bread recipes to help me navigate it. Just like I'm sure you're not going to use surf advice to figure out a way to tell your dad about your trip. Which, let me guess, you still haven't told him about, right?"

He flinched like I'd scalded with him some hot tea. Perhaps I had. "You're right. I haven't told him. I was hoping—"

"Hoping what? Watching me in the finale would inspire you again?"

Okay, maybe the tea hadn't been hot, it'd been boiling. Because he rose from the bench fast and furious. Fine. See if I care.

"You're being mean, Rubi."

"If I am it's only because I'm sick of everyone having an opinion on my life. I'm sick of everyone commenting on every single thing I do." With all the surfers riding waves, it was easier for me to ride one of my own. Instead of water, this one was made of 100 percent anger.

Anger at my mother for wanting so much from me. Dad for always teaming up with her in the end. The world and its unfairness. Even at Ryan for always cheering me on with color-blind pom-poms. Pushing myself off the bench, I rode the wave to its crest. "And I'm sick of being lectured on this from someone who could never understand."

He staggered away. Paused and turned back, frowning. "You want to know what I do understand?"

"What?"

"If you're so tired of everyone else meddling with your life, maybe you shouldn't be so quick to run away from all of your own recipes."

"Yeah? Well, maybe I should find some new *ingredients* while I'm at it too!"

Oh no. Yelling that was a mistake. Not to mention it was totally untrue. And right when I thought things couldn't get any worse, Ryan's eyes turned red. *Please let the breeze be the culprit.* With all the crying I'd done lately, the last thing I wanted was to make anyone cry. Especially him.

"I didn't mean that, at all. Please, I'm so sorry—"

With a raised hand, he cut off my mumbled, half-baked apology. His lips opened a little, but whatever he was going to say stayed behind them. He turned and walked away. I watched him disappear down the pier. Wished for him to turn back again.

He didn't. I couldn't blame him.

Tears nipped at my eyelids. I blinked them back. Refused to let them blur my world. I'd blurred it plenty these past few weeks, and where had it gotten me?

I let out a throat rattle of frustration. Kicked the side of the bench.

My toes throbbed. Good. The pain covered the aches in my chest.

Mostly.

Chapter 30

Each day spilled into the next. My parents left for work before I left for school. Classes all day. Study sessions all afternoon. At night, if I did see my parents at home, I put on my Alma cardigan. Paired it with a brave and dutiful face.

By the time I climbed into bed, my emotions were burnt toast.

I typed out a long apology to Ryan. Deleted it all. Shaky hands sent a Hey instead.

Lots of gray bubbles appeared. Disappeared. Then a Hey back.

We traded single-digit snippets of our days. No mentions of the blowout, our next tutoring session, or his surf trip. Nothing about Bake-Off either.

Drifting off to sleep, I caught myself thinking about it anyway.

The sheets rustled loudly as I pulled them over my head. Wrapped in my cocoon, memories of the past few weeks—the good, bad, and super ugly—had a harder time creeping back in. I plunged into sleep so deep it was dreamless.

I quickly came to love those bottomless black holes of sleep.

People were always so afraid of nightmares. Never realized it was dreams they needed to be on the lookout for.

In the mornings, I looked out the window. The sky tempted me with its bright vastness. Untangling myself from the sheets made me think of a butterfly emerging from its cocoon. Not that I could relate.

Because of Bake-Off though I now knew what it'd feel like to have wings.

For a moment, all I thought about was how badly I wanted to fly again. Then my legs swung from the mattress. My feet touched the floor. The sturdiness of it grounded me, reminded me to obediently tuck my wings back into place.

By the end of the week, the sharp pain of holding them back turned into a dull ache. I wondered if in another, I'd forget they were ever there.

♥ ♥ ♥

People jammed Immaculate Heart's hallways. Classmates' and teachers' voices thrummed with excitement only the final weeks of school could bring. Sunshine and warm air spilled in through the open sides of the hallways.

The sounds and smells were as familiar to me as those inside the prep room. Inside Bake-Off's tent . . .

Ugh, why did my mind go there? Again. I mean, I'd only competed in three measly challenges, so why was I still so hung up about it?

I hustled forward. Shoes slapping hard against the pathway leading to the auditorium. The closer I got to it, the closer I got to Alma.

Addison had practically confirmed it herself last night via email.

She was going to be at the debate to cheer for me and Madeline. Her colleague from the board of admissions was going to be there too, serving as a judge.

Addison not-so-casually dropped his name, instructed me to look above his jacket's lapel for a name tag, make lots of eye contact, and remember to smile.

While the rest of the team had groaned at Sister Bernadette's suggestion for one last-minute practice before tomorrow's tournament, as team vice-captain, I'd insisted on it.

For Alma's sake. Weirdly, for Bake-Off's too. Every second I spent cramming or preparing was a second not spent mourning. I pushed the auditorium's handles and walked inside.

The spotlights shot into my eyeballs. I shielded my face with a hand, ran down the familiar aisles, up the familiar steps. I blinked hard, and the team slowly came into focus. "What's with the gamma ray burst for the light?" I asked Carolina. "Lights," I corrected myself when I turned back to the gallery.

Not only had the flickering spotlight been fixed since our last practice, but it looked like every single light in the auditorium had been swapped out for newer, much brighter LED bulbs. The inside of the auditorium shone brighter than the outside did.

Before Carolina could answer, Madeline jumped in with, "It looks weird like this." She shouldered past Caro and sidled up beside me. "Doesn't it?"

Not as weird as you talking to me without a dig. The ice-blue storm clouds didn't churn behind her eyes with the same impending havoc like usual. Maybe she'd finally run out of havoc to wreak. Or perhaps she was still licking her wounds from the last practice debate.

She wasn't the only one.

I shook my head at her. The anger reserved for her was still there inside my stomach, only now it simmered instead of boiled.

Should I crank the fire back to high? Tell her to get away from me and never speak to me again?

After a moment's hesitation, I did neither. In a totally destructive way, Madeline had "helped" me finally come clean to my parents. She was like an evil dentist who'd extracted a tooth without my permission. Except the molar was rotted and needed to go so everything could heal.

I ran my tongue over my teeth, crossed my arms over my chest, and nodded. "It does look weird. Smaller than I thought it'd be. Less intimidating too, with all the lights on."

"This, team, is exactly the point I wanted to illustrate." Sister Bernadette's voice boomed from backstage. She stormed through the curtains, her habit flapping at her ankles on the march downstage. "Tomorrow, on Alma's stage, you may feel overwhelmed. You may feel nervous. If you do"—she gestured to the bright and empty gallery in front of us—"strip away the crowd, the judges, the acoustics. Strip everything away until it's only you and a big, empty room."

Like when I'm baking. I cleared my throat. "Most of your houses are bigger than this auditorium anyway," Sister Bernadette said.

Scattered giggles from the team. They nodded because in many of their cases, Madeline's especially, the joke rang true.

Sister Bernadette pushed the wire-rimmed glasses up the bridge of her narrow nose. The lens flashed against the bright light. "But in the event visualization doesn't work for you, with the spare capital from this year's fundraisers . . ." A hint of a smile bloomed at the corners of her mouth. "I took the liberty of preparing something else for you that may help. Miss Anderson." She snapped her fingers. "We're ready for you."

Miss Anderson? As in Devon Anderson?

Tires squeaked from offstage. Metal jangled against metal. Devon heaved through the curtains, wheeled a stainless-steel clothing rack to the middle of the stage.

"Clothes?!" Nat squealed.

"Oh my gawd, Sister Bernie hooked us up with new outfits!" Nina shrieked louder.

The stage rumbled with everyone rushing at Devon. I ran too, but to help her push the rack forward.

A flurry of hands blurred around us as the team searched the hangers for the blazers pinned with their name. Then the floorboards rumbled again, this time with everyone scattering to different corners of the stage to try theirs on.

"Well, this is a nice surprise," I said.

"Better than the last one I gave you?"

I smiled. "Nope. Still like that one more."

Devon grinned. She slipped the last navy blazer over my shoulders. Buttoning the round, brass-embossed buttons down the front, and drawing in the peplum waist. With outstretched palms, she smoothed the shoulder pad things.

Exactly the same way my mother had when she'd fitted me with my first suit.

My shoulders tensed at the memory. The weight of familiar expectations and duties pushed down, heavy as ever. So did the unfairness of Bake-Off having to end before I got the chance to finish it.

Devon patted my shoulders lightly. "Epaulets. Decorative insignia traditionally used by armies." The way she said it made me think she knew everything I was feeling. "You want to talk about it?"

I shook my head. "Talking about it will make me think about it."

Not talking about it made me think about it too. I was on

the brink of making the Recipe for Success finally crumb—er, come true. So why couldn't I scrub Bake-Off from my mind? The puns. The prize. The everything.

"Okay, well, I figured you needed something extra for the last debate." She rolled one of the epaulet's buttons between her fingers. "Old-school military uniforms were one of my inspirations for this look."

War uniforms were a type of armor. And armor against invading thoughts was exactly what I needed going into the last debate. I turned my attention to the team. They buzzed with a united purpose that was infectious. I straightened my spine, lifted my chin higher.

"This is perfect for the last battle. You've outdone yourself, Dev." The navy wool paired amazingly with my tan skin. "They're badass and beautiful."

"Are they?" Madeline wrinkled her nose. "I think they look like military cosplay. Something else too. I can't put my finger on it. . . ." She turned to walk away, then paused. "Oh, and speaking of cosplay, Devon, when are you going to fix your hair?" She stalked off, flipping her own tresses over her shoulder.

The second Madeline was out of earshot, Devon and I leaned into each other. We flipped my curls and her bottle-black-fading-back-to-blonde locks in faux exaggeration. "I never thought I would say this, but Madeline might be right."

"You want to make your hair great again?" I asked.

Our giggles grew to be the loudest sounds in the auditorium. After all the drama, it felt good to laugh with my best friend. Even Madeline sharpening her claws again felt good too. Things were settling back to normal. For a second there, I'd feared normal would never come back.

♥ ♥ ♥

I sat on the curb outside his house, waiting. Listened hard to the waves crashing in the distance, cars backing out of driveways, squawks of gulls. Ryan had probably already left for school.

I checked my phone for any messages before slipping it back into my pocket. Reached for the cup of Americano from the cardboard cupholder and took a sip.

No cream, no sugar, and definitely no malt.

Everything fell silent except for my pounding heart.

And then, somewhere off to my right, sandals slapped against the bottoms of feet, followed by the unmistakable sound of a plastic leash thumping across a fiberglass surfboard.

Ryan froze when he saw me. I rose on shaky legs, extended a king-sized bag of Peanut M&M's and half-melted mocha like peace offerings.

He eyed me far too warily, for way too long. My hands began to tremble, making the ice cubes jangle. "It's from Sun Goat," I said.

His face softened, and slowly he walked forward. "This is a surprise."

"A good one or a bad one?"

He shrugged, sucking air through his teeth. "I don't know yet." With his Orion-freckled hand, he took the mocha. At his fingers grazing mine, I dropped the bag of M&M's.

"Sorry." I kneeled down to pick them up. Light-headed, I flopped onto the curb. "Ryan, I'm so sorry. I was totally mean and misdirecting my anger. And that thing I said about finding other ingredients—" I broke off, nose-diving into the horrific possibility of having lost my boyftu forever. "Totally immature and not true. I can't apologize enough."

He sat down next to me. Taking the bag of candy, he popped some into his mouth before handing some over. We sat there like that for a while. Staring at passing cars. Crunching on chocolate-covered peanuts instead of talking.

"I get it." He cast a sidelong glance to the Alma cardigan I wore. "The first day we met up here, you were wearing a shirt with different embroidery."

"Rubi's Bakery." My fingers curled around the cup of coffee. I took a sip. It tasted bitter.

"You're lucky, you know, to have parents who love you so much they'd name their businesses after you? My parents?" A crack in his voice, like a leak from somewhere deep. "They'd never do that."

I didn't know if my hand-holding privileges had been revoked. I grabbed his anyway, traced the Orion constellation with my thumb. "Don't say that. I'm sure they'd name a hospital after you if they could."

He snorted. I scooted closer. "Maybe," he said, "but let's not go off on a tangent." He ran his thumb over my hand, across the deepest of my scars. "Apology accepted."

The entire street brightened. My whole body sighed. I lay my head on his shoulder, not caring a single bit about what the damp wetsuit would do to that half of my hair.

"Look, I know families are complicated, and I definitely don't know everything about your family dynamic," he said.

"No, you don't." Hell, even I was only beginning to scratch at its surface.

"But I do understand the love part though. I get why you don't want to mess with that." He was speaking from experience, that much was clear. So was his unreadiness to take the lid off whatever brewed inside. Let alone try to solve it like one of his math problems.

Then came his big, bright smile. Burning away the last shards of tension between us.

I ran my finger over the Orion freckles again, tugged at a salt-stiffened tuft of red hair. "How about we drop all of this for now and talk about me acing another quiz and you getting into USD?"

"Agreed. Change of subject."

"Good, because fighting with you didn't help how stressed I'm feeling."

The corners of his mouth stretched into that grin I loved so much. "Did you know 'stressed' backward spells 'desserts'?"

Treasonous laughter bubbled inside of me. I let the laughter explode despite myself. A moment later, Ryan did too. Together, we roared until we were breathless. "Not helping."

He shrugged. His lips parted as if he wanted to say something. I tilted my chin to the perfect angle. Silenced him with a kiss. We kissed and kissed, and when our mouths finally pulled apart, we kept our foreheads pressed together.

"Oh, I beg to differ," he said, before pressing his lips back to mine.

Chapter 31

Up the palm-lined walkway leading to Alma's main quad I went. Slowed, but definitely not steadied, by the heeled ankle booties Devon deemed "absolutely necessary" for the last debate. They clacked on the brick paving, announcing I'd made it.

Finally, I was here!

The hike up the campus left me panting. The sights at the top took any leftover breath away.

Set high above the cliffs, Alma U didn't just overlook the Pacific Ocean. It overlooked the clusters of McMansions dotting the Newport Beach Coast as far as the eye could see. All of them looked trivial compared to the buildings on campus.

Varying between Spanish Mission and Spanish Renaissance, the buildings, gardens, even the outdoor gathering areas infused the campus with a style falling somewhere between new money and old world. Dozens of red clay–tiled roofs and metallic domes soared high above tall trees.

On the far end of the campus, one silver dome glinted brighter than all. Over the palm and eucalyptus trees, through the throngs of people, it flashed like El Morro, Havana's famous lighthouse, beckoning.

I squeezed my eyes shut and tried to keep thoughts of Bake-Off's stage at bay; of imagined scents from creeping in. Flashes of pastries and phantom scents snaked in anyway. My mouth watered and my stomach growled.

Ignoring them, I turned back to the sprawling pathway in front of me. The one leading to the old auditorium. One ankle bootie clacked forward, then another. This was the right way to go. The tried-and-true path to my future success.

But I couldn't help myself. I glanced back at the new auditorium, lingering on it for a few seconds. I shook my head and kept going. Quickened my steps for good measure.

Joggers zipped through the campus from every direction. So did students, decked out in blazers and uniforms, most likely on their way to the debate tournament. There were lots of people in regular clothes too though. How many of them were headed to the old auditorium to check out the debate? How many of them were going to the new auditorium to snag front-row seats to Bake-Off's finale?

I turned away from the crowd, focused instead on the flower bed decorating the middle of the quad. It was round and ginormous. Filled with hundreds of white and red flowers spelling *ALMA*.

A huge smile spread across my face. Some of the cracks in my heart started to plaster themselves back together. I wasn't sure if it was because I'd worked so hard to get here, because I deserved to be here, or because my parents were on the brink of finally getting a return on their investment. Either way, standing here felt right.

So, why didn't it feel like enough?

I couldn't dwell on it too deeply. Not when the universe chose this moment to send my parents strolling into the courtyard. I watched my mother reach for Dad's hand. The way he linked his fingers through hers. When he leaned over and whispered something into her hair, what did he say?

Whatever it was, it made her pause. A second later, she threw her head back, cracking up. Her laughter floated over the noise of the quad. When she tipped her face down again, the tiny lines still etched it. Except now they looked laughter-lined instead of stress-made.

If I didn't know her, I would've assumed she was another student, laughing carefree in her Alma cardigan.

It felt odd to watch them interact as people and not as parents. My heart patched up even more at the sight of them this happy. I tried my best to mix in the crowd. Only Dad spotted me.

"Rubi!"

My mother's head swung in my direction and—for the first time since our blowout—she smiled at me.

We closed the gap between us. She wrapped her arms around me and crushed me into a hug. Maybe she'd finally forgiven me. I relaxed into her hug in a way I couldn't that day in the prep room. Despite Bake-Off's finale being so close, there was no way I was going to screw this up.

"The debate doesn't start for another hour," I said. "You didn't have to come this early to show your support. I mean, I'm happy you're here, but I'm meeting the team for some last-minute brushing up. I don't have time to hang out."

"Lucky for you." Dad slapped me on the back. "We don't have time to hang out either. The Boss wanted to explore the campus for a while before the debate."

"Not the entire campus." She buttoned the top of her cardigan.

"We'd miss the debate. We're only going to see parts of the west campus."

"Ohh, to see the rose gardens, again? Like we did during the tour we took freshman year?"

After the tour ended, my mother had insisted on "one more look at the rose gardens before heading back to work."

The gardens stood between the School of Business building and the ALMApreneur lecture hall. The outer walls of the lecture hall could be a garden themselves, with all the green ivy rooted to the mortar and cracks between each red brick. The vines climbed and twisted over the building. Millions of tangles swallowed most of the walls whole. My mother had stared at the vines even longer than the rose gardens.

"Yes." Her voice cracked and she cleared her throat. "The gardens."

Weird. Then again, she was probably as nervous for the debate as I was.

She tugged at the collar of her cardigan, confirming my suspicion, but not before I caught a glimpse of her eyes.

The cinnamon flecks in my eyes came from her irises, not Dad's.

How had I never noticed? "They're probably in bloom right now." I smiled; she did too.

"I hope so." Texts poured into my phone. "The team's probably wondering where you are."

"Totally. I should get going. Do you guys know where the debate is?"

"It's in the old auditorium, right? Not the new one?"

The fact that she mentioned the "new one" so casually meant she had no idea that's where Bake-Off's finale would soon take place.

The way Dad bit his lips, meant he 100 percent did.

"Definitely not the new one." My voice grew louder than necessary. "The tournament's in the old auditorium." I pointed to the right of the quad. "Over there."

"Then why are both of you looking *that* way?" She tracked our gazes—both fixed in the complete opposite direction from where I pointed.

"We were?" A single bark of laughter escaped his lips. I joined in, trying to sound natural.

My mother swatted him on the arm playfully. She pulled me in for a quick kiss on the head. "You better get going, mija. Buena suerte. I know we've had a few bumps in the road lately." She let go. "But look." She motioned all over the quad. "We're here. Only that matters now. We're so proud of you."

I was unable to form words. Dad took my arm and hugged me. "Don't forget, after the debate, you promised to introduce us to your, um, *friend*."

His not being able to say "boyfriend" made me want to burst with laughter.

"I know. I know. You'll probably meet Ryan before the debate. Devon's going to try to find seats so all of you can sit together. If not, I'll introduce you after the debate. I promise."

Satisfied, my mother walked off to the Alma flower bed. Hundreds of red buds were on the verge of blooming.

I tried to pull away from him, but his grip held. Despite his wearing clothes that'd never set foot inside the bakery, the scents of sugar and fresh bread clung to him. "Rubi, I want you to know I'll be proud of you." The conviction in his voice was palpable. So was a hint of something else. "No matter what."

Walking to the old auditorium, his words gnawed at me. *No matter what?*

What the hell did that mean?

He'd be proud even if the debate didn't go perfectly? Even if I didn't get off the waitlist? If I never baked again?

Or did he mean he'd be proud of me if I did?

Chapter 32

I pulled back a thick curtain and peeked into the auditorium. Most of the audience spilled through the aisles and out the doors. After six preliminary rounds, they probably needed to stretch their legs, run to the bathroom, get a snack. Or all of the above.

Not my parents.

Even from this distance, through the dimmed lights, I spotted them. Lips moved fast. Hands gestured faster. Faces glazing over with a mix of nervousness and excitement and pride.

I knew because I felt the same way. I scanned the rows around them.

No sign of hair like flames. No sign of Devon's almost-back-to-blond.

If she hadn't been able to find my parents in time to grab seats together, had she at least been able to find Ryan? I didn't want him to sit through the debates alone. I checked the gallery again, searching.

They weren't anywhere in the auditorium. But Addison Teague was. At the foot of the stage, she held court with the debate's judges.

Stodgy, balding, with name tags pinned on gray suits, these judges needed a huge serving of Madame Terese's style. A pinch of Johnny Oliver's edginess at the very least.

There it was. Again.

Bake-Off's spark trying to reignite. I shook my head, snuffed it out before it caught fire. Burned everything to the ground.

I took my focus back to Addison. Her eyes were fixed on her colleague from Alma's admissions board. When the other two judges left, Addison placed her hand on his shoulder. "Stunning and intelligent." A not-so-tiny wink. "And no, I'm not only talking about my marvelous niece."

I leaned into the curtain even though her voice bounced off the walls of the almost empty auditorium, loud and clear.

"Miss Ramos would be a great asset to our incoming class, don't you think, Aldrich? A background like hers is exactly what we need to enrich Alma's educational experience."

Aldrich took off his glasses, wiped the lenses with a white monogrammed hankie. "And to think she almost escaped us." He put his glasses back on, face unreadable under the glare of the lights. "If her performance stays on par during the final rounds, I agree with you wholeheartedly. She's a shoo-in for the incoming class."

A sigh filled with equal parts relief and trepidation was what should've huffed out my mouth. A bark of laughter did instead. *She's a choux-in for the incoming class.*

All right. Enough pastry talk. I pulled the curtain closed. As much as the bustle of backstage drew my attention, the large digital clock perched high on the far wall was all I could concentrate on.

In less than an hour, the debates would be over.

Bake-Off's finale would be well underway by then too.

Behind me, Sister Bernadette shouted, "Team, that's how

you decimate the first group." They rushed toward her, exploding with cheers. Nina and Carolina slapped me on the back and dragged me from the curtains when Sister Bernadette motioned us in for a group huddle.

Her lenses flashed over our heads, then back down again. "If the judges keep hitting the same types of questions, I have an inkling these rounds will continue to stay in the vein of international politics and socioeconomic policies." Her hand clasped my shoulder. "Rubi, you're up next. How are you feeling?"

How did it feel to miss out on one opportunity for the sake of the other?

It felt right.

It felt wrong.

It felt like the dark tunnel *and* the light at the end of it.

I wrung my fingers behind by back. Squeezed out leftover doubts. Kept my determination from crumbling. "I'm fine." Or I was up until a few hours ago. "I'm ready."

Sister Bernadette tipped her chin. "Really? Because the paleness of your complexion is stating otherwise."

Madeline's gaze caught mine. She licked her lips, probably tasting all the potential digs hovering at the edges of her smirk. For once she kept them to herself. A potential sign of progress? When it came to Madeline, I couldn't tell. FLOC member or not, for the first time, I didn't give a damn.

"I'm fine. I just need something to eat."

"Then do so now. That goes for the rest of you too, team. We've got a few minutes left on break. Enough time for you to visit the catering table or restroom." She rubbed her palms, taking in the commotion backstage. "While you take care of your needs, I'm going to do some last-minute recon. Rendezvous here in T minus ten." She took off in a swish of black.

"Anyone else grabbing something to eat?" I asked.

Nina shook her head. "Makeup touch-up."

"Hair." Carolina flipped chestnut locks over her blazer.

"I'm going to brush up on Chinese tariffs," Madeline said.

The team scattered in different directions. I weaved through the throng of students and down the steps leading to the backstage door.

People swarmed the hallway. Some talked excitedly into phones. Others jostled for space against walls, on floors. All around me, dozens of heads were buried deep inside books and binders for some eleventh-hour cramming. Some debaters cried into friends' and family members' shoulders. The pained expressions and gut-wrenching sobs echoed throughout the hall.

After so much prep to get here, screwing up in these rounds meant the trophy—any trophy—had slipped from their fingers.

I should've been grateful to not be walking in their shoes.

Except I sort of was. One trophy was slipping through my fingers. My tingling palms confirmed it.

With each hurried step, the pressure in my chest built. It dialed up to a hundred when another sound punched through all the noise.

Loud ticks and even louder tocks. At the end of the hallway, topping the alcove, a clock face rivaled Big Ben's. Massive dial hands sped through the seconds at warp speed.

Soon, I'd be walking onto one stage. And Bake-Off's finalists would be scrambling across another.

I darted to the catering table, hoping to finally leave thoughts of the competition in my wake.

The sandwich trays were empty. The fruit platters were too. The only remaining foods were raw florets of broccoli; the saddest snack ever.

I bit through a stalk. It crunched liked bones. Thank god

the baked goods were all gone. Who knows what a bite of sweet bread would've done to my fraying resolve.

Immaculate Heart had made it to the final rounds. I was up next.

I can do this. I can do this. I repeated the words like a mantra, waited for the moderator to call me and my opponent to the stage. Devon burst through the backstage door. Her matching ankle booties stomped all over the floorboards on her Olympic sprint toward me.

"Sorry I'm late," she panted, running a hand over her hair.

"Devon, where were you?"

"I was—um—having parking issues." She glanced over her shoulder to the backstage door. Only after seeing it'd remained shut did she exhale.

"What is it? Meter maids coming to bust you or something?" I teased.

She shrugged in response and the smile started to slide off my face. "You've got to be kidding me." My arms flopped at my sides. Maybe I was unfairly projecting some of my nerves onto her, but I couldn't help myself. "I'm freaking out, Dev. Ever since eating this broccoli my stomach hurts." It had actually started hurting before that, but still. "And Bake-Off puns are hijacking my mind." I pictured my brain boarding a small airplane, taking off to an island in the Caribbean, not so far away. "Did you find my parents? What about Ryan? He's not in the auditorium. Is he having parking issues too?"

Devon's face filled with something I couldn't quite place. She wrapped an arm around my shoulders and brought her face down to my ear. "About your stomachache, the puns, the parking—"

"Devon," Madeline interrupted, edging next to us. "I knew I'd find you here supporting our little friend."

"She's more than a friend," Devon said. "She's family."

"Ah, a family affair," Madeline said.

"A family eclair." My hand flew to my mouth. I splayed open two fingers, wide enough to whisper. "See. It's happening again."

Devon's mouth gaped, then curled into a smile. She cracked up so ridiculously loudly I had to join in. Another round of giggles. They tapered off, taking away some of the tension in my body. Made room for me to get my head back in the game.

"What did you say?" Madeline asked.

"You wouldn't get it," I said.

Madeline put a hand on her hip. "Well, I only came over here to tell you I finally figured out what these uniforms you designed look like."

"Yeah, we know," I said. "Military uniforms."

"No." Madeline exhaled, long and annoyed. "Chef's coats."

Devon's arm stiffened across my shoulders.

"'Chef's coats'?" My eyes flicked to Devon, then down at the blazer, across the long sleeves and sturdy fabric. It would be useful against splatters and stains: too warm to be used in a prep room, but considering the boxy cut and the double-breasted jacket . . .

Oh my god. Madeline's observation was spot-on.

"Out of all of us, I'm surprised you didn't see it first, Rubi," Madeline said.

I turned to Devon. "You said these were military inspired."

"I never said it was my only inspo."

"So you did this on purpose?" I blinked and blinked, peeling her arm from my shoulder. First Dad's cryptic pep talk? Now Devon playing fast and loose with these uniforms? What the hell was going on? Other than funneling down the throat of a supermassive black hole, of course. Squeezing and squeezing until only one question remained. "Why?"

"I was trying to tell you earlier—about the parking—"

"What does this have to do with parking, Devon?"

She opened then closed her mouth. Opening it again, words finally came. Only they boomed from the auditorium's speakers instead of her lips. The moderator called me and my opponent to the stage.

"Rubi, listen." She tugged back on my arm. "If you change your mind about this, there's a getaway ride on standby out front."

"Getaway ride?" I balked, motioning around. "No, Devon. Can't you see? This place, this future . . . There's no getting away."

I turned away from her and marched toward the curtains like the soldier she'd dressed. Only like a soldier. Nothing more. Especially not like a cadet-chef. That combo didn't even exist. Right?

I pushed through the curtains. Big, bold steps clicked on floorboards. I stared Aldrich directly in the eye. Took my gaze toward the podium. I was in Alma's homestretch now. My shoulders squared and my chest lifted as I got closer. Then suddenly, my steps softened.

Because underneath the layers of excitement and relief and pride there was a huge scoop of something else too. Loss.

Each step toward the podium was a step away from Bake-Off, away from Cuba.

As I reached the podium, the spotlights settled. My final answer did too.

The lights made it impossible to make out the judging table, let alone anyone in the gallery. I felt their presence anyway. I pictured my parents clutching the arms of their seats the way I held onto the sides of the podium.

Pressure pressed down on my shoulders. Thankfully, the military/chef coat's epaulets braced my shoulders against the weight of it. The moderator cleared his throat into the mic.

I nodded to my opponent and she nodded back. *Here goes everything.*

"Resolved: the United States should maintain its embargo against Cuba."

Cuba?! This hadn't been on any of Sister Bernadette's or Madeline's lists of "potential" topics. Even if it had been, I doubted I would've gone *there*.

I tried to suck in whatever air was left in the room. As vice-captain, I had the ability to debate myself out of a paper bag.

Or at least I was supposed to. Plus, maybe this question was a weird sort of blessing. If I couldn't be across campus trying to win spending a summer there, maybe exercising the immense privilege of talking about Cuba was the next best thing.

"Miss Sowers from Connelly will be arguing the affirmative. Miss Ramos from Immaculate Heart, the negative. Your time begins now."

"The US embargo against Cuba, signed by President Kennedy in 1962 and reinforced by several legislative acts, list several conditions necessary for the embargo to lift. Conditions include a commitment to fair and free elections, a free press, and the legalization of all political activity. Cuba has failed to meet these conditions. Therefore, the US embargo against it should stay," my opponent said.

I rebutted with: "The conditions listed in the Cuban Democracy Act and the Cuban Liberty and Democratic Solidarity Act are aimed with the specific intent to *pressure* Cuba to take a *different course of action*."

I couldn't explain the emphasis on some words rather than others. Maybe it was the mic, not me. I drew my face a few inches away from it, in case, and continued, "One word in these acts reveals what the US wants Cuba to achieve. Democracy."

Every word boomed louder now.

Hearing my voice project this loudly made me a little dizzy. Beneath the dizziness, there was also a hint of empowerment at how sure I sounded. The words boomeranged off the mic, bounced off the walls, rounded back, and slammed my skin with confidence. I liked it.

I liked the way it made the judges sit up straighter. The way Aldrich leaned forward, nodding as if to say *yes, yes*.

"If years upon years of a forced embargo haven't compelled the Cuban regime to shift from a communist government to a democratic one," I continued, "more years won't suddenly cause the shift the big ol' *boss* of the US wants *Cuba* to make. The embargo has failed to achieve this goal. Ergo, it needs to be lifted."

A dash of déjà vu. Why did this debate feel so familiar?

"Shifting the current political system is not the only aim of the embargo," Miss Sowers said. "Under UN declarations and charters, the US has a moral obligation to push for *better* living conditions, *better* human rights, overall a *better,* more prosperous future." She paused to let her argument sink in.

It sunk in all right. The word "better" cut deep inside me each time she'd said it. So did the argument that the only future worth living was a better one than what came before it. But who decided what was better? And what did "better" even mean? Nothing between AP covers defined it. No math equation yielded the "right" answer.

It wasn't the volume of the words affecting me but the weight of them.

I *have* had this debate before.

Alma's stage transformed into the kitchen at home. Miss Sowers morphed into my mother.

The Cuban embargo. The Ban on Baking.

In the portion of overlapping similarities, dead center, was me.

I'd been preparing for this debate my entire life.

"The embargo hurts." My voice echoed in the auditorium with a truth that rang deep.

One judge pushed his glasses up the bridge of his nose, as if he was really seeing me for the first time. I craned my head into the spotlights; maybe my parents were looking at me in the same way.

I stared out into the top row, where my parents sat.

A familiar sense of duty filled me. Only this time, it was a duty I owed wholly to myself.

On the other side of the lights, hundreds of people waited for me to speak. I stood silent until Sister Bernadette's advice began to work its magic.

Spotlights dimmed, then melted away. Layer by layer, pieces of the auditorium fell away, until the stage transformed again. And only a dark room remained.

I stood on one side of it, my mother on the other. Unblinking, I said, "The Ban has hurt people. It'll continue to hurt people as long as it stands."

The Ban on Baking hadn't just banned baked goods. It'd banned an essential part of who I was, and I hadn't realized, until now how much locking all of it behind walls had hurt me.

I wouldn't feel guilty about shattering my mother's dreams. Or tampering with the Recipe for Success. Not anymore. I couldn't do the "right" thing any longer—not if it meant hiding away entire parts of me.

The walls between who I was and who I needed to become began to crumble again.

Only this time, when the walls fell, I saw both those things could coexist.

With the rubble of them at my feet, a lightness swept over me. As different parts of different dreams combined with one another, a wholeness I'd never felt before filled my body.

I lifted my shoulders, raising the epaulets to new heights as the auditorium came slowly back into focus.

I moved my hands to the edges of the podium, no longer holding on for dear life. The smattering of scars had never been displayed so freely to such a large audience. I left them right where they were.

This was shining bright like a Rubi. This was the *real* American Dream. The Recipe for My Success.

"Under the embargo, individuals are denied certain medicines, fashions, technology. Even certain *foods*," I said. "If the *US* really wants *Cuba* to do better, and if the US has a moral obligation to ensure Cuba actually does better, then the ban should be lifted. Making all of these things readily available for the people to finally enjoy and use in the ways they see fit."

"Time," the moderator said.

The auditorium erupted into applause. The clangor of so many discordant claps filled the room with what sounded like a thunderstorm. I let myself revel in it.

As the noise tapered off, one last clap went off in my head.

The debate battle was over, but the baking war was still on.

I bolted from the stage. Hopefully there was still enough time for me to join the fight.

Chapter 33

I ran backstage as fast as I could. All the way down the small staircase leading to the back hallway. My pounding heart pushed me to go faster, and when I reached the door, Sister Bernadette yelled from behind me. "Rubi!"

I glanced back, refusing to let go of the door's handles. She stood at the top of the stairs. Madeline stayed a feet steps behind, straining her neck to get a glimpse of the action. "The last round is going to begin shortly," she said. "Then the judges will announce the winner. Your performance, while not one of your most technical, was certainly one of your most passionate."

"She's been delivering a lot of *those* lately." Without the usual acid spiking her voice, Madeline's joke was actually sort of funny. Who knew she was capable of having a sense of humor? Then again, who knew I was capable of doing all the things I'd done?

All the things I was going to do.

"Our team has shown the judges an array of skills today that the other teams didn't do quite as effectively. If Madeline keeps it up, I definitely think we have a shot of winning." Sister Bernadette tucked her hands into her front pockets. "If we win, it would be a great shame if you weren't there to accept the trophy on our behalf."

"Yes, it'd be a shame, Sister Bernadette." I meant it too. I gazed down at my hands gripping the door handle. Big and stainless steel. Like an oven's. "But it'll be a bigger shame if I don't leave and try to make it to another competition. The baking one Madeline told you about."

Bake-Off's finale had started almost half an hour ago. My chances of winning were slim, and grew slimmer the longer I lingered in the old auditorium. I smiled anyway.

Sister Bernadette did too. "Waging a war on two fronts, I see." She, like so many others, was probably familiar with the pressure behind making tough decisions. She squinted down her glasses. "And still standing in those ridiculously impractical shoes of yours. Commendable, Miss Ramos."

Yes, it totally is. Warmth rushed through my chest. "Besides, if anyone deserves to accept the trophy, it's you." I turned my attention to Madeline. "Captain, or not." Eyes back to Sister Bernadette. "You've always been the general."

She blinked hard, pink splotches blushing her round cheeks. "Well, then, Miss Ramos, there is only one thing left to say." She clicked her clogs together. The corners of her mouth pulled wide, revealing a big toothy smile. "Give them hell!"

The door slammed shut behind me.

I broke into a sprint—past students, parents, barely avoided bulldozing a few grandparents.

Hallways wound right, then left. Booties scratched against the polished floors. Screeched when I rounded the last corner.

The auditorium's main entrance. Doors came into view. My speed gathered force.

I was almost there!

Then a blur from the left. Followed by a *boom*.

Crashing into a person at full speed made my bones rattle and my vision swim. "So sorry, I didn't see you." I reached for the wall to steady myself.

"I didn't see you either." The voice was familiar. So was the hand clamping my arm.

Instantly, the rest of my vision cleared. There she was. "Mamá."

"¿A dónde piensas que vas, Rubi?"

"To the new auditorium, Ma. I'm competing in Bake-Off's finale."

Disappointment darkened her face. The grip over my arm tightened, keeping me in place. I grabbed her fingers, pried them off gently. Brought her hand to the space between us.

Her skin was cold. I wanted to hold on to it for a moment longer to warm it. At the end of the hallway though, the clock's minute hand ticked and ticked, with no signs of pausing.

"Mamá, I have to go."

She clenched her hand into a fist.

I glanced down at my hand folded over it, and weirdly the image triggered something from AP Anatomy.

The size of an adult heart was roughly that of two clenched fists. For so long our hearts—and what beat inside of them—had similarly intertwined.

Her dreams had wrapped with mine, becoming so tangled, that for a while, I'd thought they were the same thing.

I let go of her hand and reached for her gaze instead. The deeper I stared, the more the cinnamon flecks looked like embers of what was once a gigantic flame. In the dark irises surrounding them, black pools of immeasurable depths. Who knew what treasures she'd let float to the bottom? Or straight up buried under the sand.

For a moment, they softened enough for me to glimpse it.

Millions of memories swept over me. The college ranking magazine subscription she refused to cancel. All the Alma merch she wore. How cruising the campus's quad, she'd seemed so happy, so natural. How she hadn't really wanted to stroll the rose gardens, but the buildings and lecture halls beyond them. All of it translated so differently now.

Alma University wasn't only her dream for me.

"This is your dream." All breath left me in a rush. "Alma."

Her silence confirmed it.

Going to college had been her dream once. And had her life circumstances been different, she would've chosen here, Alma.

Because of them, my life circumstances *were* different. Yet here I was, rushing off across campus to bake.

No wonder it didn't make sense to her. All that mattered was it finally made sense to me. "This is my dream."

"Rubi, you've worked so hard." With each word her voice grew louder. The conviction dripping from it filled the hallway. "Don't run away from all of it for a dream."

I shook my head. "I didn't say this is my only dream." I was ready to show her all the sides of me, all the angles that seemingly didn't fit but made me whole. Ready to show her I wasn't running away from anything . . . I was running toward everything. Pa'lante, exactly like she'd taught me. "I'm doing this." If she watched me go after my dreams, perhaps she'd find the courage to go after hers. Dad stepped into the hallway. I nodded at him.

"I'll be at the new auditorium. Dad will show you where

it is." I pushed my shoulders back. "I'd love it if you guys came to watch. But I'll also get it if you don't."

Maybe it was only my overactive imagination, but right before I turned, something flashed across her eyes. A begrudging resignation bordering on respect. She was, after all, someone who had earned the nickname the Boss—and liked it. She'd transformed Dad's recipes into successful and growing bakeries. When life got tough, she believed a person should become a Boss and take care of business.

Which was exactly what I intended to do.

Dad winked as I skidded past him, running to the end of the hall. Light spilled underneath the set of double doors. Beckoning. A quick breath and I threw them open.

The pointy ends of the booties pinched my toes on the trek up the pathway. Up ahead, the line of eucalyptus trees thinned. The silver-topped dome of the new auditorium peeked out in the distance behind them.

It appeared so close, but was actually far away. At least ten minutes of track-style sprinting across hills and stairs to get there. Would my throbbing toes let me make it? With the competition already underway for nearly forty-five minutes, winning it would be nearly impossible.

Merely getting to compete now seemed like the prize.

Ah, but to win it! To bake in Havana!

I hurtled forward. Curved another pathway. Bounded another flight of steps. The heels on my booties almost snapped off as I swerved to an abrupt stop at the top of the hill.

My eyes darted from Ryan, leaning against an idling golf cart, to Devon, sitting inside of it. Her hands gripped the steering wheel, her foot on the pedal.

"Like I tried to tell you backstage . . ." She cracked up then revved the engine. "Your getaway carriage awaits."

Half panting, half laughing, I rushed forward. Devon shifted the golf cart into drive. Ryan hopped into the back seat, holding out his hand. I grabbed it. Leapt in beside him. "Took you long enough," he said.

"Better late than never, Opri-Wan."

"So the student becomes the master, eh?"

I shrugged, my mouth curling into a smile. His face moved closer and closer until the air smelled of nothing but salt and sea, until my lips claimed every inch of his.

I grabbed a fistful of his hair to kiss him even harder. Salt and sea were there too, stiffening those beautiful whorls of red. I pulled away. "You need to tell your dad you're going on the surf trip."

His cheeks flushed red. "I told him last night."

A small squeal. Then I rewarded him with another kiss.

"Kids, you mind keeping the PDA to a minimum back there?" Devon said. "I don't want any tongues bitten off. It's going to be a bumpy ride."

"Nothing any of us aren't used to." I settled against the seat, eyes sweeping around the cart. I squeezed Ryan's hand, not knowing how the hell they'd gotten the golf cart, but extremely happy they had. "We borrowed it," Ryan said.

"Do I even *want* to know?" I asked.

"I promised some of the team members a surf lesson."

"And I promised the captain a custom-made bikini for said lesson as well as—" Devon's voice broke off and she mumbled something that made Ryan explode with laughter.

"Dev, what else did you promise them?"

"That you'd bake a hundred brownies for the entire team." She shrugged like it was no biggie.

"Devon!" I yelled, but immediately cracked up with them. Now that the Ban was broken, I supposed an order this size wasn't a big deal anymore.

"Anything else you want to know?" she asked.

"What's the fastest this thing can go?" Devon honked the horn, made people jump out of our way. Pressed the pedal all the way down. The campus blurred as we wound through the twisting pathways, sped up and down Alma's slopes, swerved around fountains.

The cart went pretty fast, it turned out.

♥ ♥ ♥

Devon slammed on the brakes in front of the new auditorium. My stomach churned. With nerves, but mostly with excitement. Ryan and I hopped out of the cart. Devon stayed in it, engine idling.

The afternoon sun glinted off her honey-blond tresses. "Your hair," I said.

She brought a hand to it. Raked it loosely as she smiled. "Yep, it's almost back to au naturel. I think I'm going to rock it like this for a while."

"It'll be perfect however you have it."

She laugh-snorted. "Thanks, Rubi."

The second she jumped out of the cart, I was going to wrap my arms around her and squeeze tight. "Wait, aren't you coming in?"

"I will after I return"—she made air quotes—"this baby to the golf team."

I smoothed the front of the military/chef's jacket. Two such different inspirations had been stitched together so seamlessly. A possibility I'd been so oblivious to.

"Thank you too, Devon." I rolled up my sleeves. She'd cut

them short so I didn't have to pull them up much for the tiny scars to be on full display. "For everything."

The new auditorium's foyer was empty. Our footsteps echoed loudly. At the sight of the doors leading to the gallery, to the last challenge, I paused. "I couldn't have done this without you either, you know."

"Yes, you could've," Ryan said. "All I did was nag you."

I shook my head. "You did so much more." Grabbing his hand, I trailed the freckles that formed Orion. No wonder he'd helped me navigate the last few weeks so well. This guy was made of brightly burning stars.

"O-Ryan, remember?" His eyes shined as they moved all over my face. "Where I saw freckles, you saw a constellation."

I pressed his hand to my heart. He'd done the same thing for me. Over and over, he'd pointed things out about math, about myself, about so many things, from all different angles until something clicked.

"Then you came up with boyftu. Opri-Wan." With his thumb, he skimmed my scars. The spaces between them. "You've got a knack for combining things and making them into something new, you know."

"I guess I do, huh? Maybe that's my superpower." I pressed his hand harder against my chest, hoped he could feel how fast my heart was beating.

He smiled and I knew. Through the layers of wool and skin and bone he absolutely could. "One of many, Rubi Ramos. One of many."

Chapter 34

Cinnamon. Pineapples. I inhaled deeply. *Bacon?* The scents grew stronger with each step. As I made my way backstage, the sounds grew louder too. Ovens thrummed through floorboards. Mixers buzzed. Knives hit against wooden cutting boards. After being away from the prep room for so many days, the sounds and smells of baking rushed me forward.

I stepped to the edge of the stage. The same setup from the tent was here: shelves, fridges, screens above them to project every detail. Workstations too. Only instead of ten, there were just five.

Bakers moved around them in a blur. Or dropped to their knees to stare through the oven doors. Katherine whipped cream. Sydney and Juno rolled out fondant and dough at dizzying speeds. And there were the judges, moving from station to station, taking it all in.

I threw my shoulders back and stepped forward.

Murmurs rippled through the audience. A smattering of gasps and applause. Summer Rae turned her head, nudged Johnny Oliver in the ribs, and gestured for Madame Terese to look over. All the bakers did too.

Being in everyone's line of vision was equal parts scary and awesome.

Katherine frowned before dropping her head down to continue whisking. Sydney flashed a huge smile then returned to cutting shapes out of fondant.

Summer Rae's dress sparkled on her strut over. "Well, well, well." Her tsk-tsks boomed out of the speakers. "We'd thought you'd *desserted* us. Do you care to explain why you are so choco-*late*?" The audience cracked up at the double serving of puns.

If only the judges joined in with them. Except they didn't. Johnny Oliver folded his tattooed arms over his chest. Madame Terese tapped a red-soled pump against the floorboard. Both of them watched me intensely, waiting for an answer.

"There was something I *kneaded* to finish first." Laughter exploded from the gallery. Madame Terese bit down on a smile. Johnny Oliver let a small one show. I inched to the single workstation without a baker behind it. With all the studying I'd had to do lately, I never actually got around to notifying Bake-Off about me quitting, so . . .

"And what was it, may we ask?"

"The Law and Debate tournament across campus."

"I see." Summer Rae didn't sound very convinced. "Can you tell us one of your topics?"

"The Cuban embargo."

She sucked air through her teeth. Damn, even she knew how touchy the issue was. "Sounds very serious."

"As serious as I am about still competing. If you'll have me." *Please have me.*

Summer Rae turned to the judges. They looked at each other, then back at me.

Silence. An eternity of it.

With every heartbeat, hope trickled away.

I busied myself inspecting all the equipment at the workstation. Touching these objects, especially the apron embroidered with my name . . . "Um, Rubi." Summer Rae's heels clacked toward me. "The judges haven't said you can compete."

"They also haven't said I couldn't."

I rolled up my sleeves, extended my arms and splayed out my fingers. Angled my hand to put the pinkish-brown line on the side of my palm on display. "Pan sear, first flambé." I moved my hand again to show them its twin on the other side. "Oven rack sear, taking out the capuchinos Cubanos." Shifted again to show off a collection of small divots. "Jumping oil from the buñuelos de anís con almíbar. Anise fritters with syrup."

Bakers cast sideways glances. All of them nodded, except Katherine.

I circled a smooth swath of skin with my finger. "This part here, I really want to add—"

"You want to add more scars?" Summer Rae's jaw dropped.

"Not scars," I said. "Me."

Only then did the judges nod too. Applause broke from the audience.

"We cannot give you the hour that you've lost," Johnny Oliver said.

"That wouldn't be équitable to the finalists that were here on time," said Madame Terese.

I clung to the implications within both of their statements. "Does this mean I can start?"

"Yes, young baker," said Johnny Oliver. More cheers. Loud, but not as loud as the beating of my crazy, swelling heart. "It means you may start."

"Bon courage." Madame Terese turned on her pumps and walked to another finalist.

Summer Rae wrapped an arm around my shoulders and led

me to the shelves at the back of the stage. "Any and all ingredients you need you'll find in this pantry or the refrigerators, there and there." She pointed to the far end of the stage. "Tools and equipment are waiting for you at your workstation."

"Thank you."

She smiled, moving to center stage. "Three hours remaining, bakers!"

We all huffed in unison. Whisks, mixers, and rolling pins ratcheted up to superhuman speeds. "Three hours remain for your Jaw-Dropper Challenge. Remember the judges expect a feast for the eyes and the taste buds! Couture style and decor with delectable flavors to match!"

I rushed back to my station and dropped to my knees. Without fog or streaks, the oven's windowpane reflected my face with perfect clarity.

I was here, at Alma, competing in Bake-Off!

This impossible was possible. I turned the oven on, moved the temperature knob to 375 degrees.

The heat was high. I could handle it.

Cracked eggshells. Measuring cups. Some were dusted with flour or sugar. Others were coated with the hardening residue of melted butter and extracts. A sauté pan. Glass bowls brimming with different types of cherries. I didn't have time to clean up or put away the ingredients and equipment strewn over every inch of my workstation. Not when I wasn't even halfway through all the steps in my bake.

Every baker buzzed to complete a different stage of their bakes, so at least similar chaos reigned over their stations too. Summer Rae paused a moment and broke off from the judges, sauntering my way. "So, what are we making?"

After scoring the last dough ball, I covered the rest of them with a layer of Saran Wrap. Even under the plastic, the mini loaves spaced across the baking sheet looked perfectly symmetrical. I exhaled and wished them a quick rise. Leaning into her microphone I said, "Bolillo Bread Pudding with Malted Vanilla Sauce."

Johnny Oliver's head swung in my direction. He strode over with steady steps and propped an elbow on the top of the island. A sleeve of tattoos shifted over muscly arms.

His cobalt eyes dropped to my bolillos. He studied them before turning his attention back to me, forehead furrowing.

"I know I'm short on proving time."

"Very short is more accurate."

I nodded and wiped away the sweat sprouting at my hairline. "By shaping them smaller like this, and by upping the yeast ratio, I'm hoping it'll help them rise more quickly." Johnny O continued staring at me. While he didn't voice any approval, he didn't discount it either.

A dash of hope. "And these spotlights." I tugged at the neck of my blazer. "I'm counting on the heat to help too."

Johnny Oliver half-smiled. He looked past me to the frenzy all around us. "Well, young baker, I hope you can make these work."

"Me too."

"Bitten off more than you can chew perhaps?" Summer Rae asked.

The crowd laughed. When it petered out I said, "Always."

Johnny Oliver's half smile turned into a full one. "I'll leave you to it." He rapped the countertop with his knuckles before leaving. A moment later, Madame Terese walked over to take his place.

The bowls of cherries drew her attention more than the dough. Her dark eyes flitted between the dried sours, Maraschinos, Bings, and Rainiers.

"Have you decided which of des cerises you're going to use?" she asked. "Whether to incorporate them fresh or candied?"

The truth was, I hadn't. I could candy some for decorations. Make near replicas of the ones Dad gave me for Abuela Carmen's Rosca de Reyes. I reached for the bowl of Maraschinos. Dropped my hand halfway. Maybe not.

I gazed out into the audience. The auditorium's gallery was nearly as full as the debate's. There was Ryan. The flash of his smile sent my heart fizzing again. With him sitting right there, cheering me on, how could I not use the Bing cherries? Dark red, tart, and perfectly shaped like mini hearts.

Before turning back to Madame Terese, I glanced up a few rows to the right. No sign of my parents. Still, my Dad's voice rang loud inside my head.

Shine bright like a Rubi.

Just because they weren't here didn't mean they weren't with me. I grabbed the bowl of Rainiers. Yellow and red colored. As sweet as they were sour. Two flavors one would think shouldn't be together, but in fact, were the best couple ever.

I turned back to Madame Terese.

Instead of answering, I bit my lip.

The only reason I stood here now was because I'd refused to give up one thing for another.

I pulled one bowl of cherries closer. Then another. Pretty soon all the bowls of cherries sparkled in front of me. The tartness of one would counterpoint the sweetness of another. The juiciness in one balanced out the firmness in the other. The full spectrum of tastes and textures would explode over the judges' taste buds. Only then could they taste all the different things a cherry could be. I lifted my head high. "I'm going to use all of them."

A cloud of steam rose from the pan when I uncovered it. I turned the heat off. Inside, the cherries still simmered. Big, round, bright shades of red. Jewels, all of them.

With a slotted spoon, I transferred them onto a wire cooling rack. A dollop of syrup landed on the counter with a splat. A droplet bounced off and stuck to my finger. "Ow!"

I stuck my finger into my mouth, prodded the burn with my tongue. The edges of my lips curled into a smile. A new scar to mend some old ones.

"Time!" Summer Rae said. "Bakers, please step away from your Jaw-Droppers." Metal clanked on the countertops. Decorating tools dropped onto islands. Sighs in every octave rippled across the stage. A couple gulps of air.

I set my piping bag down. My hands shook, fingers sticky with malted vanilla cream I'd been furiously drizzling over my bake.

The whole auditorium fell silent, waiting for Summer Rae to speak. "It's been a *rocky road,* and we are nearing the end of it. Before we find out who will wear Bake-Off's first-ever crown, let's give it up one last time for International Pastry Diva Madame Terese!"

She turned from the judging table, down to the center of the stage, and waved to the audience behind her. They went wild. "And the Bad Boy of Bread himself, Johnny Oliver!" Johnny turned back and waved too. "And of course, to the fab five finalists! Give yourselves a round of applause!"

I looked down at my bake, clapped and clapped.

So the Bolillo Bread Pudding hadn't come out perfectly symmetrical. The drive for perfection gave way to having done my best. The palms of my hands stung. A small price to pay for celebrating everything I'd done today.

But not all of the bakers were celebrating. Sydney patted Nico's back, whispered something into his ear. "It's not going to be okay. I used salt instead of sugar. Salt!"

Oh no. On top of apparently mixing up the ingredients, his chocolate mousse and icing hadn't set either. The cake's top tier leaned one way; the bottom tier oozed the other; the middle one jutted forward. Each layer battled over which way to go.

Oof. Poor cake. I intimately knew where *that* led.

Madame Terese covered her mouth with a manicured hand. Johnny Oliver grimaced. The audience seemed to hold a collective breath. Which only made the *plop* and *splatter* echo even louder.

The remaining chocolate poured over the sides of the workstation, dripping onto the floor to join globs of cake. Nico burst into tears and stormed offstage.

"Gravity is a cruel mistress." Summer Rae gave an exaggerated wink. "In OC, we know better than anyone, am I right, people?"

The gesture flipped the audience's energy. Cheers and whistles rang from every corner of the auditorium. Suddenly, the lights on the stage winked out, shrouding the stage in total darkness. "Bakers, please bring your Jaw-Droppers to the judging table."

A pair of spotlights shot over Johnny Oliver and Madame Terese. Four additional spotlights beamed down across the judging table, illuminated the places where we needed to stand.

I took the spot at the far end of the table, eased my bake down. Peeked sidelong at the competition.

Sydney's three-tiered cake was worthy of a wedding at the Montage, decorated with a light blue buttercream, marzipan bumblebees, and fresh flower petals cascading down its sides.

Katherine beamed behind an edible peacock—*of course a peacock*—covered in Tiffany-blue fondant, and alternating milk, dark, and white chocolate work. Juno made an entire chessboard from what looked like every single type of cookie imaginable.

The competition was stiff. But next to theirs, my bake didn't look too shabby either.

Under the lights and malted vanilla sauce, the crust of the bolillo glittered gold, or tan, depending on how I angled my chin. Edges of the cherries jutted from the crust. Hints of all the jewels hidden inside. Shards of caramel brittle wrapped around the sides of the rectangular loaf. Jagged, semitranslucent, and slightly overlapping one another, the pieces of the brittle looked like a wall around the bake. A wall needing to be broken before getting inside everything the bake had to offer.

Madame Terese's voice broke the spell. "Sydney, this is one of the most beautiful cakes I've seen. You certainly nailed the decorations." Murmurs of confirmation came from the audience. A smatter of applause too.

I loved how the audience feasted on the cake with their eyes. It was hard to keep my attention from wandering over to Ryan again. And Devon, now sitting right next to him.

I flashed them a quick smile. She shot back a thumbs-up. Ryan mouthed, *You got this.*

More of my anxiety crumbled away. As I turned my head back to my bake, my breath caught in my throat.

There, in the middle of the third row, Addison Teague sat on the literal edge of her seat, watching the judges cut into Sydney's cake.

Each tier revealed additional layers, bursting with more

beautiful colors. More praise from the audience. Some oohs and aahs. The judges huddled closer and exchanged indiscernible looks when they tasted every tier.

Silence fell over the auditorium. The air grew thick. Addison lifted a bejeweled hand to her lips, gnawed on a pink-polished fingernail.

Johnny Oliver extended his hand across the table for the first fist bump of the finale. The entire auditorium went wild. Addison Teague roared louder than most. The sight of her momentarily letting go of her uber-posh persona made my heart flutter.

The sight of my parents sitting a few rows away stopped it completely.

Dad clapped furiously along with the rest of the auditorium. Only his gaze wasn't on Sydney, or her cake.

It was fixed on me. And instantly, I knew.

He cheered me being here. Our past wasn't going to crumble. My future would be stronger because of this. And as much as I wanted to win first place to go to Cuba, I couldn't deny feeling as if I'd already won something much bigger than the judges could ever give.

Tears blurred my eyes. I brushed them away with the wool sleeve of the jacket, determined not to let a few tears get in the way of seeing my mother.

She was the only person in the auditorium not clapping. Her gaze wasn't even fixed on me. But she was here. It was enough.

A single tear, a happy one (finally), rolled down my cheek. It landed on a smooth strip of skin between scars. My heart swelled. My pulse beat hard against my eardrums. The beating made it hard for me to listen to the judges' feedback, to Sydney's inspiration for the cake.

Something about passion fruit blending with passion. Something about saving both oceans and bees.

Katherine's judging went by in a blur too. The judges cut into the intricate fondant-molded feathers and impeccable chocolate work. Half of the audience gasped and the other half laughed when Madame Terese said, "Loads of style but no substance. I mean you used a plain vanilla Bundt cake, which was under-baked, for the core."

I had no idea what Katherine's face did when she said it. I was too amused by my mother cracking up with the rest of the crowd.

"Baking needs to be a marriage of both substance and style," Johnny Oliver said. From the edge of his seat, Dad nodded in complete agreement. "You cannot sacrifice one for another. It simply will not work."

I bit the side of my cheek, remembered how foolishly I'd once told Ryan I wasn't going to take life advice from baking. If only I'd listened to its advice sooner.

Then the judges stepped in front of me.

"I watched you meticulously shape and score the rolls. Only for you to cube and toast them." Johnny Oliver folded his arms across his chest. "Why?"

I glanced to where Dad sat. "To make bolillos any other way would be sacrilege."

"Some recipes should never be tampered with, eh?"

"Only some." Eyes drifted to my mother. "Others are begging for a tune-up."

"Well, let's dig in and see if the adjustments worked."

With the side of his knife, he broke through a shard of caramel brittle, scooped out some bread pudding, and lifted the forkful to his face for closer inspection. Malted vanilla sauce dripped down the sides of the bake, moist and rippling with the treasure trove of cherries.

"Lovely colors," Madame Terese said. She examined a piece of the caramel shard next. "Juste comme stained glass." She popped a piece into her mouth. "The brittle snaps beautifully. The sauce coats the tongue with an incroyable malt flavor before we get those different fruity pops from the different cherries. Orange zest too. Absolutely délicieux."

"Thank you, Madame Terese."

"I can taste hints of your previous bakes in this," Johnny Oliver said. He used a shard of brittle to scoop out another bite. "But I also taste something entirely new. You checked off lots of boxes with this bake."

Enough to get the second fist bump of the day?

"However, the structure of the bread is still quite dense," he said. "Despite all the proving techniques you used to make it rise quicker, there's no technique better than time. It simply needed more time to prove."

"You did the very best you could in the time allotted," Madame Terese said. "It just missed the mark from perfection."

"What about passion?" Perfection didn't matter to me the way it once did, but still. "Did I miss the mark there?"

The judges looked at each other. Hints of smiles formed at the corners of their lips.

"I think everyone here knows the answer to that," Summer Rae said. The auditorium exploded with cheers. Maybe even a few from my mother.

"Thank you, young baker," Johnny Oliver said.

"Merci, Rubi."

"Thank you both. Truly."

Disappointment, exhilaration, and relief coursed through me. Madame Terese and Summer Rae stepped down to Juno, but Johnny Oliver lingered. At first I thought he was going in for one last bite of my bake. Then his arm stretched past it.

He grabbed my hand. Shook it.

It wasn't a fist bump.

It was more.

Chapter 35

A million cameras went off, capturing the judges with the three winners. I cradled a bronze-plated whisk between my fingers. Twirling it around like a wand, all the flashing made it glitter even more.

Amazement filled my chest, then pride.

Third place! The whisk sparked with another flash. I shined bright along with it.

"Well done, young baker." Johnny Oliver's voice broke the spell. A little. "I hope to see you in the fall. Maybe sooner."

My breath caught in my throat. "Sooner?"

"Yes. Perhaps this summer? For the seminar?"

"Wait . . ." The stage swirled over my head. "I thought I had to win first place to take the seminar?"

Johnny Oliver gave a sly shrug. "I'm putting you on the waitlist."

"There's a waitlist? Does this mean I still have a chance of going to Havana?"

Another round of flashes.

When my vision cleared, the judges and Summer Rae were

halfway across the stage. They gave one last set of waves, then disappeared backstage.

"There's a waitlist . . . And I'm on it." A choke-cough turned to laughter. A few weeks ago, I would've crumbled at attempting to get off another one. Now, I knew how to rise to the occasion.

A stampede of friends, family members, and fans rushed up the stage. Devon and Ryan spilled onto it first.

"The jacket has gotten double the press today." Devon threw her arms around me, squeezing tight. "Third the nerd. Fitting, right? Oh, and the bronze whisk matches the buttons so much better than gold would've."

"I couldn't agree more." I tightened the squeeze. When I let go, Ryan scooped me up and swung me around.

"Congratulations." His breath skimmed my hair. "You were amazing."

"Thanks, Opri-Wan," I whispered into his collarbone.

He lowered me as Addison Teague shouldered her way through the throng of people swarming the stage. My parents followed a few steps behind.

I threaded my fingers through Ryan's. Held on to the bronze whisk with the other hand. The weight of both steadied my steps on the walk downstage to meet Addison.

"Rubi, who knew baking could be so exciting?" she said.

"Baking can be so many things." I said it loud and firmly, as much for her benefit as my parents.

"Hey, guys." I turned to Devon and Ryan. "Can I meet you outside in a little bit?"

"I'll head out and grab us a table somewhere at the Mix," Devon said. "This needs to be celebrated."

"Lots of things need to be celebrated." I held her gaze, then Ryan's.

"I'll wait for you right outside," he said.

He followed Devon up the aisle. Nearing my parents, she gave my mother a quick kiss on the cheek then high-fived Dad. He slapped her palm before swinging onto Ryan's shoulder, holding him in place.

Whatever he whispered into Ryan's ear, it made his Adam's apple bob faster than I'd ever seen it move before. My mother shook his hand, half-smiled like even *she* thought he was cute. All of it made me snort with laughter.

Addison followed my gaze over her shoulder. "Ah, these must be your parents."

"Yes," I said. "Mamá, Dad, I'd like you to meet Ms. Teague, Alma's dean of admissions."

A small gasp escaped my mother's lips. She squared her shoulders before reaching for Addison's hand. "Please call me Rosa." She gave Addison two short pumps then broke off the handshake abruptly. I bet she didn't want Addison to shrink away from her scars.

She shook Dad's hands next. "Addison. It's so wonderful to meet Rubi's parents." She turned to me. "Madeline told me where to find you after the tournament. Your team won, by the way."

"We won?" All my breath left in a rush. A flash of Sister Bernadette holding the gold trophy high above her head. I smiled so wide my cheeks hurt.

"Your second trophy of the day by the looks of it." Addison glanced at the bronze whisk. "You keep showing so many talents, Miss Ramos. I look forward to discovering what else you're keeping up those sleeves."

My pulse ramped up at her implication. Both of my parents tilted their heads in her direction.

"I'm sorry you didn't win first place in this competition, dear. Although perhaps this will serve as a worthy consolation prize, hmm?" She pulled an envelope from her handbag.

I handed Dad the bronze whisk, reaching for the envelope with both hands. The weight of this letter felt different than the first one. Looking down at it, I didn't wish to have X-ray vision anymore.

I had a pretty good idea of what the letter said. I motioned my parents closer.

Huddled together, I slipped the letter from the envelope.

"'Dear Rubi Ramos, Congratulations! With great pleasure we offer you admission to Alma University—'"

My head swung to Addison. "I'm in!" My heart skipped a million beats. I'd daydreamed this moment so many times, never pictured it'd arrive here, like this. But here it was, sweeter than any of us could've imagined.

"You're in!" Addison smiled. "You're exactly what Alma needs. As dean, I couldn't bear to make you wait any longer."

"Oh, mija, you did it." My mother wrapped her arms around me, hugged me the way she had that day in the prep room. This time, I didn't feel like a fraud.

I pressed the letter into her palms. Her eyes misted with tears when she read the good news for herself.

Dad placed the whisk back into my hands. "Rubi, congratulations." I couldn't tell whether he was congratulating me on Bake-Off, Alma, or both.

I was proud of all of the above.

"Your full package will be mailed out on Monday. But in the meantime, do you or your parents have any questions for me before I get back to the office?"

I looked at my mother, still fixated on the acceptance letter. The wins today made me brave. The love for her made me certain.

"I actually do." I took a huge breath. "How accommodating are your part-time programs? I don't think I'm the only Ramos who's Alma material."

My mother's eyes met mine. Her irises burned like coals so hot I almost caught fire. Still. I kept going. "Like we chatted about before, my dad's the baking genius in the family. But my mother's the business one. She's made the bakery—bakeries," I corrected myself, "what they are today." A dramatic pause. "And I really believe a *background like hers is exactly what Alma needs to enrich its educational experience.*"

Whether Addison knew I parroted back everything I'd heard her say about me, I couldn't tell. I'd promised myself when I walked through Alma's doors, I'd hold it open for people who worked in prep rooms. People from the other side of the hill. All the other places too often overlooked.

"Rosa, are you interested in the culinary arts program we offer?" Addison asked.

My mother hesitated. Her eyes shifted from Dad's face to mine. I held her stare, telepathically telling her if I had to learn to shine bright like a Rubi, the time had come for her to learn how to bloom big like a Rosa.

Bit by bit, her shoulders relaxed. "In light of my work experience . . ." Her voice was raw. It was also tinged with something that sounded like a dash of hope. "Actually . . ." A shy smile flowered across her face. "I'm more interested in an MBA program. Business law as well."

"We have amazing part-time programs in both those areas," Addison said. "I have to get back to my office. But, if you have time, I can give you a little more information about them on the walk over."

"Yes," my mother said without hesitation.

Hesitation came a beat later when she turned back to us. I caught a glimpse of the girl she might've been a long time ago. She handed me back the letter and then returned her attention to Addison. "Yes. I have time."

After some quick goodbyes, they walked up the aisle. I watched them until they disappeared out the doors. I stuffed the acceptance letter into my jacket's pocket. "And then there were two," I said.

Not like he was listening.

Mouth half-parted, Dad was too busy staring at the stations still buzzing with activity. Fans took pictures with Sydney, of her magnificent cake and gold whisk. Juno shared cookies from her edible chessboard. Some people were even on their hands and knees, picking up chocolate feathers that'd flown off of Katherine's peacock when she'd grabbed it and stomped off in a huff.

A few other people gathered around my bake, whispering and pointing, waving me over.

"Dad?" Silence. He stared hard at Sydney and Juno talking to fans, at their bakes, and mine.

"Do you think Bake-Off's coming back to OC next year? Or was this a onetime thing?"

"I think it's going to be a yearly thing."

An excited sigh escaped his lips.

"Oh my god, Dad! If it is, you should enter the croncha for the Cookie Try-Out Round! We never did get a chance to make it, maybe this summer—"

His hug cut me off. My torso would've turned to pulp if he squeezed any tighter. "Why don't you go and find out? Get the inside scoop for next year. While you're at it, why don't you go and cover my station for me? You can share my Bolillo Bread Pudding, but save a piece, okay? We can have it for dessert when I get home."

"Really?" He swallowed hard, then smiled harder. "I'll do it but only if it's okay with you."

"Of course." I chuckled, gesturing for him to go. He flew to my station.

I exhaled, took one step down the stage, and then another. When I got to the front of the auditorium, I pressed my palms against its doors.

With my parents in their own separate worlds, it was time for me to enter mine.

♥ ♥ ♥

The sinking sun lit the sky in a blaze of colors. Pink and amethyst clouds streaked the top half. Mango orange blistered from the bottom half, crowned the treetops in golden light. I ran to Ryan, waiting for me across the pathway. "Devon got us a table at the Mix—"

Before the last of his words were out of his mouth, I pressed my lips to his.

We kissed under the swirl of colors, condensed under a limitless sky. Ryan traced his Orion-freckled hand over the side of my face, across the epaulets, down my arm, over the pocket stuffed with Alma's acceptance letter, until he reached the bronze whisk.

"You won," he said.

I conjured up my superpower. Twirled the whisk as if mixing new possibilities with the best of my old plans. I felt dizzy thinking about what type of future I'd mold.

"Oh, Ryan. I did."

Epilogue

THREE MONTHS LATER

"The weather in Havana is clear and sunny, with a high of eighty-two degrees for this afternoon. If the weather cooperates, we should get a great view of the city as we descend. Cabin crew, please take your seats for landing."

I pressed my forehead against the window. Breath condensed on the pane. The plane's wings cut through thick nimbostratus clouds. A few flashes of sunlight pierced through.

My ears popped. The plane broke through the clouds, and there it was: a crocodile-shaped island in the middle of a teal-blue sea.

Cuba.

I opened the messenger bag beside me. Fingers skimmed the cake mold, brushed against Abuela Carmen's recipe book.

Some of the bakes from the margins of my Law and Debate binder lived here now. Ryan's cookies, Boss's red-velvet lava cake, and of course, the croncha. It'd taken the entire summer to figure out. Once I did, I sent the recipe to the new dean of the culinary program: the Bad Boy of Dough himself, Johnny

Oliver. Thankfully he agreed with me. I deserved a spot in the summer seminar.

So here I was. A bunch of Alma culinary students in seats behind me, an island that'd only existed in my dreams, ahead.

With a fingertip I traced the word *pa'lante* on the book's cover, then patted underneath it. No Kleenex to dab my eyes, only a ziplock bag of cherry pits.

I rolled them between my fingers.

Would they take root in Cuban soil? If they didn't, that was okay.

I had roots here already. And they went deep.

Acknowledgments

Teamwork makes the dream work. This book wouldn't exist without the teams that poured their hearts and souls into making this dream of mine come true.

Thank you to editor extraordinaire Alex Sehulster, who loved and understood these characters better than I did. I'm forever grateful for your support and for whipping this book into the best shape it could be. Thank you also to Mara Delgado Sánchez and Cassidy Graham. To Rivka Holler, Brant Janeway, and Meghan Harrington for helping get this story into readers' hands. To Petra Braun for illustrating, and Devan Norman and Olga Grlic for designing the book of my dreams. You not only captured the story perfectly, but a piece of my soul too. To Cassie Gutman and NaNá V. Stoelzle for your sharp eyes (I hope I didn't strain them too much). And to everyone at Wednesday Books who helped make this book a reality. Making my debut with you is the icing on the cake!

To my rock star agent, Jen Azantian. From our meet-cute in a cabin in the woods to bookshelves [insert happy tears gif], your unwavering attention and care has meant the world to me. You have made so many people's dreams come true, and I'm so thankful you shared some of your magic with me. Thank you to the entire ALA family: Ben Baxter for all the backstage work, Zuko for the laughs, and Brent Taylor for helping take Rubi worldwide.

To Las Musas: gracias for the inspiration, community, and mentorship. Thank you for not only breaking down doors in the publishing industry, but helping to keep them open for marginalized voices too.

A huge thanks to Nina Moreno. You changed my life when you selected me as your Las Musas mentee. Thank you for taking a chance on me, and for understanding this story so deeply.

Thank you to Brenda Drake and all Pitch Wars organizers. So many acknowledgments wouldn't be written—mine included—without you.

To my soul sisters and story geniuses: Hoda Agharazi and Stephanie Dodson. Hoda, thank you for pulling this story out from the PW submissions pile. Stephanie, thank you for walking me through the entire process. Both of your feedback has pushed me to become a better writer—and your unconditional love has helped me become a fiercer friend.

A huge hug to all of my amazing writer friends who have read my work, let me read theirs, or cheered me on, including but not limited to: Charlene Anderson, Lauren Bray, Heather Buchta, Tim Burke, Kristina Cassiano, Sari Cortiz, Molly Cusick, Mike Finch, Reyna Grande, Kalie Holford, Courtney Kae, Angela Montoya, Amparo Ortiz, Lori Polydoros, Erinn Salge, Melanie Schubert, Lyssa Mia Smith, Stacie Stukin, Elle Taylor, Melanie Thorne, Sonja Wilbert, Lennox Wiseley, and Kyla Zhao. Your talent is only outweighed by the size of your hearts!

To agency siblings and soul siblings: Clare Edge and Sara Hashem. Laughing with you every day is the sweetest of joys.

To the best friend and CP a person can have, Carolina Flórez

Cerchiaro. Thank you for reading and working on this book as much as I have. You have made my life so much brighter by being in it, and I'm eternally grateful to have you by my side. Le echamos ganas y mira, #NASC!

The deepest gratitude to all the incredible authors who took the time to read Rubi's story and so generously gave this book early blurbs: Susan Azim Boyer, Tashie Bhuiyan, Jesmeen Kaur Deo, Mia García, Romina Garber, Emma Lord, and Nina Moreno.

Thank you so much to my family and friends. A special shout-out to: Karin Lopez, Jonathan Meister, Jonathan Osterbach, Chris Pinto, Summer Shaw, and Brandon Wright. You held my hand during the most challenging years of my life—and helped me celebrate the heights of it too. I am so lucky to have you in my life. Los quiero mucho.

To Juno, Jolie, and Arwen. Thank you for keeping my lap (ankles, neck—and heart) warm during writing sessions. I'm so grateful you shared your lives with me. I miss you so much.

A special round of applause to my parents. You introduced me to the joys of books and baking. Inside the bakery's prep room, you not only taught me how to survive—but thrive—with the fire on high. Pa'lante.

A million thanks to my sister, Cindy. You have been by my side on every step of this journey, and this book would not be on shelves without your encouragement and support. Inside and out, you are "so booraafuuulll" [*Kayla voice*]. No words can express how much I appreciate you. What time should we go to Disneyland and #MO?

And most of all, thanks and love to YOU! I'm so thankful for you picking up this book. Know it is never too late to whip up a new Recipe for Your Life. Rubi and I can't wait to taste them one day.